TASHAMA

THE MAGIC OF INHERIAN
BOOK 4

TERRY SPEAR

PUBLISHED BY:

Wilde Ink Publishing

Tashama

Discover more about Terry Spear at:

http://www.terryspear.com/

Print ISBN: 978-1-63311-117-2

Ebook ISBN: 978-1-63311-116-5

UNTITLED

Synopsis

Tashama's mission is to bring peace to the kingdom—easier said than done!

Swept away and sent to a strange land called Texas when her parents were murdered, she must return to her own homeland and right the wrong. Not only does she end up in the enemy's territory, she becomes a prisoner of Prince Aleron, the man of her dreams.

Aleron is intrigued with Princess Tashama, but learns she is supposed to be the ruler of her kingdom, an enemy they have been fighting for decades. She's a danger to him, but he has no clue what to do with her. He doesn't want to give her up for anything. And she has no intention of being his prisoner but freeing her people from a tyrant and settling scores, all so she can bring peace to the region.

If you liked the Magic of Inherian series, where the women rule and the heroes drool, enjoy another fantasy set in the medieval world.

Thanks so much, Emily Darrow, for cheering me on during one of my most difficult times in my life! You really helped me through it. This book is dedicated to you!

1

―――――――

Tashama's stomach roiled with upset. She knew she had to return to her time and place, but she was happy here in Dallas, Texas. Could she really make a difference in her world? Her guardian, Balthazar, the sorcerer of her royal house, believed it was so. He had two goals—return her safely to her home and help restore her to power so she could bring peace to the region.

She'd been away for years. Everyone believed she was dead. How could she, at twenty-three, return and take over? She thought the notion ludicrous. No amount of entreaty would change his mind, though she'd tried. He was too powerful, too all-knowing. She would do as he bade.

"Can you feel the air pressure changing, Tashama?" Balthazar asked, his electric blue eyes studying her with concern.

"Yes, a storm is approaching. But you're changing the subject."

He tilted his chin down, giving her one of his annoyed teacher-to-pupil looks.

She glanced out the kitchen window and saw nothing but the cornfields bent over in the West Texas breeze. He had saved her life, then closely guarded her in this new world to keep her safe.

Which meant he hadn't allowed her any associations with the male populace, making her rebel for years. Today, as much as she didn't want to return to her medieval world of Karthland, it was her duty to set things right, to find her mate, and rule in her parents' place.

But she had finally adjusted to this world and all its amenities. And no one even knew she existed any longer. Who would care if she returned to Karthland? Worse, she knew how dangerous it would be.

Someone had wanted her dead before. How would that have changed? It wouldn't have. Not when those same powers learned she had returned.

Balthazar's beard, like white cotton candy, draped over her tiled countertop while he concentrated on a banana. Watching his bony fingers strip the green peel from the still-hard fruit, she realized then he would never taste another morsel like that again. She knew, too, she wasn't ready—not for the move she would soon have to make from Texas to a world she barely remembered—not now—not ever.

"We're in for stormy weather." She shook her head at him. "The banana isn't ripe yet."

Balthazar leaned over and sniffed the banana. "Smells just right to me." He bit into the firm fruit.

"Too hard, isn't it?"

His whiskers curled up slightly.

She stuck a coffee cup into the dishwasher. "I don't want to go back."

"You have no choice, Tashama. I've told you all along—"

"I know—I know." She mouthed the words softly. Leaning her chin in her hands, she rested her elbows on the counter. "I didn't think I would ever get used to this strange world when I first arrived —what, ten years ago when I was thirteen?" She threw her hands up in the air. "But now, well, it's different. I don't want to go back."

A sense of disquiet nudged at her. She hated to leave her friends and the new-fangled toys she enjoyed here to return to a place so foreign to her. She only vaguely remembered the screams of terror in the palace before Balthazar took her away, never again to see her parents alive.

Her computer screen, sitting in the breakfast nook, turned black, then mesmerizing zigzags of color burst across the monitor. She sighed deeply. "No television, computers, internet, or cell phones. And what of old Bessy?"

"Bessy?"

"My Pontiac Grand Am."

He shook his head. "You've taken riding lessons for years. That'll be all you need when you return."

"There's no Thanksgiving, Christmas, or Easter. No Veteran's Day Parades or Columbus Day holidays."

"They celebrate their own holidays. You must remember."

"I barely remember anything about..." *Home,* she almost said out loud. *But I have lived here nearly as long as I have lived there. So, where is home really anymore?*

"There, Tashama."

"They don't have bananas there."

Balthazar's now pale blue eyes twinkled in the bright kitchen light.

She took a deep breath. "Are you certain that in ten years they have not made any progress—"

"The war drags on there, Tashama. You're twenty-three now. Not only must you lead your people to victory, but your mate awaits you."

"There are many here that please me."

Balthazar's eyes, now the color of the cloudless sky, slimmed as his pale, thin lips turned down in a scowl. Tashama sighed, hating that she'd have to return to her medieval society, knowing whoever murdered her parents would still want her dead, too. "All right, so I cannot stay. But I don't want to go back."

Suddenly, she had a fond memory of there. "Oh, I remember visiting Princess Talamaya, and her lady companions, Lady Kersta and Mexia of the Kingdom of..."

"Damar. Aye, before things went wrong and I had to take you away."

"I must see them again."

"You will."

She tore off a paper towel, wetted it, then dabbed orange-scented soap on the cloth. She took a deep breath, then leaned over and wiped the counter, her braided hair wiggling down her back.

A strand of hair slipped from her woven tresses, then tickled her cheek. She reached her finger to twist it. She studied the golden hue of the strand of hair in the glassy reflection of the tile. "You were supposed to teach me about Karthland. Why do we have to return there first, before you tell me—"

"Seeing your home will help you to remember." Balthazar fingered his banana peel, then sighed deeply. "Well, what *do* you remember?"

She'd blocked most of it from her mind when the killing had begun, and once they'd first arrived in this new world, she'd been nearly impossible to live with—for a good year, Balthazar had said. She wrinkled her brow and leaned against the counter, pressing her mind to recall what she'd so often tried to forget. "Sand, the color of fresh snow, slipped between my toes in gritty granules while small, clawed crabs ducked into holes."

His brows tilted up in surprise. "Yes, go on."

"Thunderous waves crashed along the shore, dragging sand, seashells, and me along with it into the surf, then spat me out again upon the beach."

Balthazar's lips turned up slightly.

Twisting her mouth, she thought for a moment, then raised her finger in the air. "And a silver cart lifted me into the blackness dotted with shimmering, sparkling stars. Twisting and turning, it catapulted me through the heavens."

Shaking his head, he frowned at her. "You're remembering our trip to the Florida seacoast and Disney World."

"Oh." She stared at the countertop, then she smiled. "Yes, and the children thought you were Merlin because you wouldn't wear blue jeans like the rest of the people of this world." She walked over to Balthazar and ran her hand over the velvet sleeve of his robe. The purple fabric lightened. Smoothing it the opposite way, it darkened. "And at the Scarborough Renaissance Faire, too. I thought you were going to hold a sorcerer's convention the way the sorcerer-costumed folks flocked to you."

"They were spellbound."

"I couldn't believe you would cast spells there...a few fireworks, colored mists, a dragon illusion. If I didn't know any better, I would say you'd been drinking too much wine. Nobody even wanted to watch the tournament between the black and white knights. I think old faux King Henry VIII was a bit miffed."

Pearl white teeth glistened in a bed of whiskers. "Bit of fun." He waggled his snow-white eyebrows.

She laughed, then grew serious. "I remember caves dripping with groundwater. Spikes of rock reached up to the ceiling, while their mates reached down to them. Sometimes these would couple, forming narrow columns."

"The caves at Silver Dollar City."

"Oh." She rubbed her hands together. "They sparkled so with green gems—"

Straightening, Balthazar twisted his head slightly to observe her. "The emerald caves. Yes, yes, go on."

"Dwarves, short and stocky, mined the emeralds. They were a grouchy lot. Made Father pay to use the passage, though he bought emeralds from them."

"Where did you go after you walked out of the caves?"

"Ram...Ram..." She shook her head.

"Ramoria."

"Yes, where the Elorian elves lived." Taking a deep breath, she stared at the adobe-tiled floor. "Their ears pointed to a peak, like the mountains that ring the area."

"You remember."

"They thought me funny because I wanted to see their ears. They are not all alike, you know." She remembered. Not all, but bits and pieces like a shredded map finally taped together, only in places parts of it were still missing.

"No, just like us."

"I remember your chambers and the teaching rug." The sorcerer's room had smelled like mint and thyme, cinnamon and peaches, pleasant and welcoming. The sun's rays seemed to warm the room in a wash of golden light even on cold, gray days.

"Yes, while I served your father and mother, you learned your spells through my image there."

"And Loralee. I was teaching her a new trick when—"

"You were late for dinner."

Tashama nodded, and tears filled her eyes. Her pet dragon. Never would she see her again. Nor her family. "You came for me and took me away."

"You do realize, returning home will be fraught with danger?" His dark voice was touched with concern.

She turned her eyes up to gaze upon him. Her teacher, her steadfast companion, her protector. "We have to find the murderers and deal with them."

"You have an inner strength, Tashama, that will get you through. Always remember that."

"But you *will* be with me?" Panic tugged at her heart. "You won't desert me?" She couldn't imagine finding her killers and taking her place as leader of her people without her loyal advisor at her side. He was the only one she could trust with her life.

He inclined his head. "I've been your guardian all these many years. I'll remain your advisor 'til the end of your rule."

Returning to rule over her homelands appealed, but what would she find when she returned? An unending war between Karthland and her neighbors, the Maldovians? But worse, who were the assassins? And what about the man she was to wed? She ran her finger in a circle on the counter. "Why do I have these dreams of *him*?" Tashama looked up at Balthazar.

"What dreams are those, Princess?"

Tashama exhaled her breath, exasperated. "You know very well what dreams these are." She settled on the barstool across the counter from Balthazar and studied her long, pearl-polished nails resting on the tile top.

"He's a handsome devil of a man with hair as brown as dark chocolate, hanging in thick waves over his broad, bare shoulders. His equally rich brown eyes sparkle with flecks of amber, but seem haunted at times. He's as tall as you, too. Well, maybe an inch taller. I swear he looks like a sexy version of Hercules without the beard, smooth-faced, square-jawed, chiseled features...a gift from the gods."

She looked up and stared right through Balthazar. "He stands nearly a foot taller than me, waiting to see what I'll do. His eyes consider my lips, and I know he wants to touch them with his own."

Just as much as she wanted his mouth pressed firmly against hers, to have his fingers touch every inch of her skin, to caress her breasts, to roam lower and ease the ache that had already returned between her legs. Just thinking of the dream...

Her eyes gazed at the counter. "His mouth parts slightly as if to speak, but no words ever pass his lips. His gaze locks onto mine as if he's tied to me in some inexplicable way. Then the faintest of smiles brightens his golden complexion, but in the next instance, he vanishes from my sight."

Night after night, she wanted to be swept into his arms and vanish with him, but she couldn't follow where he must go.

"You're twenty-three, Tashama. That's why you have these dreams. Your soul aches for a mate."

"Is he the one then?" She shook her head as if to answer her own question. "He cannot be. He's not one of ours...too dark, too dangerous."

"*We must go,*" Balthazar said, though he spoke no word, and she nodded in silent agreement.

She took a deep breath and reached her hand out to him. She'd already told her girlfriends she would be leaving for Europe and wouldn't be able to return. Balthazar had never permitted her to have male friends, though she'd fought him over it for years. Now she was glad she hadn't found someone she truly loved, because she could never have taken him to her homeland when she had to return.

Balthazar's white brows knitted together, and he turned his head toward the north. "What's that sound I hear—like the gallop of 10,000 horses in battle?"

Tashama listened. "The ice maker just dumped some more ice into the—"

"No, listen."

She hurried over to the kitchen window and peered out. Boiling green clouds rolled toward them, darkening the sky. Lightning struck the plowed-under cornfields in jagged spears while their voices boomed with thunderous discontent. A blue sheet of rain grew closer, hiding the menace behind it. Taking a deep breath, she sensed the storm's power. She rubbed her forehead and concentrated on the front. "A blue norther."

The rain suddenly ceased as if a waterfall had been cut off at its source. Blackbirds caught up in the wind flew in odd patterns.

"What's wrong with the birds?" Without waiting for Balthazar to answer, her heart picked up its pace. "They have no voice... they're not birds, but...remnants of a farmer's barn."

The rotating transparent cloud of mist transformed into a solid brown mass and raced across the plowed fields. She gasped. The swirling funnel appeared like the star of the storm, ripping cottonwoods from their homes where for years they had divided the farmers' fields.

"It's...it's heading this way!" She ran to Balthazar and shoved her finger out to him, urging him to transport her to their world using his magic. "Hurry! We must go...now!"

"Your clothes! You must change them at once!"

"There's no time!" she shouted. The roar of the freight train grew closer as Balthazar touched the shimmering light from his finger to hers. The light pricked her skin. The glass from the kitchen window shattered in an explosive crash.

"Balthazar!" she screamed, her heart hammering when the high wind slammed into them, breaking the spell that he attempted to cast, ripping them apart.

Instantly, sharp pain swept through her head, and a quiet blackness swallowed her whole.

2

Aleron, ruler of the Maldovians, paced across his courtyard at the royal palace of Banff, his mood darkened by sleepless nights.

"Sire," Carissian said, his voice deeply exasperated. "As your advisor, you must tell me what ails you today. We have made much progress against the Karthlanders. The war seems to be finally shifting in our favor—"

"Damn the war. We win a battle, and for what? To lose the next one?"

"There'll be no peace, my lord, not with the current ruler of Karthland, who is adamant that he wishes to rule us or kill us. Our choice."

Aleron shook his head and stared off toward the mountains ringing the valley. "I cannot sleep properly."

He continued to pace again, infuriated that the golden-haired nymph with the emerald eyes intruded upon his sleep, night after night, without fail. So real he could taste her sweet skin and smell the floral fragrance she wore, but no matter how much he prepared to bed the woman, he would find she was no more than an illusion, and her body, none other than the goose down pillows of his bed. He growled.

"Sire, if it's the woman that still plagues your dreams—"

"Your potions don't work, Carissian. What kind of a sorcerer are you, that you cannot give some solace to your ruler?"

"I beg your forgiveness, my lord, but if you would but take a woman..."

Aleron glared at the sorcerer. "Maldovian women don't have blonde hair or green eyes."

"No, sire. Only the Karthlander women do."

Aleron began to pace again. "I cannot have anything to do with a Karthlander witch." He faced Carissian. "She must be a witch, do you not agree? How else would she be able to visit me at night in my dreams like she does?"

"I'm sorry, sire. I have tried everything in my power to learn who she is and how she's coming to you in your dreams. But I cannot stop her, nor have I come any closer to determining who the wench is. She must be a Karthlander. However, to relieve some of the...tensions plaguing you until you take a bride."

Aleron cast him a look of annoyance.

"Sire, once you are crowned king, you must choose a mate and produce an heir, or lose your title. Then your cousin—"

"I know the details." Aleron waved his hand, dismissing his advisor's comment on the subject.

"Several women have applied to be deflowered by their prince. The honor is theirs, sire, and they'll be received with higher regard by their intended mates. I beg you to reconsider. 'Twill benefit all around."

"Nay, 'tis not my desire at the moment."

"You wish the siren, Your Highness. She's like the mermaid of the sea. Beautiful, alluring, and deadly. Take one of our Maldovian ladies. Bestow upon them the honor of being bedded first by their prince. Then choose a bride. This is the way of our kings."

Aleron blew out his breath. "Fine. Find me the fairest eligible lady who has requested this of me. I'll see her first thing before the evening meal."

"To—"

"See her. I will make my decision then."

Carissian grunted. "The fairest of our women will have the lightest of brown hair. And hazel eyes, my lord. None will be blond-haired with green eyes. Of that I can assure you."

"Then perhaps we should storm Karthland in search of this woman." Aleron ground his teeth. "I will not have the woman haunt my dreams further."

TASHAMA SPRAWLED out on her back on a carpet of blue-green grass in the meadows of the mountain-ringed valley. The mountain's sharp peaks poked into clouds settling too low, holding them hostage—and they, in response, shed tears of snowflakes on the dark green daggers. Sitting up, she rubbed her eyes, then stared at the sight.

She turned her attention to the lake sparkling in the early-morning sunlight several yards away from where she sat. *There are no lakes near the mountains that ring Karthland.*

"Balthazar," she whispered. She blinked and surveyed the land for movement. Seeing nothing but a hawk soaring high above, she shook her head. "Balthazar!" she yelled, her voice betraying the fear mounting in her heart. She rubbed her forehead and tried to recall the geography of the land.

The Maldovians had a lake on their side of the mountains. Lake Cura...something. She looked back at the blue waters. "This just cannot be Maldovia," she said under her breath, the horror of the notion finally sinking in. "You've delivered me to my enemy, Balthazar!"

Unsteadily, she rose to her feet. A stinging sensation crept across her arms, and the sleeves of her red turtleneck were riddled with cuts. She pulled one up with a cautious movement to find her arm streaked with blood. After finding the same with the other, she hurried to the edge of the lake, then crouched on the white-powdered, sandy beach.

She dipped her arms into the lake, then washed the cool liquid over the cuts. The blood mixed with the water, stinging her to the marrow of her bones, and she gritted her teeth against the pain.

Whispered voices filled the woods nearby.

She paused to listen; the voices abated. Except for the rippling of water at the tips of her running shoes and the dancing of the fresh green leaves on the branches of the elms, everything was quiet—too quiet.

She dipped her hands into the lake again. The reflection of the dark-haired man from her dreams shimmered in the water while he seemed to tower over her. Startled, she glanced back. No one was there.

She took a deep breath, relieved to see she was alone. Turning her eyes back to the water, she found him watching her again.

"Balthazar, what does this mean?" she whispered, and stretched her finger out to the man's reflection.

The image of a ten-inch-tall butterfly flapped above her head in the mirror-like lake, and she looked up as the translucent blue-winged creature fluttered before her face. "Water sprite—I didn't remember you."

The creature darted around her head. "They come for you, Tashama! They come for you!" She circled around Tashama's head again, then grabbed a strand of her hair. "A good catch for the dark-haired ones, you'll make. Your emerald-green eyes—a mermaid, they'll think you be!" Her tinny voice dripped with laughter, then she darted with a splash back into the lake.

Tashama stared at the ripples forming concentric circles, then the earth shook beneath her feet. Looking south, she saw a cloud of dust headed in her direction. She jumped up and dashed for the cover of the filtered shade of the forest.

"They come for you, Tashama." The voices rustled with the breeze of the leaves. "They come for you."

Covering her ears, she dodged branches and ran into the heart of the forest. The woodland sprites taunted her until the shade lightened and the forest gave way to a man-made clearing in the woods.

Tashama drew close to the forest fringe and gasped when she saw a group of about thirty men clad in armor, sipping ale beside a campfire. "Maldovia knights," she said under her breath and moved behind the broad trunk of a tree, hidden by the leafy lower branches of the tree, and tall green ferns at the base.

The smell of ale on the soldiers' breaths and the earthy male scent of unwashed skin carried on the breeze, making her wrinkle her nose.

"His Highness said the war will go on for another ten years at this rate. We kill them—they kill us, and for what? Neither of our kind has made any progress for years." The breeze shifted, and the soldier threw his dagger carelessly into the earth, but another touched his arm and said, "What's that smell on the breeze? There's a sweetness in the air."

The men grew quiet and tilted their noses up, trying to smell the fragrance the soldier had noticed. Tashama held her breath while the beating of her heart pounded wildly in her ears. Before anyone could make a move, a tall gray-haired man sauntered over to their location and cast a wary glance in her direction. Her heart nearly stopped.

The men all nodded at once. With as gentle a manner as they could muster, they set their tin cups on the ground and stood.

Tashama's cut arms stung when the hair prickled in anticipation. They knew she was there. *Damn it.* Why hadn't Balthazar prepared her better?

The old man standing with the soldiers, dressed in flowing midnight blue robes—sorcerer's robes—bowed his head in her direction just once. As the armored men ran toward her, she bolted back through the woods in the direction of the lake. The branches tore at her arms, and she yanked her sleeves down to protect her wounds.

Hushed laughter rippled through the light-green leaves while the metal of armor clanked and crashed through the web of branches behind her, sending her heart skittering in panic.

She tugged at a spindly branch that grabbed her long braid. She wrenched the offending limb from its trunk and threw it to the ground while she gasped for air to fill her aching lungs.

The ground shook with the men's approach. She dashed off again.

Soon she reached the lakeside clearing but stopped abruptly as men on horseback in leather tunics—at least a hundred, she surmised—filled the area.

One of the men chasing her from the clearing grabbed her wrist with his armored hand. She screamed out in surprise.

"Is *this* what we were called here for?" the leader of the cavalry shouted, jumping down from his horse. "For *this*?" He grabbed Tashama's free arm and held it high in the air. Then he dropped her arm and grabbed her braid. "What *is* it even?"

Her feelings bounced around her like a ping-pong ball on a tennis table, back and forth, from fear to anger. She wanted to slug him for touching her, but at the same time, she wanted to run away as far as she could from the enemy of her people. Unprepared for being caught, she felt her stomach knot in frustration. How could she let them catch her so easily?

Deadly silence ensued—no whispered voices—not even from the wood sprites now. The cavalry officer tossed her braid aside and stared at her clothes. "Is *this* what they send to fight their battles now?"

She glared at him, matching his scowl. He considered her turtleneck a form-fitting shirt that accentuated her feminine figure. "It's female—that's for certain." Then his eyes dropped to study her brass-buckled belt. His black bushy brows furrowed, and he ran his ruddy finger over the inscribed letters etched into her oval buckle.

His lips mouthed the letters in silence, then the armored men standing nearby parted briefly. The gray-haired man stared at her.

"I cannot read these strange symbols. What does it call her, Carissian?"

Carissian peered into Tashama's eyes, and though she fought to turn her head from his stare, she found she was unable to do so.

"Dallas." A whisper of a smile touched his lips. "But my saying so amuses her."

Tashama struggled to clear her mind. He explored her thoughts as if fingers touched the most sensitive parts of her body.

He arched his brows in response. "She's very clever—this one. Take her to his lordship at once."

"A Karthlander female? What would Prince Aleron want with the likes of her?"

Carissian's stern look made the warrior grunt in response. He grabbed Tashama's wrist, then yanked her toward his closest mounted cavalry officer. Tashama cried out when he lifted her off her feet with a sudden jerk of her arm.

"Careful, Oshon. Be careful with this one." Carissian vanished.

"Sorcerers—they'll undo our realm!" Oshon yelled, jumped into the leather of his saddle, then waved his men toward the direction of the royal city.

～

WITHIN THE HOUR, the cavalry rode into the marbled city of Banf. Tashama assumed the rest of the men dismounted to take care of more pleasurable business, while Oshon rode straight with his captive, her, to Prince Aleron's palace. Golden spires, fifteen in number, reached for the clear blue skies while white marble walls connecting the towers shimmered in the sunlight.

Tashama studied the steel gates as they opened, then glanced up at the wall walk. Guards roamed about on top of the wall, though several peered down at her to see the prisoner. She was led into the inner courtyard, where pages hurried to take the men's mounts. The cavalry officer dumped her onto the grassy grounds.

Before she could recover from her unceremonious dismount, he jumped down beside her and yanked her to her feet. She fought crying out this time. She would not allow them to think of her as weak.

The two men hurried her into the palace, and she reached up to tuck a loose curl back into her braid, unraveling from the blue ribbon that once bound it. She studied a royal guard's shining gold trappings when he saluted Oshon with his spear.

When she caught sight of his leering gaze, she quickened her pace to her escort's surprise, and they hurried to catch up to her. Her rubber-soled shoes made nary a sound on the polished ivory floors. Still, the clicking of the metal-edged boots of Oshon and his officer echoed off the peach-tinted, variegated-marble walls, making their arrival all the more pronounced.

Young girls in flowing gowns of opalescent sheers covering opaque satins in vibrant blues, burgundy, purples, and golds fluttered up and down the cris-crossing hallways like butterflies flitting in a marble garden. They stopped only briefly to stare at the oddly dressed prisoner escorted through their residence, then floated away. The sweet-scented, jasmine-like waters they wore drifted in the air with their departure.

Male servants walked toward her, wearing white satin robes

nearly touching the floor like garments worn by the early senators of Rome.

They did not wear trousers like her own people did. She would never have thought... She shook her head. She never realized everything would be so different in Maldovia.

They seemed a pleasant enough people, except for this Oshon, leader of the cavalry and a total brute. But if they learned she ruled the people that were their enemy, or would when she set things right, how would the Maldovians then treat her? Torture her for tactical secrets? Use her to ransom her kingdom?

She shuddered at the notion. For now, her best defense was to keep her lips sealed tight.

When Tashama and her escort arrived at the entrance of the throne room, the royal guard bowed low to Oshon. "Prince Aleron is expecting you in his chambers."

"Surely he wouldn't wish for me to bring *this* to him there." He lifted Tashama's cut arm slightly.

"Carissian is already there and has advised His Highness concerning the prisoner. They're expecting you at once."

Oshon grumbled his displeasure, then pulled Tashama down the next corridor. When they arrived at Aleron's apartments, a man greeted Oshon and turned to Tashama. "I'm Acholuria, the prince's personal guard." He motioned for them to enter.

Satin pillows in a rainbow of colors were piled high in a corner of the room, and a long wooden desk rested against the opposite wall. Taking a deep breath, she tried to calm her sense of fear and frustration. Level-headedness was what she needed to see her through. *How, Balthazar, am I to get myself out of this?*

"Well, what have we here?" a broad-shouldered man asked, stalking into the room. His deep, dark voice drew her in, though she fought the feeling, and she avoided looking at him, innately fearful of what she might see.

He's your enemy, Tashama. Remember that.

"Prince Aleron," Acholuria announced. "Bow before His Highness," he ordered Tashama.

If he were in her palace, he would bow to her, so she had no problem doing so before him in his own palace. She curtseyed the way she remembered to do when she was young. It surprised her to find her memories slowly returning, but it felt odd to curtsey in a pair of jeans and not a gown. She felt like she was in a medieval movie script; she was an extra who had forgotten to dress properly for her role in the film.

The prince sat down on the edge of his desk, then flipped his gold-trimmed, royal-blue, satin cape off his shoulders while he dangled his bare legs over the side.

Her eyes roved over the short cut of his tunic, hiked up some. Muscular legs, like a runner might have, spread apart, and she couldn't help but eye the shadows centered between his legs underneath the tunic. What did men wear under their tunics? Codpieces? Or just some kind of a wrap?

Or like the Highlanders of Earth world, who went commando, did they wear nothing at all? Having spent way too much time considering the matter, she found lifting her gaze from the forbidden area proved harder than she imagined.

His lips smiled almost imperceptibly. Conceited bastard.

She studied his dark hair and eyes. Her breath caught in her throat, and her legs felt like they'd turned to boneless mush.

He was the one from her dreams. *He* was the ruler of Maldovia?

Her heart thumped hard. How could he be the one whose lips tantalized her so? She studied his perfectly muscled arms. Not muscle-bound like bodybuilders, but just developed enough to hold her tight.

Knowing he was not the one for her, she couldn't understand why she wanted him to wrap his arms around her and squeeze so hard she would lose her breath. She...his enemy? What would he want with the likes of her? Did she only imagine he desired her as well? She was disgusted with herself for feeling any wanton desire for her enemy.

You have gotten me into a fine pickle here, Bal... She glanced over at Carissian when he walked into the room. *Ballerina...figure that one out, oh seer of naught. You were trying to read my thoughts from the prince's...* She glanced into the other room. *Bedchamber.*

Her brows lifted slightly, then her gaze shifted to the prince. How could she possibly find a mate and lead her people to victory here? She should never have left Texas.

Carissian cleared his throat. "She's curious about your bedchamber."

The prince's lips curved up maliciously. "Oft you have told me I need to take a love slave, to work off some of the pent-up frustrations I have over this everlasting war." He stood up from the desk, then walked over to her. "The lady I met with earlier, who requested my blissful attentions, did not meet with my expectations. But this wench..."

His love slave! If he even thought for one moment that she would go along with such an absurd notion...

He touched her hair, but she swung her hand to slap his away. Instantly, he caught her wrist. Her heartbeat thundered out of control, and the palms of her hands grew sweaty. The heat of his grip sent electrical charges swirling through her veins at hyperspeed. Resenting his controlling her, she tried to break free, but a devilish smile elevated his lips and reflected in his dark eyes.

"She needs to be stripped of her clothes and scrubbed clean first. I wish to consider her further. I couldn't bed someone as unkempt as this." He stared at the skin around her eyes, then turned to face Carissian, his voice changing instantly from amusement to barely contained anger. "The area around her eyes is darkened like a raccoon's. I thought it was merely dirt, but it appears she has been injured. Did my men do this to the woman?"

"Nay, sire," Carissian said quickly. "We found her like that, watching us from the woods near the lake."

"She looks similar to the one..." Aleron quit speaking and shook his head.

"Karthlander women all look the same," Oshon growled from the threshold.

Tashama swallowed, her throat feeling as parched as if she'd crossed the Arizona desert without a drop of water to drink. Had the prince shared the same dreams with her? Did he recognize her from them?

"What do you think, Carissian?" He touched her cheek.

She meant to swat away his hand, but he seized her free wrist and raised a brow. Clenching her teeth, she fought the urge to tell him to go to hell.

"I think, sire, you will find the siren a deadly advisory in bed, or otherwise. My advice to you is to select a genteel lady from our staff. Send this one to your castle in the south, under strictest guard."

"Clean her up." Aleron released her and folded his arms. "I haven't had a good battle for a fortnight. We will see who the victor will be."

Carissian spoke to Aleron in private, though Tashama read the words on his lips. "And if she is the witch of your dreams, sire?"

Aleron glanced back at her. "Then she'll earn her pay for keeping me awake one more night."

3

A leron leaned forward on the desk. "Truly Carissian, she doesn't look to be much of a threat to me." He stared at the discoloration around her eyes and frowned. "You are sure my men did not injure her?"

"We found her like this, sire. She was alone."

He cursed the interest he had in the woman. Would his soldiers not see him as weak for desiring the wench, an enemy of his people? "Are we certain she is a Karthlander?"

"Yes, sire, she's very much a Karthlander. I would be wary of this one," Carissian said. "She's dangerous to you and the realm."

Aleron took a deep breath, wondering how the woman could be a danger to him. She wore no weapon, had been injured, was of slight build, and...

His gaze shifted to her breasts. "What *are* these garments she wears?"

Carissian shook his head. "I've never seen anything like it before."

"Does she speak?"

"She hides her thoughts from me. I gather bits and pieces, but she veils them in other notions. Still, I feel she's mystified at her circumstances." He rubbed his smooth chin. "Something has gone wrong, and she's not supposed to be here."

Aleron laughed out loud. "Even *I* could have figured *that* out. Why was a female Karthlander caught so close to the palace? Is she a spy?" But her clothes, and the scent of her skin...provocative, luring, and goddess, yes, the same as the woman from his dreams. Yet the blackness around her eyes had disguised her, confusing him at first. "What *is* that fragrance she wears?"

He sniffed at her neck. She tensed her posture, making him smile. "Sweeter than neferatu—more powerful than barberessa, but subtler than agathan. I cannot tell what it is."

Tashama wrinkled her nose at him. Joy, but their primitive people would never be able to produce such a heavenly scent. His breath warmed the sensitive skin of her neck, tantalizing her to distraction. *Caress me further, prince of my dreams.*

Carissian folded his arms. "Joy, is what she says it is."

Glaring at Carissian, she attempted to clear her thoughts. *Meddling sorcerer.* Her sensitive touch felt the heat from the prince's body so close to hers. Closing her eyes, she took a deep breath and enjoyed the spicy scent he wore. *Joy is what I feel when you are close to me.* She looked at Carissian and said, "*Not! Begone, oh sorcererly one!*"

Again, she tried to hide her feelings from the sorcerer's probes.

"Joy," the prince said. "Appropriate." Glancing down at her turtleneck, a perceptible smile crept across his face. He looked at her pale blue jeans, then turned back to Carissian. "She wears the oddest shaped men's leggings of an indescribable cloth, but then is clothed in a tunic to reveal her feminine stature in bountiful proportion. If she were trying to disguise herself as a soldier, why would she wear something so revealing as this?" Aleron waved his hand at her, brushing her nipples with a light touch.

She ground her teeth, fighting the flame that surged through her body with his fleeting touch. Didn't he know how that simple form of intimacy had weakened her knees and created an ache she craved to have satisfied?

He considered her shoes. "Her feet have little protection, she wore no weapons—I'm to understand, and yet," he said, then grabbed her arm and studied her torn sleeve, "she has been wounded in battle."

"I cannot read her thoughts, my lord. They're confused and scattered. I see strange signs she voices in her mind—Scarborough Renaissance Faire, Waco, 45 miles, *Dungeon Siege*. She feeds me these unreal images of buildings towering into the sky, blocking out the sunlight with their translucent structures.

"Wagons move without the pull of horses, rushing down seamless stone roads. I hear strange beats in a primitive form of rhythm through her ears, perhaps a new sound that leads her into battle. She fights my presence. I've never known one of their kind to have that type of ability."

Aleron caught sight of gold glittering through the torn sleeve of her right arm, then he lifted the cloth, revealing a gold chain hugging her wrist. He fingered the bracelet linked together in golden wedges like the shape of geese in formation, then frowned.

"What metal is this?" He peeled back the sleeve of her left arm, then touched the emerald and diamond-studded gold bracelet on her left wrist and shook his head.

"The metal appears to be the same, except it's smooth in part and intricately crafted into tiny chains that connect the rest. I've never seen anything like it." He glanced up at Carissian, who shook his head in response. "These stones come from our mountains nearby. How could the Karthlanders have stolen our precious gems without having paid the price?" The prince examined the clasp that bound each of the bracelets. "Have you seen anything as odd as this?"

"No, sire."

"I want them removed at once." He walked around Tashama in

a narrow circle and turned to his sorcerer. "Why would a woman warrior be wearing such things? Only the nobility is allowed to wear jewelry."

"I've never heard of the Karthlanders resorting to using women warriors, sire." Carissian examined one of the bracelets. "Perhaps one of our metal workers could determine what the metal is."

The prince motioned to his sorcerer. "Remove them then."

"I'm not sure how to remove them. They're not long enough to slide over her wrist."

"Remove the chains, prisoner!" the prince demanded.

She complied in the slowest manner she could manage as the two men looked on. *I should have taken martial arts like I wanted to, but nooo. I had to work on potions and spells.* She sighed deeply. *A little Kung Fu and I could have given this better-than-thou prince a little what for.*

Twisting her mouth in annoyance, she shook her head inadvertently. *Couldn't do that though, could I? Not befitting the soon-to-be ruler of...*

She glanced at Carissian whose eyes slimmed as he studied her. *"Ruler of naught...put that in your peace pipe and smoke it, oh sorcerer, reader of minds, discerner of nothing."*

"How did she do it?" the prince asked, when she dropped the first bracelet into his outstretched hand.

Her skin touched his briefly, and the warmth from his touch made her shudder. He was her enemy, and yet, she desired nothing more than to have his lips pressed hard against hers. *What spell is it that binds me to you, prince of Maldovia?*

"It appears to have some kind of a clasp. Our head jeweler can examine the bracelets and tell us how they've done such a thing."

Aleron shook his head when she dropped the second bracelet into his greedy palm. He pocketed the bracelets into a leather pouch tied to his belt, then touched Tashama's cheek where dried blood crusted in a streak. His fingers lingered longer than was proper, and Carissian frowned at the gesture.

The prince quickly dropped his hand, then turned to his personal guard. "Acholuria, bring me my sword and yours, too."

His guard disappeared into the prince's bedchambers, while Carissian asked, "What do you propose to do, my lord?"

"I'm curious about this warrior woman. Would she fight as well as a man? I would think not." He took a deep breath and studied the Karthlander, an enemy of his people. How could she be a menace to him, Ruler of all Maldovia? Women were meant to provide a man pleasure, nothing more. How could she be a danger?

Still, Carissian had never been wrong before. She clasped her hands together. She appeared so hardened, so unbending, and yet, there was a sweet softness about her. Did she give this other outward appearance because she feared him?

Acholuria reappeared with swords in hand, and after offering Aleron's jewel-encrusted sword to him, he waited for further instruction.

"Give her your sword, Acholuria." Aleron pointed his sword at her chest.

Carissian cleared his throat. "Do you think it wise—"

"Do it!"

The guard handed his ivory-handled sword to Tashama, but when she folded her arms in response, Aleron laughed. "Make her take it!"

Acholuria grabbed Tashama's arm, but she cried out in pain, and he glanced back at Aleron. The prince rubbed his chin and considered her disheveled appearance. "Perhaps our healer should—"

Carissian shook his head. "The Karthlander's healer should see to the woman. However, from what I can see, her injuries are negligible."

The prince nodded and motioned for his guard to get on with

the task. Acholuria shoved the sword into Tashama's hand. Aleron readied his sword while he planted his feet apart and raised his free hand slightly in the air. She frowned at him and dropped the sword on the marble floor with a resounding clatter.

The prince stared at her for a moment, not believing she wouldn't even try to fight him. "She's no threat to me." The prince handed his sword to Acholuria. "If she wishes to presume to be a warrior, house her with the rest of her kind. A woman like that would not be worthy for a prince to bed."

"Would sending her to the prison camp be wise, my lord?" Carissian considered her appearance. "A woman amongst all those men and dressed as provocatively as she is…"

"She is dangerous—so you say. What else am I to do with her, Carissian?"

"She'll be even more dangerous to you there, I predict."

"I would bed the wench if she were a Maldovian." He folded his arms. "Perhaps she should stay in the tower in case the witch invades my dreams tonight." He reached over and stroked her jaw with his fingertips.

When she fisted her hand and tried to strike him in the chin, he quickly caught her wrist. "Then she could relieve my anxiety, when the other cannot." He laughed, released her, and motioned to Carissian. "Take her away to the enemy prison camp."

BLACKNESS BLANKETED the region when Tashama rode on horseback to the walled-in tent village, confining over a hundred Karthlander soldiers. She studied the prisoners sitting about the small campfires scattered about the campsite. Eerie twisting fingers of light crept into the shadows while the fragrance of burning hickory scented the air.

Oshon motioned to his officer, who, in response, grabbed

Tashama's arm and threw her to the ground. She landed on her backside with a thud and stifled a cry.

"Rot here with the rest of your compatriots," Oshon scowled, then turned his horse with the other and headed beyond the gates, their horses clip-clopping out of camp. For the first time since her nightmare had begun, she felt truly afraid.

"Balthazar, how could you have forsaken me?" She took a deep breath. She hadn't remembered the war. He was right in saying she had to lead their people to victory, but...

She shook her head when her thoughts reverted to the palace of Banff. Even now, she could see Aleron's dark eyes studying hers. What magic was his that he used to hold her hostage?

Tashama pulled her torn sleeves down over her arms, the lacerations now burning in the cool breeze. She remained seated in the dark, afraid to move from the small comfort she drew from the deep shadows. She cringed at the sound of the crunching of boots on the graveled path that headed in her direction.

She shivered from the cold when more boots tromped her way, but couldn't force herself to get up and move away from the menacing sound of their footfalls.

4

"What is it?" a gruff man asked, leaning down to look at Tashama. She shrank deeper into the shadows.

"I cannot tell. It's too dark over here."

Panic coursed through her blood, worried when they discovered she was a woman. Then what?

"Is he wounded? Why doesn't he speak?"

"What is that sweet scent?"

One of the men touched Tashama's shoulder, and she cried out to their surprise and her own. "It's a woman." He took a step back.

"You're mistaken. They wouldn't have thrown a woman in here like this."

"Are you hurt?"

"I'm—I'm all right," Tashama said.

"Can you stand?" He touched her arm.

"Ah!" she cried out when his jagged fingernails poked at the cuts on her arm.

"She's hurt." His voice was shadowed with concern. "Get the healer."

"No, no, really, I'm all right." She tried to stand.

"No, miss, just sit."

"Who is she?" one of the men whispered.

"Tashama." Her voice was soft and high compared to the men's deep voices, and she felt more out of place than before.

Deadly silence prevailed, then hushed voices encircled her when the word soon spread concerning the woman in the prisoners' midst.

"That name is forbidden to us."

"Where is she?" a hurried voice asked, his light footsteps treading on the ground close by.

A torch was brought to bear on her. She squinted at the sight of the bright light and covered her sensitive eyes. A renewed rush of voices ensued.

"She's not one of us!"

"Yes, but she's not one of them either."

"What is she?"

The healer leaned over her and touched her hair, tangled in her ribbon now with more of it undone from the braid than not.

"My arms." She stared into his blue eyes as dark and deep as the lake she'd been to earlier. His ash-blond hair hung loosely about his narrow shoulders. "They were cut by…"

"They attack our women now!" one of the men shouted.

The cry was repeated throughout the gathering crowd. Sentries rushed to double the guard, and several shouted orders on top of the high walls to watch for trouble.

The healer rubbed his smooth, pointed chin. "Carry her to my tent."

"I can walk, for heaven's sakes." She attempted again to rise.

One of the men grabbed her up, then cradled her in his arms. He headed toward the healer's tent, ignoring her protests. His lumbering gait rocked her back and forth like a rowboat on an unsettled sea. "You're not one of ours," he said.

Tashama frowned at the bulky brute of a man. His body odor repelled her. She tried not to breathe. "Who is in charge here?"

"General Karam. He'll wish to question you, but after the healer has seen to your wounds."

Nearing the tent, she observed a circle of fair-haired, strapping men wearing brown leather tunics and leggings, standing around the lighted area, gaping at her. She was carried inside the hospital tent, where twenty cots were lined up across the back. Only two were empty. Several of the wounded prisoners sat up on their thin mattresses when the man laid her in one of the vacant beds.

"She's shivering hard," he said.

Tashama's teeth chattered when she opened her mouth to speak. "I must lead my people."

The slightly built healer nodded and pulled up her sleeves, using caution. "She's delirious. Cover her with the blanket, Sergeant." The healer motioned to a shelf filled with woolen blankets. "You, there, Private," he said to a man peeking through the tent entrance, "make yourself useful and get some of those aloverat leaves for me."

Tashama wrinkled her forehead. "I cannot stay here."

The sergeant pulled the blanket over Tashama, while the healer grabbed a candle and shone it into her left eye. She closed her eyes.

"Hand me a cup of that tea," the healer ordered.

"But the general wishes to speak to her, and it'll make her..."

"Yes, yes. Do as I say."

The sergeant shuffled off to get the tea while the private stood by with the aloverat leaves. "Wet them down in the solution in that pan," the healer said.

When the sergeant brought the tea to him, he helped Tashama to sit.

"What is this for?" She breathed in the minty-moist fragrance. The steam rose to the tip of her nose.

"To warm you."

She nodded, then sipped the concoction. "It tastes like mint julep." Her face warmed, then her body slowly heated as the mixture circulated through her system.

You thought I would be mistreated here, Aleron, but my people are good to me. They warm me as the heat of your body did.

She swung her legs over the edge of the mattress.

"Whoa." The healer grabbed her arm and pushed her legs back onto the cot. "You must stay in bed and drink the rest of the tea."

"I feel warmer already." Her words sounded slightly slurred.

"More," the healer insisted.

"I'm not able to drink..."

"She's not like our women at all." The sergeant shook his head.

"Drink the rest, miss."

Tashama studied the sergeant's light blond hair, cropped short in a military manner, and finished the tea. Her eyes met his amber ones, then she touched his hand. "You'll be free soon."

The healer helped her to lie down, but the sergeant's mouth gaped open. The healer shook his head. "Her words are not her own."

"Are you sure she has not the gift, Healer Throckmorton?"

"She hasn't." He studied her left arm and brushed away the glass still clinging to her skin. She closed her eyes. "She's sleeping now."

In a dreamlike state, Tashama found herself listening in on the conversation of the men while her body felt imprisoned on the hospital bed.

"What do you make of her?" the sergeant asked.

"I don't know." The healer brushed the glass from her right arm. "Get me the green box on top of that chest."

She opened her eyes, only able to see their actions in a hazy, ghostlike fog.

The sergeant returned with the brass box and handed it to the healer. He dug around in the container, then pulled out a thread and a needle. Afterward, he slipped the threaded needle through her skin. The silver sliver moved in and out...in and out...with a calm, methodical manner. She turned her head when one of the wounded men climbed off his bed.

"They're not injuring our women now, are they?"

The sergeant folded his arms. "She's not one of us."

Tashama opened her lips slightly to speak, but found the words wouldn't come. *I am too*, she tried to say.

After wrapping her arms in the leaves and covering them with a linen wrap, the healer moved his chair next to the cot. She stared at him through the mist, and her eyes locked onto his. *The prince...why can he not be kind like you?* Her thoughts drifted to the palace where Aleron had sat on his desk.

Muscular legs with just enough hair to make them sexy...not beastly. She sighed deeply.

"Is she awake? She cannot be. Nobody can stay awake after drinking *the* tea." The sergeant shuffled his feet.

"She's not awake. Just dreaming." The healer turned to the private. "Give me some of those cold compresses."

"But her eyes are half open. She watches you; she watches me."

The healer shook his head. "She hears not a thing, nor can she see. When she awakes, she'll remember nothing."

Balthazar, where are you? Tashama wrinkled her nose as the pungent odor from the compresses touched her nostrils. *You could have given that sorcerer of Aleron's a taste of his own magic.* She smiled broadly. *Then again, I could have, too. No, Balthazar said, be careful...be careful. But he wasn't supposed to abandon me either.*

She tried to roll onto her side. The healer and sergeant turned her onto her back.

The healer applied the cool compresses to her eyes. "These will help to draw out the discoloration from her skin."

"Did they beat her?"

No, Tashama attempted to answer, but her lips wouldn't obey.

"I cannot imagine so—they don't beat our men."

"Where's the woman?" a voice boomed.

"Lower your voice, General," the healer warned.

A cold, wet cloth wiped her cheek.

"Did they do this to her?"

No, Tashama tried to respond.

"She's sleeping. I had to sew her wounds. Questioning her is *your* line of business."

"*Fighting* is my line of business."

Tashama felt the warmth of the general's body drawing close. *Aleron*, she thought, *your body next to mine...your breath on my cheek. How I long to be held tightly.* She reached out to touch him. Hands pushed her grasping fingers away.

"The damage?"

"She had cuts on her arms—some deep enough to require the needle."

"From swords, daggers—what?"

Glass.

"We're not certain. I've never seen such a weapon before, like shards of ice that don't melt."

"Who is she?"

Tashama, her mind tried to force her tongue to say.

"She used a name forbidden to us, General."

She waited with great anticipation to hear the forbidden name.

"*Tashama*," the sergeant said, his voice a harsh whisper.

EARLY THE NEXT MORNING, Tashama listened to the sounds of men's murmured voices in the tent hospital. "They say she is Tashama."

"She cannot be. She's dead."

Her brows lifted slightly. Light drifted toward her, and she opened her eyes while the veins of leaves screened them. The leaves were pulled away, and the light burned her eyes. She quickly closed them.

When she opened them again, she watched the healer study her face. He nodded. "The discoloration is gone. You certainly look more human today." He unwrapped her left arm. "I'm afraid I was so busy attending to your wounds, I neglected to ask your name."

"It's..." The healer touched the stitches he had sewn, then, recalling the fuss her name had caused the last time she mentioned it, she said, "Mary."

The healer's eyes grew big, he sat back in his chair, and stared at her. "Mary?"

"Well, yes, isn't that all right?"

"I've never heard of such an unusual name before." He examined her right arm. "How old are you?"

"Well, if a woman will tell you her age, she'll tell you anything."

The healer frowned at her.

"It's a joke. I'm twenty-three."

"Are you linked?"

"Linked?"

"Do you have a mate?"

"I'm supposed to have."

"Who?"

"I don't know. Bal...Balfour was supposed to tell me who this prince of my dreams would be, but then again, he wasn't supposed to have dumped me in the middle of Maldovia either."

"Balfour?"

"My dear friend."

"What happened to him?"

"I'm not certain." She winced as Healer Throckmorton touched the deepest laceration.

"You're not a Maldovian then?"

Tashama stared into the healer's blue eyes. "Do I *look* like a Maldovian?"

He shook his head. "You're too fair. But you're not one of us."

"Because?"

He fingered the sleeve of her turtleneck. "Your garments. I've never seen such strange clothes in my life."

"I got used to it just fine."

"What village do you hail from?"

"I don't remember."

The healer eyed her suspiciously, and she shrugged. "Bal... Balfour was supposed to instruct me..."

"Instruct you?"

"Reintroduce me to my people. I've been away for a while." Tashama squirmed on the cot. Her answers must have sounded strange.

"To?"

She said nothing in response.

"We don't know what to make of you, young lady."

"I want to see the general."

"Our women don't make demands of us."

"Oh?" Her eyes grew round. Standing up from the mattress, she grew dizzy. She grabbed the healer's shoulder, and he helped her sit on the bed.

"You might feel a little groggy until after you've eaten."

"Can I eat soon so I can see the general?"

"Our jailers will feed us soon."

The rumbling wagon wheels rolling into the compound announced the meal was on its way. Not long after, a young man hurried to bring Tashama's pewter plate to her.

His hand brushed hers, and she glanced up to study his eyes for a moment. "You'll help lead the revolt." She looked at the roasted chicken, stewed tomatoes, and garden lettuce sitting on the plate. "I expected wormy bread and potatoes—nothing like this."

"What does she mean?" The soldier stared at her.

"She has the gift," one of the wounded men said.

The healer attempted to change the subject. "They feed us well —as we feed their prisoners in kind."

She took a bite of the chicken. "With food like this, who would want to escape?" She licked her fingers of the lemon-and-pepper spices flavoring the home-grown fowl.

The healer shook his head. "Nobody is to escape, miss. It's just our way."

"Does she truly have the gift?" the soldier asked.

"You have other wounded to feed." The healer motioned for the soldier to leave the tent. Healer Throckmorton turned his attention to Tashama. "You should not say such things to the men, miss."

She poked at her stewed fruit with her three-pronged fork. "You're not serious? You mean, no one has tried to dig tunnels or slip under the food wagon when it leaves the compound or wear the guards' uniforms to make their escape?"

"Of course not, miss."

She grimaced and lifted a lettuce leaf off her plate. "*I won't* stay here any longer than *I* have to."

"How do you propose to leave?" The healer's voice rose slightly as if surprised.

"I would have to check out the lay of the camp first—watch the comings and goings of the guard—that sort of thing." Tashama had seen enough World War II prisoner-of-war movies to know how it was done.

Several soldiers entered the tent with the remaining wounded men's plates, and one offered to take Tashama's empty dish. When she held her plate up to him, he grabbed her wrist, startling her. She looked into his eyes. "You have a new baby boy."

The man stared at her and stuttered, "It...it's true. She has the gift."

The healer studied her, but before he could speak, a soldier rushed into the tent. "The prince has arrived!"

"Aleron?" The healer's brows knit together, and he quickly stood up from his stool.

"Yes." The man motioned to Tashama. "They say it's because of the woman he comes."

The healer licked his lips. "He has never made an appearance here before, and I've been the healer at the compound for over a year."

"The general says she's not to be trusted. He says…"

"I don't care what the general says. Leave us."

Tashama stood and found her legs steady again. She walked over to the tent's entrance and peeked out.

The prince sat tall in his saddle. The brilliant red tunic he wore shimmered in the golden rays of the sun, contrasting with his dark brown hair. His sandal ties, made of black leather, intertwined up his well-developed legs, matching the swirls of ebony thread that twisted in intricate patterns on his tunic.

A shirt with blowsy sleeves in gold accompanied this, while he wore a gold sash across his chest. His jewel-encrusted sword rode at his side like his ever-faithful companion. His dark eyes searched the prisoners standing in packs while they watched him.

Tashama's heart pounded way too rapidly. Annoyed with feeling so affected by his presence, she gripped the tent flap fiercely. Her fingers hurt from the pressure of the heavy cloth. She tried to refocus her thoughts from admiring the sight of the prince to the pain tormenting the tips of her fingers. Her desire was torn between wanting to run as far away from him as she could and having him hold her close so she could feel his heartbeat thumping against hers.

The healer joined her. "He searches for you."

"Can you cover me up in my bed, and I can pretend to be asleep?"

"One of the guards has pointed to the tent."

She sighed deeply. "I don't want to see this tyrant of a man further."

"He has spoken to you?"

"Certainly." She scratched her head and looked around the canvas room. "Maybe I could hide under the bed."

Several of the wounded men laughed. One said, "You may hide under my covers with me, my lady."

Her cheeks warmed. "Thank you, no."

A shadow stretched across the floor, and she turned when the prince stalked through the entrance.

5

———

Three of his royal guard joined Aleron while one shoved the healer out of his path as he entered the healing tent, intent on learning how the woman fared.

"You have no right," Tashama said with indignation.

The healer interrupted her, "I'm all right, miss."

Her words were feminine, like she was, though harsh with condemnation. Aleron studied Tashama's face with amazement at the transformation that had taken place from the last time he'd seen her. Now, he was sure she was the witch who visited his dreams, but last night she had not come to him.

Was it because of her injuries? The healer would have given her the tea to help heal them. Did that make her incapable of coming to him in the night?

He should have been grateful, but all it did was force him to come to see her again today, to ensure she was all right. To ensure she was not a figment of his overwrought imagination. Even though she had not slipped into his dreams, he still hadn't slept well at all because of worrying about her safety.

He reached for her hand. She stepped back. He motioned to his guard, who grabbed her arm, then held it out to him. Glancing at the healer, the prince tilted his head slightly, causing the healer to step forward and pull her sleeve up. The prince caught her twisting her mouth in annoyance while she frowned at him. Stifling a smile, he signaled the guard to show her other arm to him.

Aleron's fingers touched her skin with the gentlest of caresses, avoiding contact with her wounds. Without Carissian objecting, he enjoyed prolonging the gesture. After examining her injuries, he opened his mouth to speak, then closed it.

Reconsidering, he said, "You have a tongue."

"Certainly, and you have yet to hear it."

He tilted his head back slightly and considered Tashama's ivory complexion and gem-quality green eyes. His eyes roamed over her naturally blond hair, striated with fine strands of gold and honey drifting over her shoulders now in ruffled waves past her slim hips.

His smile returned when he studied her turtleneck drawn snugly over her breasts. His brows rose slightly in amusement, then he chuckled when her full pink lips pursed with irritation.

She was lovelier than anyone he could have imagined, although she was only a Karthlander woman. Yet there was something more about her. Even Carissian sensed something unusual. His gaze rested on her inviting mouth, and he shook his head. Since her capture, he'd been unable to think of anything else.

He sighed deeply. His women wore colored waxes to enhance the appearance of their lips, but this woman needed no such coloration. Perfectly formed and pink as the frizolan when in full bloom, she didn't need to improve their luscious color. With just a little persuasion, he knew her lips would succumb to his.

He motioned for her to sit on the bed. She folded her arms. Aleron waved to one of his guards, who yanked her to the mattress. Sitting on the bed, she glared back at Aleron.

He sat on the stool the healer had used and studied her further. "Who are you?"

The question wasn't meant to be answered...just his thinking out loud. He rubbed his silky chin.

"My jewelers are baffled by the chains you wore. Only royalty can wear such a thing." He furrowed his brow. "Are you a thief?"

The healer and the other prisoners waited on the edges of their seats for Tashama's answers. Aleron shook his head. "You are nobody."

~

WHY HAVE you come to see me, then...a nobody...when you have never before visited the compound? Why do you sit here undressing me with hungry eyes? A nobody wouldn't be worth a smidgeon of your time, great prince.

Tashama was glad Carissian wasn't around to read her mind. She'd hold her tongue in the prince's presence with her own people sitting in audience, but she could think as freely as she wanted.

Aleron touched the ribbed edge of her doubled-over collar. The prince's fingers stretched the material. *You're as curious as that silly Maine Coon cat I used to have. But I'm not your mouse to play with.*

She studied Aleron's gaze while he seemed to take in every measure of her figure...the spread of her narrow shoulders and her slim hips, then his focus centered on the points of interest beneath her turtleneck.

The wounded prisoners watched his attentions to her. "You're no threat to me." The prince rose, turned on his heel, and stormed out of the healer's tent.

"Just you wait and see," Tashama said under her breath. *And yes, despite realizing my feelings for you are wrong, I want to share your bed. But, it will never be, prince of Maldovia.*

She turned to the healer. "I noticed when I arrived last night that the guards had only a few posted when it would be easier for our people to escape. Why is this?"

"I do suppose they feel we would never be able to find a way through the mountains to Karthland."

"Nonsense. Our people can do anything they set their minds to do."

"They'll get themselves killed."

"They'll be free. Living here kills the spirit. If this war goes on forever, won't the body die here, too—never knowing the freedom to live? Never to be with family and friends? I lost that freedom once." Tashama looked down at her hands. "I never realized how much I longed to be with my family and friends until I was torn away from them. I didn't realize it until now. I was just as much in a prison where I was, hiding until I was able to return and resume..." The words she almost said died on her lips. "I *will* return home."

"To a place you do not know."

She took a deep breath. "I will remember it again."

"To find a mate you know not."

"In time."

"Do you truly have the gift?"

"They seem to think so." Tashama waved her hand at the camp.

The healer gave her a small smile. "If nothing else, you sure have been entertaining, miss."

Tashama peered out of the tent. The prince and his entourage mounted their horses at the gate, and she walked out into the open. Several of the prisoners caught sight of her, and an unexpected roar of cheers erupted. The prince and his men turned to watch her.

She motioned for everyone to be quiet. A guard uniformed in the same manner as the palace guard at Banff caught her eye, and she shuddered to see the sight.

"What's wrong?" the healer asked.

"Who's the guard standing on the wall walk?"

"Aleron's own palace guard."

She took a deep breath when the prince and his men headed

out of the compound. "They're watching me. They'll come for me soon, I fear."

"To what end?"

"That—I don't know."

Tashama walked back into the tent with the healer. "Was a mapmaker taken prisoner?"

"Yes, miss, but..."

"I don't believe the general will allow me to speak to his men. Will you have the mapmaker illustrate enough maps for"—she counted in the air—"fifteen men?"

"Will you lead them?"

Tashama smiled. "A woman? Surely you jest?" Walking over to the cots where one of the wounded men rested, she touched his shoulder, felt his essence, his future life in the palm of her hand. "You'll live long enough to marry your girl back home and spend an eternity with her." He beamed, grabbed her hand, and squeezed it tightly.

She made her way to the next bed. She touched the man's cheek and smiled. "You have a new young'un at home, and you'll soon be there to bounce him on your knee."

"A boy? After six girls, I'm finally going to have a boy!"

"Do not touch me, woman!" the next man scowled. "My life grows dimmer with every breath I take." Though she intended to pass him by at his request, he grabbed her wrist and twisted it hard.

"Ah!" she cried out, tears filling her eyes when his fingers dug into her cuts.

"Let her go!" several of the men shouted from their beds.

"What is this?" the general demanded, storming into the tent.

"You're hurting my wrist!" Tashama cried out and tried to pry the man's fingers from her arm when they dug deeper into the wound. His thoughts intermingled with hers; her heart thundered. The general grabbed the man's hand and wrenched it free, while the healer administered a sedative to the patient. "He murdered his very own family," Tashama said under her breath and sank to her knees.

"Stay away from my men, woman!" the general shouted as the healer helped her back to her bed.

"Are you General Karam?" she asked, not to be cowed.

"You're not to speak to anyone here, do you understand?"

"She has the gift, General," one of the patients said.

The general shook his head. "She's tricking you."

Tashama stood. "I must leave here. I cannot stay. I must find Bal, Balfour. I cannot understand why he has not come for me before now." *He would know what I have to do.*

"This Balfour...is he one of Prince Aleron's men? Why has he sent you here?" the general demanded.

"What?" Tashama stared at him in disbelief. He thought she was a spy for the prince? She headed for the entrance of the tent, then turned to face him. "You may be a great leader on the battle-field, but you have a lot to learn about diplomacy."

Tashama hurried outside, where the men had dispersed according to the general's orders. She walked to the west wall and began surveying the perimeter of the camp. A quarter of the distance around the barrier, she noticed the guards on the wall walk studying her movements.

She took a deep breath, then turned to find the prisoners watching her while they stood in clusters about the camp. Turning her gaze back to the wall, she ran her hand over the moss-covered stone structure. When she came to a set of stairs winding up to the top of the wall walk, she made a mental note of its location.

A bird nestled in an alcove caught her eye. *Aleron cannot keep you here any longer than he can imprison me.* She paused, envisioning the sight of the prince sitting proudly upon his steed. *You could not stay away from me, oh prince. I didn't think I would have such an effect on you.* She grabbed a curl tickling her cheek and tucked it behind her ear.

What did you think, prince of my dreams? That you would send me here to silence me? The tips of her fingers touched the sun-drenched moss. *Your skin is as soft and warm.* She closed her eyes. *Your fingers on my skin stir longings I dare not reveal to your sorcerer. If he were to know I am the true ruler of Karthland…* She shuddered. *I could be a pawn used to obtain concessions against my very own people.*

"Sire, you're scheduled to see the Alsate's ambassador," Carissian said.

The prince continued to pace. "Tell me why the Karthlander woman is so dangerous. You haven't given me one good reason." He stopped only long enough to glower at his advisor. "You should have seen the way her people cheered her. I've never seen a woman affect a group of men so. Never." He renewed his pacing.

"Sire, the—"

"Her green eyes distract me."

Carissian shook his head. "Sire, you—"

"She shouldn't have been taken to the compound. She's stirring up trouble there, don't you sense it?"

"The woman is a—"

"She is nobody. How can she rouse the men so?" The prince took a deep breath. "The Karthlander healer cared for her injuries adequately, but she shouldn't have been left there." He sat down on his throne.

"Should I have the ambassador shown—"

The prince jumped up from his seat. "She cannot stay there. You should've advised me better, Carissian." He strode out of the throne room.

Carissian hurried after him. "Sire, I can see what you have in mind, but—"

"Then you already know what I will do."

BY LATE AFTERNOON, Tashama had surveyed the grounds. Now, she sat on a stone bench to monitor the movements of the guards.

"Are you really going to try to escape, miss?" a voice said from a little way off.

Twelve men stood ten feet behind her.

She nodded, then turned her attention to the gate when a wagon rolled into the compound. She noted the time as the men lined up for supper. "All very civilized."

"Do you have the gift?" one of the men asked.

"We're not to converse, gentlemen, by order of your general."

"Are you really Tashama?" another asked.

"Really, gentlemen, I wouldn't wish you ill tidings."

Before she could join the others for her food, the first one in line hurried to bring the plate to her. "Why, thank you." She took the plate from him, and as she touched his hand, her eyes grew big.

"What's wrong, miss?" He steadied her plate.

"She touched you. She has the gift," one of the men hurried to say, growing closer to Tashama.

"What did you see, miss?"

"Your general—he doesn't want me to speak with you—any of you."

"What did you see, miss?" the man persisted.

She smiled. "You'll escape from here in two days."

"And me?" another said, grabbing her arm.

"Oh!" she cried out.

"Forgive me, miss." He dropped to his knees.

"Yes, you, too, only my arms—they still hurt."

Another knelt before her. "And me?"

General Karam, his blond hair and beard striped with gray, his face appearing to redden as he stormed across the compound toward her. "Please—gentlemen, the general is headed this way."

"We want to know, too," several said.

Tashama shoved her plate into the man's hands who had delivered it to her, then ran her hand over several who stood before her. "Yes, all of you. And you'll return safely to your villages, too."

"And you?"

She shook her head and sat on the bench. "I cannot see what fate awaits me."

The men all stepped back from her. The general closed the gap between them. He folded his arms across his broad chest and glared at her. She reached for her platter, and the general commanded, "You'll return to the healer's tent at once!" He surveyed his men for a moment, then turned to her. "You screamed out in pain when one of my men accosted you."

"He hadn't meant to."

"Return to the tent, now!"

"You have no business telling me what to do." She tilted her head in defiance. He pointed to the tent, and she nodded. "For now, you'll have your way, but not for long, General."

She would do what he ordered, only because she didn't want Aleron's guards to get wind of the fact that she was Tashama, rightful ruler of Karthland.

LATER THAT EVENING, Tashama met with the fifteen men at the eastern wall. "Seven will leave tonight. If all goes as planned, the others will escape tomorrow night. They don't do counts of our people, so they won't notice when people are missing."

After the guards changed shifts, Tashama led the men up the wall walk stairs and, finding their way clear, she motioned to the parapet where they hurried to tie the braided hemp. She stared in the direction of Banff and the palace where she assumed Aleron would be settling in for the night.

What do you wear when you slip between your princely sheets? Do you have thoughts of me when you close your dark eyes? She frowned. *Even when my eyes are wide open as they are tonight, I can see only you.*

"What about you, miss?" the last of the men said, holding the rope out to her.

Startled, she glanced at him. "I'll join you and the others as soon as I can."

The men took turns dashing into the tall brush near the prison walls. They disappeared into the moonless night, and she gave a tentative sigh of relief.

"The guards," one of the lookouts said, quickly removing the rope.

Tashama and the men scurried down the steps and hurried away from the wall. "Tomorrow night at the same time."

The healer joined her. "The general is on his way to do a bed check, miss."

"A bed check? For everyone?"

"No." He smiled at her. "Just for you."

Before she was halfway across the compound, the general blocked her path. He glowered at her, seized her wrist, and dragged her to the hospital tent. "What do you think you're doing, young lady?" He shoved her to her cot.

"Aiding my people to escape, such as you should have done since you've been imprisoned here."

"I will not escape from this place, as it is not our way. Those who do will soon be recaptured and sent to a compound where they will be starved or worse for their disobedience."

"You won't escape from here, General, but you're the only one.

Tomorrow, there'll be an officer exchange. You'll be returned to Karthland then."

A surge of shouts beyond the tent muffled the clanking of metal boots as they neared the canvas entrance.

Her heart hammering, Tashama stood up from the cot. *Aleron.* "He has come for me."

6

The tent flap jerked aside while torchlight cast shadows into the hospital. The royal guard studied Tashama for a second, then announced over his shoulder, "She is here, Your Highness."

Aleron walked into the tent dressed entirely in black. His smile stretched across his face, and she folded her arms.

Oshon entered the tent, and the prince motioned to her. "Bring her with us." He hurried outside.

"You're to come with me." Several of the prisoners had taken up position at the entrance of the tent, and Oshon said to her, "If you make any trouble for us, we'll start killing prisoners."

Tashama kissed the healer on the cheek. "I'll see you again."

Cheers resounded when she waved her hand at the men while the royal guards flanked her. "We *will* be free!" she shouted, then walked with the royal guard, the crowd following her to the gates.

The camp guards doubled their numbers and bolted up the stairs to the wall walk while the ones in the compound unsheathed their swords.

Aleron watched the imprisoned soldiers stir into a frenzy. Oshon boosted Tashama into the saddle of a horse. As they rode from the compound, the guards rushed to close the gates while the prisoners surged toward them like cattle being prodded into a pen.

A cry of "We will be free!" was raised by the prisoners, and the prince kneed his horse to a canter. Tashama kept pace with him and studied his facial features. She turned her head from his view when she caught his eye, demurely, more like the way he expected his women to act.

Riders, a few horses in front, carried torches of flame, casting an eerie glow in the dark. The fragrance of pine scented the air, and an owl hooted in the distance.

"What am I to do with you?" Aleron asked. "You are dangerous left to your own cunning ways in the compound, so my guards have told me, but Carissian assures me you are just as much of a threat to me should you return to the palace."

"Then he is feeble-minded. How can a mere woman be a threat to a"—Tashama hesitated, and considered the cut of the prince's tunic—"powerful figure such as yourself? Why do you listen to such a man?"

He noted the sarcasm in her voice and dismissed it. "Carissian didn't wish for me to come for you. He wouldn't say why."

"Yet, you came anyway. Release me, Prince Aleron. Let me return to Karthland. I didn't believe Maldovians or Karthlanders, for that matter, took women hostage. In taking me prisoner, you've violated the rules of war."

"I think not." The prince rubbed his chin in thought. "If you would be dangerous to me here, then you would undoubtedly be more of a threat to me there, though I'm at a loss as to how this could be so."

"You do not truly believe I'm dangerous to you."

Her fingers were unadorned, and he assumed she could not be mated. "How old are you?"

"Old enough." The breeze tossed a loose curl in her face, and she tucked it behind her ear. "I've heard it said you have never visited the compound before."

"The time was right." Aleron studied her fingers and added under his breath, "You are not linked."

BY EARLY MORNING, Tashama was escorted into the palace. This time, the guards deposited her in a room where peach and gold sheer silks billowed out from a ten-square-foot window. Reaching the floor, the window served as an open doorway into gardens.

The gold doors leading back into the palace were shut behind her, and Tashama ran to the window and gazed at the garden. Pink, blue, purple, and yellow colors of numerous floral varieties filled islands that dripped into the peach-tiled walkways, and the smell of heavenly flowers scented the light breeze.

Movement on one of the paths caught her eye. She frowned when one of the members of the royal guard walked off the walkway, followed by Aleron. He smiled at her. She tilted her head up in defiance. Feminine voices caught her attention as three women, dressed in gaily colored shimmering sheers of blues and golds laced over opaque satins, entered her room.

Tashama's back stiffened when they hurried to join her.

"Come with us, miss." The one smiled at her.

"Where to?"

The ladies tugged gently at her arms, then, feeling her resistance, pulled her into a room off the main one.

"In here." The lady waved at a Roman-style bath of marble. Fudge swirls whirled about the glassy surface of the ivory tiles covering both the tub and the surrounding floor and walls. Tashama was reminded of her favorite ice cream flavor—fudge ripple.

"A bath." Tashama hurried to pull her turtleneck over her head.

Then, as the woman gasped at the sight of her lacy bra, she held her shirt in front of her breasts. "Could I have some privacy, ladies?"

"We're to help you, miss." The lady yanked the shirt from Tashama's grasp, then tossed it to another.

They pushed her to sit, then as one helped her off with her shoes, another poked at her bra. Tashama reached behind her to unhook the fastener. She pulled it off and covered her naked breasts with her hands.

"And those." One of the ladies pointed at her jeans. She unfastened the belt. The lady touched her jeans button to her annoyance. "I can do it!" But the ladies soon had unbuttoned and unzipped the zipper despite her protests. She pulled off her jeans.

The ladies stood back to study her lace bikini-cut panties. Tashama turned her back to the women, slipped her panties off her feet, and then hurried into the bath. "Oh." She dove under the blanket of roses, dipping in the water with the waves she'd made, then she resurfaced. "It's so warm."

"She can swim like a water sprite," the one whispered, and the others nodded.

"Shampoo? Soap?" Tashama asked.

The ladies leaned over a wicker basket and pulled out a bottle of jasmine-scented soap. One of the ladies handed her the container. Tashama ran the slippery, sweet-smelling fragrance over every inch of her skin. She lathered her hair with a rich, golden soap and rinsed it thoroughly. Studying the shape of the bath, she observed bubbles bumping the roses in one corner.

Slipping beneath the rose petals, she swam the length of the pool to the corner of interest. She surfaced and touched the bubbles with the tips of her fingers, smiling. Melting into the built-in seat, she lay against the jets, forcing the warm water onto every inch of her back. She closed her eyes and rested her head against the pillow attached just above the water line.

Her mind drifted to thoughts of the prince as his fingers

touched her arm lightly. He ran his hand through her hair, but he'd never done such a thing, and she opened her eyes in surprise.

Carissian and the ladies stood near the entrance of the bath. His pale gray eyes studied Tashama's thoughts. He was touching her. Not the prince.

Angered, she imagined a blank sheet of paper and wrote across it in heavy black ink: GET OUT! He shook his head and motioned for the women to dry her skin. He vanished in a puff of white mist, and they lifted towels from a basket.

Tashama jerked one of the towels from the lady's grasp. "What kind of a sorcerer is he to witness a lady bathing? He's a bad one, I can tell you!" Not seeing her clothes, she said, "Where are my things?"

"You must wear these, then you must have an audience with our prince."

"Once in a lifetime was enough for me." They held a sheer, pink silk, sleeveless gown out to her. "There's to be more than this for me to wear, surely."

The ladies giggled. One grabbed a miniature fan and shot the air into Tashama's hair. "They say the clothes you came here in are just as revealing. But there is an undergown to go along with it."

"Hogwash." Tashama considered the gown.

"It has been said," one of the ladies replied, as she pulled a pink satin slip under the sheer one, "our lord had you monitored every minute of the day at the prison camp."

"Oh?" Tashama pulled her hair out of the dress. "And what do his spies say?"

"You move the men like no general can. They were afraid of you, miss. They said no good would come of your being there."

Tashama smiled. "True."

"They say, Carissian cannot read your thoughts. He fears you may be as powerful as he is. I've never seen him so concerned over a mortal before."

"We want to know how you did it."

"Did what?"

"Moved the men, miss."

"Don't let them rule you, for one. I mean to say, you can let them think they do, but in the end, make sure you have your own way."

Two of the women giggled, but the third remained silent. "And the sorcerer?"

"I'm not mortal." Tashama smoothed out her skirts. "But then I imagine, Carissian already knows that. He has been forewarned."

One of the ladies pulled a blended, pastel-colored sheer, lacy overdress over the satin one Tashama wore.

"Can I not have my undergarments?" Tashama touched her bodice. She examined the other ladies' gowns. "The style of your gowns sufficiently covers your bodices." She looked at hers and frowned. "I'm revealing much more than I want in this." She touched the silky edge. It barely covered her breasts.

"The gown is as His Highness wishes it."

"I will not see him then."

One of the ladies gasped. "You cannot refuse to see His Highness, miss. It just isn't done."

"I can," Tashama said as one of the ladies fastened a veil to her hair. "Come, ladies, get me another gown, or one of you switch your gowns with me. Then I will see your prince and all will be well."

"He had the gown designed specifically for you, miss. If you don't move around too much, the gown is not all that revealing."

Tashama folded her arms. "Very well, I'll stay here."

The royal guard appeared at the door, and one of the ladies said, "He's ready for you, miss."

"I'm not ready for him." Tashama sat in an oversized, pale-blue, velvet chair.

She sank into the goose-down pillows, and the lady motioned for the royal guard. The leader of the escort waved to two of his men, who responded by grabbing Tashama's arms and half-dragging her to the door as she grasped at the doorframe.

One of the ladies frowned at her. "If you would go calmly, you would reveal much less than you desire."

She motioned for the men to take Tashama to the prince's chambers. They yanked her from her tentative grip on the doorframe. Tashama glanced down at her bare feet. "I don't have any shoes."

"He would rather you were without." The lady walked beside the guard.

"What? He likes his women barefoot and..." Tashama stopped her speech as the ladies all turned to hear what she had to say. She closed her mouth and said nothing further.

"Barefoot and what, miss?"

"Nothing," Tashama said.

"Barefoot and nothing doesn't make any sense," the lady said.

Seeing her nipples pressed against the thin satin, Tashama shook her head. "The prince is not a gentleman."

They walked into the prince's apartments, and the ladies directed Tashama to sit on the colorful pillows in the corner of the room. She shook her head.

"He wishes to dine with you here."

"On a bunch of pillows? Not at a table?"

"Sit please, miss."

Tashama backed up to the door.

7

"He's not going to poison you, miss," the one woman said to Tashama.

"That's *not* what I'm afraid of."

"What *are* you afraid of?" Prince Aleron walked into the room. The ladies quickly curtsied. He motioned for them to step aside. Holding his hand out to the pillows, he waited for Tashama to comply.

"If we are to dine, can we not sit at a table?"

"Sit," he said.

"Do you often bring prisoners here to dine with you?"

He took her arm and nudged her toward the cluster of pillows. After he encouraged her to sit, he sat beside her. He studied her eyes, then passed her a goblet of wine. "Drink." He touched his gold cup to hers.

"To what?"

"To the end of hostilities between our peoples."

"All right." She took a sip of the wine, then smiled. "It tastes like mint julep with a sprig of...cinnamon."

"I'm pleased you like it." He handed their goblets to a waiting servant, then said to another, "The first course."

Fruits and cheese were served, and Tashama leaned back on the pillows slightly. She pulled off a cluster of blue grapes, then held it over her head. After grasping a grape between her teeth, she lifted the branch above Aleron's head. He smiled at her, then grabbed the grape with his teeth.

When they'd both eaten a slice of cheese and several more grapes, he reached for the goblets. He handed Tashama hers. She sipped some of the wine, then said, "Can I try yours?"

"It would taste the same as yours." The low-cut, form-fitting bodice of Tashama's gown caught his eye. He raised his goblet. "A toast."

"To?" Tashama raised her drink.

"To you."

"Why me?" She lowered her goblet.

He reached under her veil and touched her blond hair as it curled about the pillows. "I've never seen such beautiful tresses."

"A different toast." She pulled a pillow over her bodice.

"To the end of the war!"

"To the end of the war!" she repeated with enthusiasm, then drank her wine.

The prince reached for her goblet. She reached for his, and he smiled. "We'll have the next course of the meal."

When sausages and rice were served, the prince spooned a sample for Tashama, but when he took a spoonful for himself, she grabbed his wine cup from the steward. She took a sip of his wine. "It doesn't taste as good as mine. Here, taste mine and see what you think."

"I think," the prince said and handed the goblet back to the servant, "we can only handle one course at a time."

Tashama sighed deeply. "That's why we should have sat at a table while we ate."

She lay back on the pillows with her outstretched arms above her head. He motioned to a servant to bring the next course.

Carissian nodded to him from the doorway. The prince buttered a slice of bread for her. "What were you doing all alone at Lake Curaca when my men first found you?"

"Washing the blood from my arms." She pulled the veil from her hair, then tossed it aside.

The rainbow-colored cloth fluttered to the floor.

"Yes, but why were you there?"

"A mistake. He made a mistake."

"He?" Aleron's dark brows rose.

"My dear friend, yes."

"His name?"

She stared at the floor for a moment and tried to recollect his name. When it wouldn't come to her, she shook her head.

"Where was he?"

"Who knows?" She rocked her left leg back and forth. "I was there, and he was not."

"You were spies then?"

She turned over on her side, then smiled at Aleron. "You have the warmest eyes—dark brown with golden flecks—the same oval shape as the hart's." She reached up to pull a wavy strand of dark brown hair behind his ear. He kissed her hand, then laid it on the pillow in front of her. He faced Carissian. "Well, does she speak the truth?"

Carissian frowned back at him. "Every word, my lord."

The prince turned when she touched the golden threads that circled in intricate swirls on his tunic. Her slender fingers traced the maze along his chest. He twisted his mouth in thought. "Will you remove your gowns for me?"

She rolled over on her stomach, then covered her head with a pillow. Carissian grumbled, "I didn't expect this kind of questioning of the prisoner, my liege. You're supposed to distract her while I probe her thoughts."

"What was she thinking when I proposed the question?"

"You wouldn't want to know."

"Her answer was no, then."

Carissian motioned for the servants and ladies to leave. The room emptied. "She desires to, yes, sire. If you think we can get further with the questioning this way—"

"You mean for me to have my way with her when she's not truly herself—"

"Perhaps in the throes of passion, she will quit blocking my attempts to win her thoughts."

"Is she blocking them now?"

"No, the drink has muddled her thoughts. A thick fog fills her mind now."

"What is she thinking?"

"She's curious whether your chest is as smooth as a cow's teat or as hairy as a goat."

The prince wrinkled his brow when her fingers caressed a satin pillow nearby. "I take it she doesn't like hairy chests."

"You have no problem in that regard."

"What else is she thinking?"

"She envisions you in the garden when you caught sight of her when she stood in the window. Your smile, dark hair, and eyes enthrall her. Her own people are all very fair."

The prince folded his arms. He leaned over and pulled the pillow away from her cheek. "She's asleep."

"She dreams."

He touched her blond curls floating over her cheek. "What does she dream of?"

"She's talking to someone in a strange room. I cannot see his face because she's looking out the window now. A massive black funnel shoots down from the dark clouds above. I've never seen anything like it. Then she observes a blue-winged butterfly—no, she realizes it's a water sprite—something she hadn't remembered before now."

"At our lake?"

"Yes, her arms hurt, and she's trying to wash them in the lake. She doesn't like Oshon. He hurts her arm. She's confused about you, however. You're angry with her, and she's distressed. But then you seem to like her, and she feels renewed hope."

"Renewed hope for what?"

Tashama rolled onto her back.

"She's waiting for you to kiss her. She has never been kissed before, and she wants to know what it would be like from your lips."

The prince stared at Carissian. "Have her taken back to her room."

"She's dangerous—this one. One of the maids said your prisoner could swim like a water nymph in our great lake."

"Mortals cannot swim. The woman was mistaken."

"As I said. The prisoner explained to the ladies that she wasn't mortal."

Aleron stared at his advisor in disbelief. "What do you think?"

"Of course she's mortal. Her arms were cut, she was in pain, and she was bleeding. She dipped her head under the water of the bath and walked along the bottom, that's all. Beneath the cover of the roses, the women assumed she was swimming when, indeed, she had her feet on the tile floor of the bath the whole time. But the point is she's extremely cunning."

"You think she's still dangerous, then?"

"I haven't discovered her true identity. The healer told our guard that her name was Mary, but it was not correct. Dallas is not either. She hides her identity from me like a turtle who ducks into the safety of its shell." Carissian motioned for a servant to remove the prisoner. "She has the confidence of her people—she's an emergent leader, despite being a woman. Sending her to the compound was a mistake. Even with her being spirited away from there, much unrest has been reported at the camp."

THE NEXT DAY, Tashama stretched in bed, realized she was naked, and then opened her eyes quickly. She pulled the sheer curtains around her bed aside. An auburn-haired lady sewed on a tapestry in a chair nearby. "Where am I?"

"At Prince Aleron's palace, miss."

"No, no, what room is this?"

"Your room, miss, for the time being."

Tashama collapsed back in bed. She rubbed her bare arms. "Where are my gowns?"

"On the peg on the wall over there, miss."

Tashama held her covers to her chest and peered at the gowns. "Who removed them?"

"We did, miss."

"We?"

"The other ladies and I."

"Oh." Tashama lay back down.

"Would you like to dress now?"

"In the same gowns?"

"Yes."

"Can I not have my own clothes back?"

"They're being examined."

"Examined?"

"The cloth is not like anything we've ever seen before. The prince's head tailor is examining the material as we speak."

"All right then, help me to dress."

The petite lady lifted the gowns off their satin padded hooks. "The prince said you were awfully agreeable last night."

"What did he mean by that?" Tashama hurried to slip the shift over her naked figure.

"I wouldn't know. Carissian dismissed us."

"Carissian was there?"

"Yes, midway through the meal."

"But you say you were dismissed?" Tashama pulled the satin gown over her head with the lady's help.

"Yes, it seems the business with you was to take a more personal direction, and we were not allowed to witness the outcome."

"Does the prince often interrogate his prisoners in such a manner?" Her voice irritated, Tashama's face grew hot.

"You are the first he has had in his chambers."

"Prisoners, you mean."

"Well, I cannot say about the prince's personal interest in women, miss."

The young lady tried to fix the veil to Tashama's hair, but she brushed it aside. "I don't wear such a thing on my hair. Take it away."

"But, miss, the women always wear their hair veiled. To not do so, would entice the men entirely too much."

"Fix it to your own hair then. I haven't worn one since I arrived at Maldovia, and I've found the men have not come unglued over me here."

"Unglued, miss?"

"Too interested in me—enticed—whatever it was you said, for heaven's sakes."

The lady shook her head as she put the scarf back on the peg. "That's because you looked so strange before."

"Strange?" Tashama moved to the window and stood in the breeze.

"Yes, well, your attire for one, and your eyes were blackened like the raccoon. Your arms were shredded. You really were a sight. But now—well, now, it would do well for you to follow our customs."

"I'm not one of you."

"No, but your own people have the same custom."

"They do?" Tashama turned to face the lady.

The lady's lower lip dropped slightly. "Why would you not have known this?" She took a step backward. "Breakfast will be served shortly. Wait here."

The lady hastened out of the room. Tashama walked through the glassless window onto the tiled path and hurried down one until she came to a wrought-iron gazebo shimmering like white lace in the sunshine. She took a deep breath, then backtracked and headed down a path intersecting with the first. Picking up her pace, she traveled a reasonable distance before voices stopped her dead in her footsteps.

"You let me kiss you yesterday, why not today?" the distinctive deep voice of the prince said.

"You entertained that Karthlander woman in your chambers last evening, I was shocked to learn."

"Carissian believes she's a threat to our realm. I'm forced to take extreme measures to learn how so."

"By wooing her in your chambers? That's the lamest...oh," she said, then giggled. "Stop it." She laughed. "You cannot kiss me in that manner. I forbid it."

Boots running in the direction of the prince made Tashama take a step back. "The Karthlander prisoners have revolted at the Sheian Compound," Oshon said.

"And?"

"They made their escape."

"But the woman wasn't there to aid them."

"They found her plans left behind in the healer's tent."

Boots clicked on the tile pavement, then the prince said, "How do they know she wrote them?"

"Carissian has examined them, sire. He said it was the same as the writing he had seen her use before."

The prince stormed down his path with the men, but another ran to intercept him. "The Karthlander woman has slipped out of her room, sire!"

"Find her!" The prince continued on his way.

Tashama ran back along her path and crossed the intersection. This time, she headed straight until the path dead-ended at a ten-foot-tall blue door. She stared at the brass handle for a moment, then touched it. She envisioned the sorcerer's eyes meeting hers when she felt his presence on the door handle, and she pulled her hand away. Voices headed in her direction, and she turned back to the path.

"She has to be in the gardens! Her door into the palace was guarded!"

She grabbed the handle and twisted, then as the door opened, she hurried into the darkened room. After closing the door behind her, she ran her hands over the knob in an attempt to locate a lock. Not finding any, she hurried into the center of the room. She paused to get her bearings, but couldn't see anything in the abyss.

Taking another step, she gasped to find the floor had vanished beneath her feet.

8

Tumbling down a great stone staircase with one jarring thump after another, Tashama rolled until she hit the bottom with a thud. She lay still in the dark, then a dim light appeared in the room above.

She held her breath when a man whispered, "I cannot see anything in here. Carissian wouldn't wish for us to disturb his quarters."

"What if she's in here?"

"He'll find her soon enough."

The door shut the light out, and Tashama closed her eyes as her whole body ached from the fall.

"Tashama," a small voice whispered. "Tashama, they'll soon find you."

She covered her ears and whispered back, "Go away."

Dripping laughter followed. A pesky water nymph—if she could hear their voices, water would be nearby. Tashama tried to sit, but her ribs hurt with the effort, and she groaned and lay down.

"Tashama," the tinny voice said. "He comes for you."

For some time, Tashama breathed in the wetness of the air. With the methodical drip of water, she drifted off to sleep. A few minutes later, the flutter of wings aerated her breathing space, and she opened her eyes. Darkness was all she saw.

"Tashama, sleep, and they will find you."

She sat up, and pain filled her chest. She touched her bruised ribs, then wrapped her fingers around the railing beside the stairs. The entrance to the stairwell was dark and foreboding, and she pulled herself off the cold, wet floor. He'd come soon for her, she knew.

Then she turned toward the gloom looming before her. Reaching her hands outward, she took a baby step, searching for a proper footing with her toes as she inched away from the stairs.

The soles of her feet touched wet moss as it carpeted the stone, and she knelt. Reaching forward with her hands, she crawled along. Her ribs ached with every wiggle of her hips, and her hair touched the floor, snagging under her knees. Pain shot through her scalp. Then warm water rippled at her fingertips.

A small voice said, "He's coming for you now, Tashama."

Tashama knew. She felt his presence as he moved about his chambers, but without being in the same room with her, he couldn't know her thoughts, her pain, her whereabouts. He was trying to sense if she'd been there, but he couldn't know such a thing—not like she could.

She smiled at the notion, and the deep breath she took made her wish she hadn't, as her ribs ached as though they'd been broken in two. She slipped into the water and relaxed her tense body in the warmth. *Perhaps I cannot escape from you yet, but it pleases me just the same that I have upset your plans.*

Tashama pulled the water behind her and swam slowly across the underwater lake. Voices from far away made her pause. "No, she's not here!" The sorcerer slammed the door shut. His soft-shoed footsteps ran down the stairs as she reached the other side of the cave.

Diving beneath the surface of the water, her fingers probed the thick stone walls for a passage. A dim light wavered nearby.

For some distance, she followed the spark of light. When the flicker illuminated a narrow underwater tunnel, she resurfaced to take a breath. A light shimmered off the surface of the dark waters as the sorcerer ran along the edge of the lake. Over the water, he stretched a lantern dangling precariously on his staff. The bobbing light grew closer. She disappeared beneath the water and headed straight for the tunnel.

Her hands touched the rough surface of the stone as she frantically pulled herself along the tunnel wall. With only the tiny light to guide her and her lungs ready to give out, she attempted to shove the panic from her mind. A pocket of air suddenly appeared, and she pushed her face above the water and gasped.

She floated with her nose nearly touching the formation inches above her face as she attempted to steady her breathing. Despite her efforts to calm herself, she couldn't stop her heart from thumping rapidly in terror because of the closed-in space. She pushed against the rock and propelled herself through the tunnel, floating on her back toward the exit she hoped she'd soon find.

"Does it exit?" Tashama whispered, and her words bounced off the enclosed space. *Does it exit...exit?*

Her head bumped into the rock formation dipping into the water again, and her eyes filled with tears. She paused as she took a deep breath. Not ready to make the dive, her heart pounded hard against her painful ribs, and she exhaled the stale air. *Calm yourself, Tashama.* She took a deep breath, closed her eyes, and saw the prince's lips curve up as he touched her hair. *You had me drugged you, you deceiver of women.* Then she took another deep breath and dove.

Pulling the rock walls past her, she swam until her head fuzzed with the lack of oxygen. Then she burst into another enclave of air where the ceiling lifted higher. She bobbed in the water and gasped at the moist air. "Have you tricked me, water sprite?" *Tricked me, water sprite...sprite?*

Their tinny laughter followed. She took a deep breath, then dove again.

After swimming several yards, her lungs screamed for air. Then strands of her hair were yanked forward. Kicking her feet and pulling at the rock with her hands, she finally made it to another shallow airlock. She caught her breath and shook her head. A tear mixed with the water droplets on her cheek. "*I cannot do it.*"

Do it...it.

Tiny impish giggles ensued, then silence.

The water lapped against the edge of the rock, and the sweet fragrance, like perfume, touched her upturned nose. "*What* is it?" she whispered.

What is it...it?

She took a deep breath and exhaled again in exasperation. "You can do this, Tashama!"

Do this, Tashama!

"Do it, Tashama!"

Do it, Tashama!"

"They search for you, Tashama," a tiny voice said, as a spark illuminated her small space.

"Water sprite, how much longer must I endure?"

I endure...endure?

"They come for you."

Tashama filled her lungs again and dove under. The water swirled before her, its surface shimmering with the flutter of translucent blue wings, bubbles dancing with light. *I won't make it.*

She closed her eyes and gave up the struggle. *I cannot make it.*

The prince's dark brown eyes studied her as his image appeared before her in the blue light. Her slender fingers reached out to touch his lips as they parted slightly for her.

"They come for you, Tashama," the sprite bubbled in her ear. "You'll never make it."

I'll never make it.

Tiny hands pulled at her gowns and hair, and all at once her face broke the tranquil surface of the water. She gasped for air, and a voice laughed. "You escaped them, but *he* won't let you go." The water nymph splashed back into the water.

Tashama stared at the lake she recognized as the one she'd encountered when her nightmare had first begun. She crawled onto the sandy beach and eyed the ring of mountains in the distance. *How can I make it through the mountains?* She shook her head at the thought. *I'm not sure I can even make it off the beach.* She rested her head on the shore.

ALERON STORMED through the hallway to the sorcerer's chambers with one of his royal guard. "She cannot have left the palace grounds! She couldn't have gotten past the guards!" He glared at two guards who hurriedly bowed to him in the hall as he strode on past them. "Why did Carissian want me at his chambers?"

"Sire," the guard said they turned down another passageway, "he's concerned she may have drowned in the underground lake."

The prince stopped. "You didn't say this to me before."

"No, sire. I was afraid you would be angry. We don't know what to think, really. Carissian found a slip of cloth belonging to her dress at the bottom of the stairs."

Aleron shook his head and quickened his pace. They turned down another corridor. "Why would I have been angry? If she has..." He rubbed his chin as his brows furrowed. "She would..." The prince shook his head as the notion disturbed him. *I should be pleased with the notion. She's a danger to me, is she not?*

What is there about this Karthlander woman that stirs the beast in me so? No other woman has ever made me feel this way...to spawn such longings. He studied the floor, then shook his head. *She is more powerful than Carissian has ever been.*

His guard waited for him to finish his sentence, and he took a deep breath. "She would no longer be a threat to me." His words were said in a hurry as if to reassure himself, but his tone of voice hinted at concern with the prisoner's well-being instead.

"Yes, sire."

The prince turned onto another path. "I've told Carissian he shouldn't live so far from my wing of the palace!"

After another ten minutes of maneuvering through the maze of passages, the prince walked into Carissian's chambers. A guard greeted him. "We're looking for any signs of the woman in the water, as much as we can, sire."

"How? No one can swim."

"Several men are on makeshift rafts as they hold lanterns close to the water." He jogged down the steps after the prince.

"Is there no sign of her?" The prince waved at Carissian.

The sorcerer shook his head. "I found blood on the bottom step and this." He lifted the fragment of sheer cloth up to the prince.

"Has it been verified that the cloth belonged to the lady?"

"Yes, sire."

"Why was she not being watched? A lady was to stay with her in her room."

"Princess Listra sought me as she grew concerned the prisoner didn't know about the custom of her own people concerning the wearing of veils. She used unusual words, such as 'unglued.'"

The prince stared at the black waters as the lantern light reflected off its surface. "Has she drowned, do you think?"

"If she tried to swim through the tunnel—"

"You said she couldn't swim...mortals cannot swim."

"But if she did make it to the tunnel..." The sorcerer shook his head. "It's just not possible."

"Can you not tell where she is? You did once before."

"I saw her in the shadows of the tree." Carissian stared at the waters. "I cannot see her in the waters."

"But there's nowhere for her to go—"

"A tunnel empties into Lake Curaca."

Aleron motioned to his guard. "Get thirty men together. We ride to the lake at once."

"She wouldn't have made it, sire. The tunnel has air pockets to be sure, but she couldn't swim. She's just a mortal," his sorcerer said.

The prince hurried to the stairs. "Are you so certain?"

"He comes for you, Tashama." The water sprite fluttered in Tashama's face.

"I hurt too much to move."

"Then they win."

"No." Tashama sat. Horses' hooves pounded against the earth, making it tremble beneath her legs, and she groaned as she stood. Then she walked stiffly toward the forest.

"You'll never make it, Tashama." The sprite dove into the water with a splash.

Tashama winced with every step she took, then reached the shadows of the forest as the fingers stretched out to her. She walked into their beckoning arms, and the voices renewed.

"Tashama, Tashama, Tashama," the woodland sprites taunted in a whispered hush. "You're back and they're coming for you... *again.*"

"Shhh." Tashama touched her temple as it throbbed. She walked deeper into the forest and shuddered as the horses snorted at the lake.

"There's a small footprint over here—a woman's, I would think, sire!" a man shouted from the beach.

"She was barefoot." The prince studied the print.

"The beach is wet here—there's an imprint of a figure in the sand, sire. She must have lain here for some time."

"She must be near here. Spread out and search the woods!"

The men cantered their horses into the woods. The prince and two of his guards soon spied Tashama leaning against a tree, staring at her feet. "Call off the search," he said to one of the men, then walked his horse close to her. "Bind her wrists."

After dismounting, the man grabbed hold of a rope, then approached Tashama with caution. She stood still, staring at the ground. The soldier pushed her blond hair aside as it hung about her wrists. He lifted her hands to tie them, and she cried out in pain. The prince blinked.

He'd forgotten she might have been injured. He hardened his stance. She shouldn't have escaped. He motioned for the guard to proceed with the task, while the remainder of the guards joined them.

The man tied her hands together and waited for the prince's direction. "Remount your horse. She'll walk behind you to show what we do to her kind who escape from our good graces."

9

The man remounted his horse and kneed him to walk. After his horse took several steps, the rope grew taut, and Tashama was pulled from the tree where she leaned. She cried out again, but when the soldier stopped his horse, the prince hesitated. How would his men view him if he showed mercy to the prisoner?

Weakness, that's what it would indicate. He was only seven when he ascended to the throne and began his reign as ruler of Maldovia. Carissian had drummed into him how important it was not to show any weakness when dealing with the enemy. But she was only a woman. The pained expression on her face made him motion to the guard. "Carry her on your horse."

One of the men dismounted from his own, then lifted Tashama to the other's saddle. Aleron tried to ignore her, to be hard and unyielding, but his gaze more than once drifted back to her. She was the most stubborn woman he'd ever met and the most enticing. Her golden hair dripped over her shoulders in wet curls.

His brows rose slightly as her nipples poked at the drenched fabric. Her eyes met his, and he stiffened his back. Her alluring green eyes narrowed at him like a wildcat preparing to pounce on its prey. He tilted his head up and turned away.

Now what? He couldn't return her to the compound. She couldn't go back to her chamber. She would just escape again. The tower. He pursed his lips. Women didn't go to the tower. For her, he would have to make an exception. She couldn't run away from there. At all costs, he didn't want to lose her. He had to know who she was.

When they rode into the courtyard, the man handed her down to another guard, then jumped from his horse. He held the rope tied to her hands while he waited for word from the prince.

"Take her to the tower." The prince waved his hand in the direction of the prison. "She'll find it difficult to escape from there."

"But, sire," one of the men said, "shouldn't your healer see to her first?"

"You should not have stolen away like you did." The prince glowered at Tashama, then he turned to the soldier. "Have the healer see her in the tower." Then he stalked off to the great hall.

When the prince disappeared, Tashama's guard asked, "Where do you hurt, miss?"

She stared at the floor in silence.

"I must know where you're injured to apprize the healer…"

Tashama shook her head.

"You're limping. You must have cut your feet on the forest floor. The stickling burs are bad this time of year if you're not wearing boots." He reached for her leg.

"Let go of me," she growled. If the prince was going to treat her badly, she would deal with it in her own way. And here she had a tender spot in her heart for him. *No, more. He is my enemy. Learn your lesson well, Tashama.*

"Let me see your feet." He lifted her foot as if he were examining his horse's hoof. Shaking his head, he pulled three burs. He moved to the other side, and one of the ladies joined him.

"What's happening to the prisoner?" she whispered.

"The tower, Princess Listra." The man tried to lift Tashama's left foot, but she lost her balance and grabbed Listra's arm to keep from falling. Listra gasped in surprise when Tashama cried in pain.

"What's wrong with her?" Listra held Tashama's arm while he pulled off the stickers from her foot.

"The thorns have left a poison in her feet."

"No, she hurts elsewhere."

"She won't tell me."

"I'll get the healer right away."

He tucked the burs into his leather pouch. "See if you can get some salve for the poison from the burs."

"I don't understand why she's being sent to the tower."

The guard shook his head. "Carissian says she's a danger to our people. The prince feels she cannot escape from there."

WHEN THE GUARD arrived with Tashama at the round, stone tower, he set her on her feet while she gripped his arm. The black-haired and bearded tower guard frowned at her. He looked like a grizzly bear, barrel-chested, thick-necked, with beady black eyes. "What's the matter with you?" he said to the royal guard. "Women don't come to the tower."

"By the prince's orders, Toscarlo."

The tower guard grunted. "She won't be safe in there."

"The prince's orders. Find a place where she's safe then. Be careful with her as she has been injured." The guard untied the rope from her wrists.

"She must have murdered the prince's best friend to have earned a room in this place. Wounded prisoners don't come here."

"She escaped from the palace."

The tower guard's bushy black brows arched. "Why would anyone want to leave the palace?"

"She's a Karthlander prisoner."

"Oh," he grunted. "I must be dense—didn't even notice her fair features." Then he scratched his head. "What would a Karthlander woman be doing as a prisoner of the prince? Only the men are taken prisoner."

"This one is special—apparently."

"So special she gets the tower." The tower guard shook his head. "Well, come on, you." He grabbed her arm and pulled her toward the room. She cried out in distress as pain filled her chest and the wooden floor pressed against her sensitive, swollen soles.

"She's injured, I tell you." The soldier raised his voice in irritation.

"All right, all right. I'm not used to having a woman...an injured woman...and a Karthlander up here to boot."

He walked her into the cell where several male prisoners loitered in the expansive round tower. All eyed her suspiciously when the guard made her sit near the window. She lay down on the straw, and the guard turned to the prisoners. "Stay away from the woman, prince's orders. Anyone who bothers the lady will be flying out yonder window. Since we're ten stories high, it wouldn't make a pretty sight on the stone pavers beneath the window."

The tower guard hesitated when he considered Tashama, then glared at the men. "Don't test my resolve in the matter."

Before he left the room, the healer hurried into the cell. "I understand you have a wounded prisoner."

The massive hulk of the guard moved out of the way and waved his hand at Tashama. The healer gasped. "A Karthlander woman. What is *she* doing here?"

"Prince's orders."

The healer hurried over to Tashama, then knelt at her feet. He examined the punctures already swelling with the effect of the poison. After rubbing a salve on her feet, he wrapped them with cloth. Then he touched the rope burns on her wrists.

"I don't understand why the prince is so angry." He applied medicine to her wrists, but when he lifted her arm higher, Tashama groaned in pain. "Where do you hurt, miss?" the healer asked when a tear rolled down her cheek.

"My heart hurts, Healer."

The man touched her lower rib cage, making her cry out. He nodded and felt the rest of her ribs. Convinced there were no breaks, he turned to the tower guard. "I want to give her something to help her bruised ribs heal, but it'll make her sleep through just about anything. She'll be more vulnerable."

The tower guard nodded. "Do what you must. I'll ensure the lady's sleep is undisturbed."

The healer gave her the tea, and Tashama reacted to the drug as before. In a haze, she watched the guard tie the men together. He looped the rope to a metal rung on the wall opposite her.

"You breach our rights!" one of the men shouted.

"Write up your grumble and send it to the prince." The tower guard turned to Tashama as she closed her eyes. "Sleep well, miss."

Before he could take a step out of the room, Carissian appeared. She felt his presence at once and opened her eyes. Carissian folded his arms when the guard blocked his path. "I want to see the prisoner."

"She's asleep, Carissian."

"Then I will wake her. I want a word with her."

"She was wounded."

"Yes, I'm well aware of this." A muffled laugh escaped his lips when he observed the prisoners tied to the wall. "Close the door," he ordered the guard.

"You want to be alone—"

"Close the door," Carissian reiterated, his voice growing low.

"Of course."

Tashama closed her eyes before Carissian could turn to face her. His footsteps grew closer. Feeling his mind probing hers, she could sense his frustration.

"You've been drugged. I can see nothing of your thoughts. Yet, it is as though you read mine." His knees creaked when he knelt beside her.

He unwrapped her right foot while one of the prisoners said, "The prince made her walk on the poisonous burs of the forest. Even a prisoner condemned to die wouldn't have been made to suffer so."

"Go to sleep."

"The healer said her ribs were bruised. Did the prince have her beaten as well?"

"Sleep. And do not disturb the lady."

"She says her heart is broken."

She opened her eyes slightly when the sorcerer tilted his head in surprise. "Who did she say this to?"

"To the healer, when he asked her where she hurt."

"I wonder." Carissian tapped his chin with his finger. "Sleep," he commanded the prisoners.

Tashama sighed deeply, wondering where Balthazar was and if he would ever help her out of this mess, when Carissian's footsteps hurried out of the room.

THE PRINCE RECLINED in his bed as the stars filled the night sky. He shook his head when Carissian walked into his chambers. "It's a little late for sorcerer tales, is it not?"

"Sire, the lady shouldn't have been made to walk on the poisonous burrs. The notion is quite barbaric."

"Who tells such lies?"

"I've seen the wounds myself, sire."

Her feet were bare and softened by the water. "I hadn't realized—"

"How long do you intend to keep her locked away in your tower, sire?"

"As long as it takes."

"As long as what takes?"

"To break her, of course. Once she's broken, she'll be no threat to me."

"She wasn't any threat to you, sire, while she was in her room."

"She escaped—remember?" The prince motioned for his servant to leave the room. "What are you getting at? You have told me she is dangerous to me."

"The woman is injured; she's remanded to the tower where women are never sent. What are you thinking?"

"You said she's dangerous to me. She won't be able to escape from the tower. Isn't that so?"

"Yes, sire."

Aleron stared at Carissian. He'd never known him to advise him wrong in a matter before. But his contradictory behavior toward the woman made him wonder what was going on in his mind. "Why is she so dangerous to me?"

"I cannot say, sire. I just haven't been able to fathom who she is or what makes her so different. Call it sorcerer's intuition."

Aleron left his bed and walked over to his window. He'd never distrusted his advisor before, and sorcerers were known to be highly loyal to the ruler they served, yet... He turned as Carissian watched him, listening to his thoughts. "Well, what did she say?"

"She was asleep when I saw her."

"And her dreams?"

"She had none."

"None?"

"No, sire."

"All right, then. I'll see you in the morning."

"I believe she's growing more of a threat to you all the time. She says her heart is broken, sire. I believe she refers to you."

The prince stared at his sorcerer, then took a deep breath. "I didn't realize you had a sense of humor, Carissian."

"She is dangerous." Carissian vanished.

Aleron swore under his breath.

Later that evening, Aleron arrived at the guard tower, and the guard nearly knocked his stool over in his haste to stand. "Sire."

"I want to see the prisoner."

"The woman?"

The prince glared at him.

"Yes, sire." He fumbled with his keys, then finally unlocked the door. Pushing it open, the prince brushed past him.

"Pretty wench, ain't she?" one of the men bound to the wall said.

Aleron ignored him and walked over to the straw where she was sleeping. With the moon clinging to the black velvet in a shimmering sphere of white, casting a light into the room, he knelt beside the window and touched Tashama's cheek. *How will you hurt me?* He ran his fingers over her soft skin. Her lashes fluttered, and he nearly fell backward.

Regaining his balance, he lifted her hand from her breast and touched his lips to her fingers. He'd never desired a woman before like this one. What made her so appealing? Besides her looks, of course...then the thought occurred to him. She wouldn't bow down to him. That's what it was. She wouldn't bend to his desires. He smiled. She was the most significant challenge he'd ever faced, and he loved a challenge.

EARLY THE NEXT MORNING, darkness hung like ebony drapes at the naked window, and Tashama stirred. She focused on the shadowy forms of the men bound across the room, then she attempted to sit.

She breathed deeply, relieved to find that her ribs were no longer sore, but when she tried to stand, the tea had made her dizzy.

"I have to have food," she said under her breath. Her soft voice woke one of the men, and he sat up to observe her.

"I do not believe you're as much of a threat to the prince as he seems to think," the gruff voice said.

Tashama touched her left foot and gasped as the sole was still painful to the touch. She rolled onto her knees and hands, then made the slow crawl toward the prisoner. His eyes grew big, and a slight smile appeared on his lips.

"Would you like a good-morning kiss?" He puckered his lips.

"What are you in here for?" Tashama made it halfway to his location. If she could, she would set the prisoners free. All she could think of was getting back at the prince. Served him right. He would not keep her enslaved.

"Thievery."

"And the others?" Tashama studied their sleeping forms. One, a young boy dressed in blue, couldn't have been older than sixteen.

"The same."

"No murderers or well...or other sorts are here?

10

Tashama wasn't about to release murderers or rapists from the cell.

"No, miss, there are only thieves among us." The man shook his head, then leaned against the wall. "What are you doing?"

"I'm going to free you and your friends."

The man chuckled. "And the prince is afraid of you!"

"I'm serious." She touched his wrists bound with sisal, then her fingers twisted at the rope.

"Who are you?" the man asked.

"Tashama."

He nodded with no sense of recognition that she was the daughter of the royal family of Karthland, who had warred with his own kingdom for twenty long years. She smiled as the knot untied. "Now undo the others."

"Are you not afraid of us? We have not been this close to a woman in weeks." He ran his fingers through the strands of her hair, then lifted them to his bulbous nose. His smile stretched across his face. "Water lily."

"You must free the other men, then ensure the rope is secured to the metal rung over there. You can slip down to one of the tower windows below and make your escape. From there, it'll be your business to leave the palace."

"The sewers—we know them well." The man released Tashama's hair. He hurried to untie the other men as he shushed them while they grumbled about his waking them in such a gruff manner.

Tashama crawled back to her bed of straw.

One of the others asked, "What's going on?"

"She has aided our escape. As soon as the last man is untied, three of you will climb down to the farthest window we can reach. After that, bind anyone in the room. I'll follow with the woman and the others."

Tashama lay on her straw, then shook her head. "I'll only slow you down. I can barely stay awake, and I cannot walk a step."

"We'll carry you then. You'll be punished for helping us to escape, miss. We wouldn't leave you behind."

The youngest of the men knelt at her side. He touched her cheek. "She's nearly asleep with the drug they gave her. We'll have to leave her."

The man motioned for three of the others to make the climb. "She'll sleep in a bed as her kind should then. At least we can do that much for her, Jaren."

"But they'll know which window we'll climb into. They'll find her before very long."

"Then we'll leave her in a room several floors down."

"She'll get us caught for certain."

"She made our escape possible in the first place."

The man lifted Tashama. Her stomach muscles tightened into a knot. Heights and narrow spaces...both she dreaded.

The man made the arduous climb with her draped over his broad shoulder, and she closed her eyes. When his feet landed on the wooden floor, he pulled her from his shoulder. She opened her eyes and frowned as a man and a woman, bound and gagged with their shredded satin sheets, sat on their bed, wild-eyed in the large chamber.

"Fear not," the big man said. "We're only rescuing a damsel in distress." He bowed slightly to the couple as they wiggled against their restraints, then he headed out the door with the rest of his gang.

The thieves climbed three flights of stairs before the man motioned his head at one of the doors. With the tools of the trade, one of the thieves poked a long, skinny metal object into the keyhole. Within a matter of seconds, the men entered the lavish apartment. One of the men fingered a jeweled clock.

The others hurried to shred the sheets on the man's bed. After tying him to his bedpost, the leader of the thief's guild said, "The lady deserves a bed of luxury." He touched the spongy goose-feather-filled mattress and smiled. "This one, in fact."

After he laid Tashama in the bed, he turned his attention to the man. "Do not disturb the lady's sleep. Advise the prince's guards that the lady was taken against her will. She did not desire to join us."

"He's a clockmaker," one of the men said and pocketed the clock.

The six men slipped out of the room like shadows in the dark. The door clicked behind them, and the clockmaker twisted his shoulders as he grunted, "Eh, eh."

Tashama smiled as she squirmed to get comfortable on the goose-down-filled pillows. Soon she was running along the gray beaches at Galveston Island, breathing in the fishy fragrance as the gulf spray touched her cheeks. *I am free! Free!*

WITHIN THE HOUR, warning bells rang throughout the palace. Aleron woke from his slumber, and a guard rushed into his chambers. "Sire." He bowed low.

The prince frowned at the interruption of his dreams and rubbed his bare chest as he glowered at the guard. "What is the trouble that you barge into my chambers like this without invitation?"

"The prisoners in the tower have escaped, my liege."

Aleron scratched his head for a moment, then turned to his manservant. "Get my clothes!" Turning to the guard, he asked, "What has happened?"

The servant helped the prince with his tunic, and the guard said, "They escaped by climbing down a rope and dropping into a window three stories below their own."

"The woman couldn't have made such a climb."

"She did, sire. She's gone as well."

"And the room where they entered? What of the occupants?"

"They were bound and gagged, sire, with their own bed sheets. We assume the thieves entered the sewers and have already made their escape."

The servant helped the prince on with his sandals as Carissian appeared at the prince's chambers.

"Sire." He bowed low. "The lady and the rest of the prisoners have made a successful escape, I'm obliged to inform you."

"She couldn't walk. You said so yourself, Carissian."

"The occupants of the room where the men first alighted said the woman was carried over the leader's shoulder."

The servant buckled the prince's belt, and the prince said, "We've lost her then."

"Yes, sire."

"She couldn't have helped the men escape. How did they do such a thing?" The prince paced across the floor.

"The tower guard tied the men to keep her safe from harm.

Apparently, they found a way to untie the rope, though he was at a loss as to how they could have done such a thing. He assumed they took the woman against her will."

The prince stormed out of his room, and the guard and Carissian followed him. "I want her brought back here at once!" He turned to Carissian. "Did the healer drug her?"

"Yes, sire, because of her injuries."

"Did he not know how dangerous it could have been for the lady when she was drugged like that...to be left alone with the prisoners...defenseless?"

"The tower guard tied the men together to ensure they couldn't reach her."

The prince shook his head. "And they used the rope to escape and got to her anyway."

"The men are searching the sewers as we speak, sire," the guard said.

The prince stormed to the tower, and Carissian said, "The men would have taken her to their mountain hideaways by now. We won't find her, sire."

"Whose side are you on, Carissian?" The prince jogged up the stairs. "You say she'll do injury to me."

Carissian cleared his throat.

"Come, come, tell me what you're thinking." The prince scowled at his adviser.

"I believe the woman aided the prisoners as she aided her own people to escape."

"But her clothes...they are unlike anything we have ever seen. She speaks strange sentiments. Are we certain she's really one of them?"

"She has the same coloration as the Karthlanders, sire, yes."

"She is not immortal." The prince reached the seventh floor without missing a breath.

"No, sire, her injuries are very real."

"And yet she swam when none of our people can do such a thing? Nor can hers, for that matter, and she blocks your thoughts. How can she do this? Even *I*, ruler of all Maldovia, cannot block your thoughts, should I wish to."

The sorcerer shook his head. "I've considered she may be a sorceress."

"A sorceress? Only one per royal house can exist. You know that. Balthazar was the sorcerer of Karthland. Though I've heard tell that his whereabouts have been unknown for some years. Valmor has taken his place."

They reached the tenth floor, and the tower guard jumped to attention. "Sire." He bowed.

"How could you have allowed the prisoners to escape?" The prince dashed into the room. He studied the hefty weight of the hemp, then leaned out of the window and stared at the dizzying height to the ground. "Show me the room where they entered from down below." The prince hurried to the door.

While they jogged down to the next floor, the prince said, "Carissian, could she be a sorceress from a different region?"

"They only serve a royal family, sire. If she were a sorceress, she would not have been on her own like she was near the lake in any event."

The prince rubbed his forehead as they reached the landing three stories down from the prisoner's tower. "Would she have replaced the Karthlander's sorcerer then?"

Carissian shook his head. "They don't believe in using sorceresses any more than we do. The Karthlanders don't trust a woman's emotions—too volatile. Valmor is still their sorcerer, so I understand."

"But she could swim." The notion bothered him. He walked into the room where the thieves had taken refuge briefly. The husband and wife quickly bowed to the prince. "Tell me what happened here." He folded his arms across his chest.

"They were like shadows, moving without sound in the dark. Before we knew it, they'd dragged my wife and me out of bed, then covered our mouths with their hands while another hurried to rip our sheets into strips. Within seconds, we were bound like ancient Calathian mummies, then they tied us to the bed. Two ran to the window and motioned to the others. Soon three more followed.

"The biggest one of the lot carried a golden-haired goddess draped over his shoulder. I couldn't imagine where the men had come from, or where they were bound with the woman. The big man said they had rescued the damsel in distress, then hurried out of the room with her. About half an hour later, the bells sounded. Within minutes, the royal guards barged into our room and found us tied and gagged."

The prince peered out the window and studied the rope still dangling before it. "I cannot imagine how they could've done such an escape without the aid of light."

"They are thieves, sire." Carissian joined the prince at the window. "They steal under the cloak of darkness. It is their way."

"And they intended to carry the woman throughout the palace grounds?" The prince turned back to the man and his wife.

"It appeared so, Your Highness. He didn't seem to want to give the woman up."

The prince shook his head. "Then she would have slowed them down. To the sewers, men."

11

"Do you wish to suspend breakfast, my lord?" Carissian hurried after the prince. The prince glared back at him. Carissian nodded, then motioned for a servant in the hall. "Tell the chief steward, breakfast will not be had this morning."

"Let it be known that the escape of the Karthlander woman is the reason." The prince ran down the flight of stairs to the basement.

They approached the sewer grate for the upper sewer levels, and the guard hurried to open the lock. Then the guard climbed down the ladder to the walkway alongside the sewer flow. The prince wrinkled his nose as he climbed down after him. They spied guards searching the corridor ahead of them. One of the men ran toward the prince.

"We've found no sign of them, save a couple of skewered rats. They've been down this way, but for over an hour, we've found no other indication as to which of the tunnels they continued into, sire."

The prince shook his head as he joined more of his men. They walked for nearly two hours as water dripped perpetually, casting a shiny gloss on the moss-covered walls. Rats squealed out in the tunnels when soldiers ran across the critters along their path, and the smell of sewage and decaying matter permeated the air.

When they arrived at an outlet in the vast countryside, the prince took a deep breath of fresh air. He studied the landscape as one of the guards said, "We've investigated the path leading from here. Though it is well-worn, there's no indication feet have passed this way recently." He pointed at the blades of grass poking out of the black soil. "Not a blade has been tromped on." He walked onto the grass, then stepped back. "The grass doesn't spring back, you see. If a man walked on it, we would see the imprint."

"All right, not here then, but through one of the exits." The prince reentered the sewers.

"Yes, sire, there are well over seventy. They will all be investigated as soon as possible."

The pattering of footsteps on the stone-cut path made everyone turn. A servant, offended by the smell of the sewers, held his nose as he tiptoed on the path. "Sire, they've found the Karthlander female."

"What?"

"She has been sleeping in the clockmaker's bed."

"What?" The prince grabbed the man's arm and headed for the nearest exit from the sewers.

"Should we call off the search, sire?" a palace guard asked.

"No! The thieves must be apprehended!" The prince turned to the servant. "Tell me what happened."

"The clockmaker never arrived at work this morning. He's been known to sleep late on occasion...so there was no concern for quite a while. But when the time grew close to the lunch hour, one of his helpers grew worried that something was wrong."

The prince exited the sewers into the basement, and Carissian said, "Perhaps His Highness would prefer a bath before we investigate the matter further."

"She's back in the tower, sire," the servant said.

"How did she end up in the clockmaker's bed?" The prince quickened his step as he headed for the clockmaker's apartments.

"He said several shadows entered his room, tied him, then gagged him. All the while, the biggest of the group cradled a golden-haired woman in his arms. He laid her in the bed next to him, while she slept the sleep of the dead. She didn't even wake up until the clockmaker's helper entered the room. Then she seemed confused and frightened. Of course, the helper was just as terrified as he feared whosoever had bound his employer might still have been in the chambers. Why else would the young lady have still been there?

"The helper hurried to untie the clockmaker, then once the man was freed, he told his helper to call the guards while he watched over the woman. Her feet were bound in cloth, and she wasn't able to walk on her own. The tower guard soon came for her and carried her back to the tenth floor. Why would a woman like that be taken to the tower, we all wondered?"

The prince reached the clockmaker's apartments, and the royal guard opened the door for him. "Sire." The clockmaker ran to join the prince. "The tower guard took the woman to the prison, but she shouldn't have been taken there. The lady didn't do anything but sleep in my bed, for heaven's sakes. One of the men took a jeweled clock. They were thieves to be sure. But the lady was drugged, of that I'm certain. She couldn't have done anyone any harm."

The prince grunted, then left the room. He headed for the stairs as Carissian motioned for the guard to leave them. "Sire, what do you propose to do?"

The prince forged up the stairs like a salmon headed upstream and didn't say a word.

"Sire—"

The prince walked more slowly now in the direction of the tower. "If she cannot walk, as several have said—"

"You do not think we should remove the woman from the tower, Your Highness?"

"She will stay in the guest chambers ."

"But—"

The prince glowered at him.

Carissian sighed deeply. "Yes, sire."

The tower guard jumped from his seat when the prince walked toward him. "She's back in the tower, sire." The man bowed low.

"Notify a palace guard to remove her to the guest chambers at once."

"Yes, sire, right away, but there's no one here to guard the prisoner in the meantime."

"Do you think perhaps Carissian and I might thwart her in the event she has an urge to flee?"

"Of course, sire." The man bowed and hurried away.

The prince walked into the room and frowned at Tashama as she lay on the bed of straw. Her eyes met his. She glared at him, then looked away. He turned to Carissian. "What thoughts has she?"

"She's angry with you, sire."

"And I with her." Aleron folded his arms. "Why do you treat my kindness with an attempt to escape from the palace grounds?"

She twisted a piece of golden straw in her fingers, then snapped it in two. "She says, Your Highness, she won't be a caged animal. She says you drugged her and tried to take advantage of her in her delicate state."

"I did not!"

"You deny you drugged me?" She turned to him as her green eyes heated.

"I did not take advantage of you, nor did I make any such attempt, young lady."

Tashama stared at the gray eyes of the sorcerer. "All right then. Your sorcerer confirms you speak the truth."

The prince looked at Carissian. "She can read your thoughts?"

"I'm not certain, sire. She blocks my trying to read hers, but... well, I'm not sure."

"You cannot swim," Aleron said to Tashama.

"If you say so."

"She's swimming in waves of the ocean, sire. I see her diving under the frothing, foaming breakers."

"She's tricking you into seeing this. How can she perform such a feat?" He circled Tashama as he studied her. "What does she wear while she swims in the ocean? That strange tunic she wore with the unusual leggings? What?"

"Something similar to what she had on underneath the leggings and tunic, only instead of white and lacy, they were shimmering blue, trimmed in sparkling gold."

Aleron studied Tashama's gowns as he tried to visualize her wearing such a garment, then he frowned at her. "Why would you wear such a meager garment as that? Were you trying to catch the attention of the mermen of the sea?"

Tashama smiled. "A prince on the beach would have been more like it."

Aleron exchanged glances with Carissian. The prince said, "You thought you could ensnare me?"

"Ugh." Tashama closed her eyes, then opened them. "Heavens forbid. I had no intention of enticing one as mean as you."

"You were being punished for your disobedience!"

Tashama wrinkled her nose as the breeze carried the scent of the prince's clothes to her. As two palace guards arrived at the tower, the one said, "You wished the prisoner relocated, Your Highness?"

"To her guest chambers and have the healer look at her injuries again. And post a guard." Then he stormed out of the room.

TASHAMA WAS TRANSPORTED to her chambers, as Carissian followed close behind. "What is it that you see, Carissian?" she asked.

"How can you swim?"

"I taught myself."

"Mortals cannot swim."

She smiled. "So you say."

"Did you free the men?"

"Of course."

"You answer my questions freely now."

"Now you don't try to steal the answers from me. Ask me what you will."

"The prince will want to hear your answers to my questions."

"Will your abilities not be lessened in the prince's eyes if he realizes I will answer your questions without your sorcerer ways?"

"Are you a sorceress?"

"What do you think?"

"I'm not certain."

"It must be difficult for you to have to deal with one like me."

Carissian smiled. "You amuse me."

"You don't fear me? The prince seems to."

"You move men, like the Gods move mountains. Who would not fear a woman who can do such a thing?" He stared at her hair as it swept around her hips, then shook his head. "Any other woman would have been at risk in the presence of the male pris-oners—both in the compound and in the tower, but not you. In neither situation have the men shown anything but compassion in your disposition. How can this be? You confound me, woman."

"I have not eaten. I'm dizzy."

Carissian stopped the guards. He thought for a moment, then a slight smile appeared. "Take the lady to the prince's chambers."

She sighed deeply. "He won't like that you do this."

"He will hear your answers to my questions while you dine in his chambers."

"Does he always dine there?"

"When he entertains."

"The ladies?"

"Only one at a time."

"He will not like this."

When they arrived at the prince's chambers, the men hesitated to enter the room. Carissian insisted and motioned for them to lay Tashama on the pillows. He excused the guards as the prince walked into his bedchambers wearing a gold towel around his waist.

Aleron only saw his sorcerer at first in his outer chamber and said, "I can see by the smile on your face that the woman has revealed something about herself to you."

"She wishes to answer our questions." Carissian waved at Tashama, who studied the prince's muscular figure as a fine smattering of water still dotted it. She smiled at the sparse growth of dark hair covering his chest, running down his stomach in a narrow trail.

The prince's mouth dropped open, then he stormed back into his bedchambers. "What were you thinking by bringing her here, Carissian?" The prince shouted at his servant, "No! The blue one!"

"She needs to eat, Your Highness."

"So feed her!"

"She wishes to answer our questions. I thought you might like to hear what she has to say."

The prince walked back into the room as he buckled his belt over his pale blue tunic trimmed in gold. Tashama touched one of the satin pillows with her fingertips as he turned to his servant. "Have the steward fetch us a meal."

He paced across the floor for a moment. "All right, ask her something."

"Do you not wish to have a question of yours answered first, my liege?" The prince considered Tashama's golden curls draped over her shoulders. Carissian shook his head. "I mean about who she is."

Aleron glared at his sorcerer. "Stop reading my mind. Read hers!"

"She won't allow me to, but she promised to answer our questions." The prince stared at Tashama. Carissian laughed. "All right, since your mind doesn't seem to wish to focus on the questions that I believe need answering, I'll ask a question or two of the lady myself." Carissian folded his arms across his chest, then tilted his chin up slightly. "Where do you come from?"

"Oh." She pushed her curls behind her shoulders. "I'm really famished, and I'm having difficulty concentrating." She frowned at the prince. "It has something to do with a certain kind of drink I've been plied with."

"See, she will not answer our questions! She dallies with us."

The servants hurried into the room with trays of cheese and apples. Tashama smiled. "Are you not going to join me?" She picked up a slice of cheese and wrapped her full pink lips over the snowy-white morsel. Aleron studied her. "It's excellent. To answer the sorcerer's question, I don't remember the name of the village."

Aleron glowered at her. "She's not answering your question!"

"She doesn't seem to remember the place of her birth, sire."

Carissian offered her a goblet of wine.

"It's not drugged, is it?" she asked.

"There is no need."

She took a sip and nodded. "This is what the prince drank before." She ran her finger over the top of the cup, then slipped her finger into her mouth as she sucked the wine from her skin. Her brows rose when Aleron followed her movements with intrigue. Picking up a slice of blue apple, she ran her tongue over the length of the fruit. "I hadn't remembered it tasting like peppermint." She took a bite and savored the crispy, sweet fruit, then lay down on the pillows. "Are you afraid of me?" she asked the prince.

"Who are you?"

12

"You have not asked this of me before. Nobody has asked me who I am. I'm an insignificant Karthlander—a woman. Why do you fear me?" she asked.

"She has not said who she is, Carissian. What does this mean?"

"She says she taught herself to swim."

"Mortals cannot swim!" The prince paced. "Put her in my bath."

"What of her wounds?"

"Have my healer look at her injuries. I want to see her swim."

The servant was dispatched to find the healer, and Carissian said, "Since you cannot tell us your birthplace, where did you live before we found you at the lake?"

"Texas." Tashama reached for a slice of bread. She savored the scent of garlic-soaked butter coating the bread, then took a bite. "Hmm, the food here is very good."

"Does she speak the truth?"

Carissian nodded.

"I know of no such place. Why will she not tell us what she is called?"

Tashama ignored the prince as she sucked the flavored butter from her fingertips. Then she lay back down on the pillows. "Are you not hungry?" she asked the prince.

Carissian leaned against the edge of the desk. "You've never been kissed before."

"What an odd thing to say to me. Of course, I've been kissed before."

Carissian eyes grew hard as he studied hers. She shook her head. "Quit trying to read my mind!"

"What is it, Carissian?" The prince tensed. "Who is she?"

"She has not been kissed before by a young man, but family members have kissed her. There was someone, I couldn't see, who wouldn't allow anyone to get close to her. But her thoughts drifted back to an earlier time, and I could see a hazy memory of her mother and father kissing her cheeks. She has not seen them for many years."

Tashama grabbed her goblet from the servant. "You do not play fair!" She drank the remainder of the cup, then lay back down.

The servant glanced over at the prince, who motioned for him to refill the goblet. Then Carissian said, "I asked you before if you were a sorceress, but you answered me with a question. I ask again, do you meddle in sorcery?"

Tashama motioned to a servant to bring her a slice of fish. She lifted the white meat to her lips, then savored the lemon-pepper flavored filet. "I answered—do you think I am?"

"I don't know what to think."

"Okay, I'm not a sorceress."

The sorcerer rubbed his chin, then shook his head. "You seem to be telling the truth in part, but a human cannot block her thoughts from me as you're capable of doing."

"Yet you say mortals cannot swim. I swim, so therefore I must be immortal."

"You are not immortal!" the prince said.

"No, Prince Aleron, I am not."

"You cannot swim!"

Fine lines beneath her eyes appeared as a smile stretched across her face, like the sun's rays shining on a peach-colored morning.

The healer walked into the room, and the prince motioned to Tashama. "Tell me if she can enter the bath." The healer stared at the prince. "Tell me!"

The healer knelt at her feet and unwrapped the cloth binding them. "How are your ribs feeling this afternoon?"

"You have healed them, healer, and I thank you for your kindness."

The healer pulled off the bandage of her left foot and shook his head. "She needs to keep her feet dry for at least another day while the wounds heal."

"Another day?" the prince said.

"Yes, sire. In another day, I believe her feet will be well-healed."

"Leave us."

The healer rewrapped her foot, then hurried out of the room.

"You have been saved from the bath for the moment." He sat down on the pillows and waved for a goblet of wine. He drank the entire goblet of wine.

"Do you always drink your wine so quickly?" She stretched her arms above her head. "It would all go to my head." The sorcerer smiled. "But my thoughts would be unclear for you to read."

"So we've found," Carissian said.

The prince studied her hair, then turned and waved for a servant. The servant offered him the tray of cheese and apples. The prince picked up a slice of cheese. He bit into it as Tashama touched his free hand. She frowned.

Carissian's brows furrowed as he leaned forward. "What are you attempting to do?"

"Nothing, sorcerer." Tashama lay back down.

Carissian shook his head, then walked over to the pillows as the prince and Tashama stared up at him. "What is it, Carissian?" the prince asked.

"She was trying to read you somehow."

She rested her hands on her waist and nestled her head on a plump purple pillow. The prince stared at her, then touched his fingers to her hand. "By touching me? What could she read?"

"I'm not certain."

"What were you doing?" the prince asked Tashama.

"I have the gift. Did you not know?"

"The gift? What gift?"

Carissian reached down and examined Tashama's hands. He shook his head. "I don't know."

The prince drank from his goblet, then motioned for the servant to offer more wine to Tashama. She shook her head. "I've already had too much."

The prince reached for a slice of apple. "Whatever you were trying to do, it didn't work."

"If you say so."

Carissian nodded. "You're right, my prince. The lady couldn't read you like she wished to."

"Good. At least someone cannot do so."

Carissian touched Tashama's cheek. "She cannot do so because her feelings for you are getting in the way."

Tashama's cheeks reddened as she brushed the sorcerer's hand away. "What a ludicrous thing to say."

Carissian laughed as the prince studied her reaction. "Her cheeks are blossoming like the white neleron when it blushes pink in the springtime. She needn't say a word—her skin tattles on her just the same."

The prince smiled. "What feelings does she have for me?"

"I've told you before, she wants you to kiss her."

"I do not, sorcerer." She sat up and scooted away from the prince.

"She doesn't speak the truth," the sorcerer said. "She's intrigued by your looks. Your smooth chest tantalized her as you left your bath. She barely took a breath as she studied the towel wrapped around your waist. Her..."

She hurtled a pillow at the sorcerer, and the prince and he stared at her for a moment, then both burst out laughing. The prince held his chest for a moment as he caught his breath. "Do tell, what else interests her about me?"

Carissian shook his head. "Now she's so flustered, I cannot say."

The prince stared at her, then smiled. "Tell her I desire to kiss her, too."

Carissian took a deep breath. "Should I leave the room, Your Highness?"

"No!" Tashama shouted. "You've read my thoughts wrong! Your prince needs to replace you, sorcerer, as your mind grows feeble."

The prince's eyes sparkled with mischief, and then he motioned for his staff to leave the room. The servants hurried to remove the platters of food, and Tashama folded her arms. "I cannot walk."

"Our prince doesn't want *you* to leave, just the rest of us." Carissian vanished.

The prince finished his goblet of wine, then set the empty cup on the floor. He stretched out on the pillows as he leaned on his elbow to observe her.

"You've hardly eaten anything," she said.

"Are you afraid of me?"

"Of course not."

"Even without Carissian's saying so, I can see you are. I won't harm you." He rolled onto his back, then studied the mural of the ocean painted across the twenty-foot-high ceilings of his chambers.

She lay down to consider the swirling aqua waters with sugary spray spilling from white caps as mermen intertwined their emerald-scaled tails with mermaids in the milky foam. She turned her head to see what part of the painting the prince was looking at, but he studied her bodice instead. She pulled a pillow over her chest and turned back to consider the mer-creatures further.

"It's the mating ritual." The prince touched her hand.

"How would you know?"

"Sailors have captured such visions for our artists to paint for centuries."

"Why can't we be at peace?" She looked over at him.

"Your leaders will not allow us to take them over, and of course, we will not allow them to do the deed to us."

"Why does one have to take over the other? Why can we not live in peace?"

"It has been this way forever." He touched a handful of her hair to his face, then breathed in deeply and smiled. "The fragrance of the blue water lily coats your hair from your dip in Lake Curaca. I imagine the mermaids in my mural tantalize their companions in much the same way. Her hair is as golden as yours, and her skin as ivory. If you truly can swim, perhaps you're really a mermaid."

"I don't have a tail." She studied the painting again.

He looked down at her skirts as they draped between her legs. He smiled. "You're so right about that." She watched him, and he touched his finger to her lips. "I wish to kiss you."

"You kissed another in the gardens yesterday when she forbade you to. If I forbid you to kiss me, will you disobey me, too?"

"Women have no say in such matters. Should I desire to kiss you—and you already know that I do—the choice would be mine to do as I pleased."

"You cannot be serious." She sat up quickly and furrowed her brow at him. "Your sorcerer has made a mistake about my interest in you."

"I *am* the ruler of Maldovia."

"You do not rule over me!"

"I don't know how things can get so quickly muddled between

you and me. The truth of the matter is, you desire me to kiss you, and I wish to oblige you. It's as simple as that."

"I want to be returned to my room at once!"

The prince stared at her for a moment, then sat upright. He jumped to his feet and hollered, "Guards!"

"Yes, sire?" two of the palace guards chimed in as they both hurried into the room at once.

"I'm retiring to bed. The prisoner will make her bed on the pillows here tonight. Make sure she doesn't leave here this evening."

"As you wish, my lord," one of the men said.

Aleron turned to Tashama. "Women do not make demands of men. And in particular, *no* woman makes a demand of me!" He strode back to his bedchambers.

Tashama grabbed a pillow, but before she could fling it at him, the guard grabbed it from her grasp. "You're courting disaster, miss." The guard tossed the pillow behind her.

"You sure are full of yourself!" she shouted to the prince as she collapsed on the pillows. She listened to the sounds of his mattress creaking as he slipped onto his feather-stuffed mattress.

The guards exchanged glances. One turned to her and said, "What does that mean, miss?"

"I wasn't speaking to you!" She twisted to get comfortable on the pillows. "I need a blanket."

"Sire," the guard whispered into the dark chambers of the prince. "Would it be all right for the prisoner to have a blanket?"

"No!" the prince yelled from the abyss.

"You are a tyrant!" she screamed back.

SOMETIME BETWEEN THE late-night hour and the early morning one, Tashama woke to find Carissian leaning against the desk, observing her. "The metal workers say the bracelets you wore were made of some gold alloy. Where did you get them?"

"The Virgin Islands." She rolled over on her side, then closed her eyes.

"Is it an uncharted island somewhere off your coast?"

She shook her head. "If it were uncharted, it would not be named."

"What is your name?"

"Dallas—you have said so yourself."

The whites of Carissian's knuckles showed as he gripped the edge of the desk with his fingers. "Dallas is a fanciful place. Your thoughts betray visions of the buildings scraping the sky as they loom toward the sun. One in particular fascinates you as its blue mirror-like sides shine in the sunlight. And again, I see the shiny, bright-colored, horseless wagons darting about their business on black stone roads, cris-crossing in such a maze it's similar to our palace corridors—in one respect."

She pushed the wayward wisps of hair back off her cheek. "What are you going to do with me?"

"The prince hasn't said."

"But you advise him. What will you tell him to do?"

"I can suggest."

"And?"

"Keep you here, close at hand for the time being." She shook her head slightly. Carissian laughed. "You envision stepping into your village amidst cheers from your people. Why does a woman think she would have such an effect on the Karthlanders? You're quite attractive, to be sure. But a woman—any woman—would never have much of a say in a man's world."

She rolled onto her back and glared at Carissian. Hearing the mattress creak in the room adjoining hers, she twisted her head in that direction. "He's already awake," Carissian said as he stood tall. "He's been listening to all that has been said."

"Balthazar is cleverer than you!" She knew as soon as she said it, she'd made a grave mistake. It was the early morning hour that tripped her up.

"Balthazar," Carissian said as his eyes narrowed. "Balthazar," he repeated as he took a step toward her. "What would you know of the Karthlander's sorcerer? He vanished with the rest of the royal family many years ago. Only now a cousin rules in their place. Valmor is the sorcerer who has taken Balthazar's position."

Tashama sat up on the pillows and stared at the floor. "A cousin?" she said to herself. Had he murdered her family for the power?

13

"You search for the missing pieces. You're trying to recollect who the Karthlander king's nephews were—but the names and even the faces elude you. *Who are you?*" Carissian asked Tashama.

"An insignificant Karthlander woman—so you have already said yourself."

Carissian bowed as the prince entered the room. "She has ties to Balthazar, the cagey old fox, sire."

The prince stared at her. "She must have been part of the royal staff then." He turned to Carissian. "Are you *sure* she's not a sorceress? Perhaps he was training her—"

"No." Carissian shook his head. "Balthazar was a royal sorcerer. He only saw to the..." Carissian paused. He glanced down at Tashama's cotton-wrapped feet, then took the prince's arm and led him from the room.

"What?" Aleron said, his voice raised.

The sorcerer's muffled voice mouthed a few sentiments she could not decipher, then he spoke out loud, "Yes, sire, I'm almost certain."

"Very well, have the healer check at once."

Tashama sighed deeply as she pulled her hair back, then began to wind it into a braid. The prince paced back and forth while Carissian said to a servant, "Have the healer brought here at once."

"At once," the servant repeated and hurried out of the chamber.

"When do I get to return to my chambers?" she called out to Carissian and the prince.

The two men walked back into the room, and both looked at her differently this time. She frowned at them, then continued to twist her hair into a rope as she turned her gaze to the floor. "Has your sorcerer told you I want to kiss you again? He lies, you know. He's only feeding your big ego, you do realize."

"How old are you?" the prince asked.

"I've been asked that an awful lot of late. Do you not know that asking such a thing of a woman is truly impolite?"

"She's twenty-three," Carissian said. "She's rattled and is having a difficult time blocking my exploration into her thoughts."

"Then she would be the right age." The prince took a deep breath.

"Balthazar would have stayed with her when the king and queen passed on."

"If she's the one."

"The one what?" Tashama finished twisting her braid. "Does anyone have a ribbon for me to tie my hair with?"

The prince considered Tashama further as she caressed the tail of her braided hair. "If she's the one, what should we do with her?"

"I'm not certain. She'd be a great pawn," Carissian said. Aleron studied his sorcerer while the old man rubbed his chin. "Loran is well entrenched in his role as leader of the Karthlanders. I doubt he would want the woman, if she is the one, to remove him from such a lofty position. And his sorcerer, no doubt, would be a great obstacle as well. However, it wouldn't hurt to ransom her. Then Loran can dispose of her as he will."

"Dispose of me?" She tilted her head to the side as she still held her braid tightly in her fist to prevent it from unraveling. "That sounds rather ominous."

"The notion doesn't seem to disturb her. Why is that? He surely would throw her into the sea, should she be the one, and we were to return her to him," Aleron said.

"Perhaps she believes Balthazar will rescue her."

"Balthazar," she scowled.

The healer hurried into the room and quickly bowed to the prince. "Sire, you would like to see me?"

"Inspect the woman's ankle and see if she has a dark heart-shaped spot on her skin."

"Which ankle, sire?"

The prince and Carissian turned to Tashama. She shrugged. "Don't look at me."

The healer hurried to unwrap her left foot, then examined both ankles. He shook his head. The prince motioned for him to continue. The healer unwrapped her right foot and examined the left ankle, then the right. He nodded as he twisted her leg hard to the side for the prince to get a better look.

"Ow! Let go of my leg!"

Carissian nearly bumped heads with the prince as they studied the tanned spot forming the perfect heart-shape on the crest of her ankle, the size of a dime.

"You *are* Tashama!" Aleron turned to his sorcerer. "She was thought to have died with the rest of her family."

"Apparently not." Carissian beamed. "The mystery is solved."

"She's no longer a threat to me, then." The prince considered Tashama while the healer rewrapped her bandages.

"The lady doesn't realize it, but for the moment you're her savior."

"Savior!" She glowered at the prince. "Why, he's no more my savior than Balthazar is."

"Where *is* Balthazar?" Carissian asked.

"How should *I* know? If he were here now, you would not be questioning me."

The prince smiled. "Tashama, princess of Karthland, and the true heir to the throne." He turned to Carissian. "She was being brought back here to find a mate. She's of age. Somehow, Balthazar sent her to the wrong place, don't you think, Carissian?" He studied her. "He was trying to reinstall her in Karthland, but she cannot lead without a husband."

"Ha!" She released her braid. The golden strands quickly untwisted, and she tried to stand. The memory of the painful burs digging into her water-softened feet etched across her mind, and Carissian grabbed hold of her arms and made her sit. "You cannot walk yet." His brows furrowed deeply.

"I can do as I please!" She scowled at the floor.

"Wherever this Texas is that she has lived has certainly made her unruly. Our women would never behave as she does. She wouldn't be a suitable wife for any man!" Aleron stared at her hair, then said to one of his servants, "Have one of the ladies veil her hair. Her hair should not be exposed as it is, especially since she is a princess."

"Why so ever not?" Tashama ran her hands through the silky strands. "Does it entice you too much?"

Carissian smiled as the prince frowned at her. "I told you she was wily, sire."

"What *are* we to do with her?"

"Let me give it further thought, Your Highness. In most probability, we should send word to Loran that we have his cousin here under guard and see how he responds."

"He was a spoiled brat and a veritable bully, the last I recall of him." Tashama ran her hands over a satiny pillow while she rested her cheek on her knees. "He was always an angry little boy—mad at the world because my father, not his, was king of Karthland.

Since he has continued the war, I assume he's still angry with the world. Being the ruler of Karthland changed not a thing."

The prince knelt next to her and touched her hair. "If you were the ruler of Karthland, would you stop the war?"

"Of course. I've already told you that I didn't feel it necessary. The soldiers are weary of fighting. I even heard your own armored knights say so the day I was taken prisoner by your lake. It's time to end the war. I doubt Loran will feel the same way. He won't stop until he's proclaimed emperor of the entire region."

"What is the gift you spoke of?" He lifted her chin and studied the golden flecks in her green eyes.

"I can see the future for some—not for all though."

"And you can read thoughts as Carissian can?"

She smiled. "Sure."

The prince looked over at Carissian, who shook his head. "She's blocking my reading of her thoughts again, sire. She's very good, this one."

The ladies walked into the room with veils and pins in hand.

Tashama shook her head at them. "I will not wear those."

The prince stood, then motioned for the women to get on with the task. She sat quietly while the maids attached two rainbow-colored sheer veils to her hair. They stood back to admire their handiwork. Tashama pulled the pins out, folded the veils, and then placed them neatly on the floor. "I thank you, ladies, for helping me with my hair, but my hair was just fine without."

The ladies looked over at the prince, who motioned for them to veil Tashama's hair again. The prince and Carissian leaned against the desk with their arms folded across their chests while the ladies attached the veils to Tashama's hair again. When they walked away, Tashama pulled the pins out and dropped the veils to the floor.

Everyone looked over at the prince, who rubbed his chin in thought. He leaned over to speak to Carissian in private, who stared back at the prince. The prince nodded, whereupon Carissian walked out of the room.

When the sorcerer returned, a guard followed him with a rope. The prince waved his hand at Tashama, but the guard said, "But she cannot stand."

"Make her lie down on her stomach then. Just get on with it."

The guard knelt by Tashama. "Miss..."

"Princess to you, sir."

The guard looked at the prince, who nodded.

"Princess, would you please—"

"Why certainly." She turned on her stomach and placed her hands behind her back. "I will do anything for you, kind sir, since you ask so sweetly."

The guard hurried to tie her wrists together, then looked for the prince's direction. "Make her sit up so the ladies can veil her hair."

"Yes, sire." The guard helped her to sit, then the ladies hurried to attach the veils. Once her hair was veiled, Tashama got onto her knees and began to walk toward the door.

The ladies giggled as the men all laughed. "You are making a fool of yourself," the prince said.

"No, sire, you are showing your people how cruel you can be to a royal princess who is your captive."

"Carry her to her quarters," the prince said, "and untie her there. In her own chambers, she can wear her hair as she pleases."

The guard lifted Tashama off the floor and the ladies hurried out of the door. When they were all well out of the range of his voice, Carissian shook his head. "You should attempt to pacify the lady, sire, so that should we be able to reinstall her on her throne, she would look more favorably toward a peace treaty with us."

"Her husband would be the one to make such a decision. How can she have a husband if she will not obey one? She is a lost cause, that one. If I'm able to tame her ways, her husband will thank me for the training we've provided here." He paced across the floor, then smiled. "I have work to do."

"Yes, sire. I will consider what to do with the lady concerning Loran in the meantime."

"Do." Aleron headed down the hall. When he arrived at Tashama's chambers, the guard knocked on her door. Princess Listra answered it, and Aleron said, "What is the princess doing now?"

"She's sitting in a chair next to the window. She seems to enjoy the fragrance the breeze draws into the room."

"Is her hair veiled?"

The lady shook her head.

"Have her hair veiled, and she can sit with me in the gazebo now."

"Yes, sire."

Princess Listra reentered the room, and Tashama said, "Sit in the gazebo? Very well, I would like that." There was some silence, then she said, "No, I don't want the veils on my hair. When I return to Karthland, I will abolish such a notion. You would do well to revolt against such an archaic..."

The prince strode into the chambers. "Either she wears the veils, or she stays in her room."

Tashama smiled. "I'm enjoying the gardens from here, thank you, sire. Perhaps some other time we could sit in the gazebo."

Aleron glared at her, then turned and stormed out of the room.

"Oh, my lady," Listra said, "you shouldn't treat the prince in such a manner."

"I'm a royal princess in my own right and ruler of my own kingdom. He has no right to tell me what to do." Tashama folded her hands in her lap.

"But you're a guest in his—"

"Prisoner, you mean. Are guards at my door?"

"Well, yes."

"A prisoner, I tell you." Tashama stared out the window and saw a dark-clothed figure walking along the garden path. "What is that?" She pointed at the sight.

"She's with the religious order of the Bachavin."

Tashama studied the woman, clothed in a black gown and veil, her face hidden beneath a black cloth, allowing not even a glimpse of her eyes. "How absurd. How can she see in such a contraption?"

"She can see. She's wed to the king of the gods, Bachava. No mortal man may view a woman of the order."

"And this god lives on Mount Olympus, I suppose."

"Mount Olympus?" Listra furrowed her brow in concentration as she tried to recollect such a place. "No, Mount Monadanock."

Tashama sat back stiffly in her chair as she spied the prince sauntering along the path with a dark-haired woman, arm in arm. The woman's familiar voice scolded the prince lightly as it carried on the breeze. "You had her in your chambers again. What am I to think of such behavior?"

"She's only a means to an end, Daveal. She'll have a home here for the time being until she can be of no further use to us."

"Did you kiss her?"

"Why would I want to kiss a Karthlander woman?"

The voices and footsteps faded away, and Tashama's cheeks warmed. "I want to take a bath."

"The healer said you're not to get your feet wet."

Tashama reached down and unwrapped the cloth on her right foot as Listra ran over to stop her. "Leave me be! I wish to see how my foot is faring after that brutal prince injured them so."

"You shouldn't have run away." Listra tried to grab Tashama's hand to stop her.

Tashama scowled, "They are my feet. Let me see them."

"They're not to be unwrapped."

"By the prince's orders?"

"No, the healer's."

Tashama pulled the cloth free from her foot as Listra hurried to the door. "Get the healer! The princess has removed the cloth from her foot."

"Cloths from her feet," Tashama corrected as she pulled the other free.

"Do hurry," Listra said to the guard. She returned to Tashama's side and wrung her hands as Tashama studied the puncture wounds, still red and swollen. "The air is not good for the wounds, my lady. That's why your feet must remain wrapped until the healer says otherwise."

"Nonsense. I'm tired of seeing my feet bound like I'm being mummified. Even if the soles of my feet are a sight, at least the rest of my feet look nice and normal. Besides, the healer said they should be fine by tomorrow."

The guard pushed the door open, and the red-faced healer hurried to her side. "Word has been sent to the prince," he said to Listra. Then he turned his attention to Tashama. "You must keep the bandages wrapped around your feet, my lady."

"But you yourself unwrapped them earlier today—not once, but twice."

"By the prince's orders, but against my better judgment."

"Well then, by the princess's orders, my feet are to remain unbound. They feel hot and sweaty in those bandages. The cool breeze feels fine between my toes." She wiggled them slightly.

"This is a foolish notion, my lady, and can be dangerous to your health."

"I wish to have a second opinion!"

"The prince is coming," the guard warned.

14

"The second opinion," Aleron said as he stormed into the room, "is that you will have your feet bound as before, and if you don't mind the healer's orders, your wrists will be tied as well to keep those mischievous hands still." *How can she be so beautiful, but as cantankerous as an untamed filly at the same time?*

A slight smile crept across Tashama's face. "Was the lady very offended that you abandoned her to visit me in my chambers?"

"Rewrap her feet, healer." Aleron wrinkled his brow as the healer reapplied salve. Once the healer finished rewrapping her feet, Aleron motioned to the door. "Everyone, leave us."

Listra followed the guards and healer out of the room and closed the door behind her. Aleron folded his arms. "You *will* obey me and those who speak for me."

"Of course." Tashama relaxed.

"My personal business is none of your concern."

"Are you marrying the woman?"

He couldn't believe his ears. Hadn't he just told her that Daveal was none of her business? "You seem to have difficulty interpreting the spoken word."

"She won't like it that you spend so much time with me."

"She knows her place, unlike you." How could he, ruler of all Maldovia, put up with such insolence from this woman...a mere prisoner? Yet, even now, his loins ached for her.

She toyed with a golden curl. "My place is as the ruling head of Karthland—not under your thumb."

"Your place is beside your husband. I already feel sorry for the poor man." He could only imagine what her husband would face if he risked linking with her. Still, he couldn't take his eyes off her.

"He'll be a kind sight nicer than you, that's for certain. And he'll get all the kisses he wishes." Tashama puckered her full lips slightly.

"He'll get a lot more than that from you."

"Of course." Tashama tucked the curl behind her ear.

"I meant that tongue of yours."

Tashama laughed. "You know, you say the funniest things even though you don't realize you say them. So what are you going to do about my dear Cousin Loran?"

"We've sent a dispatch to him already. The sooner he takes you off my hands, the better." He was annoyed with her, but he didn't really feel the sentiments he spoke. If he could, he would keep her here, under his thumb, as she said. No, under the weight of his body, full of desire. How could he feel this way about her? His enemy?

His heart increased its pace as he tugged at his tunic. He didn't want her to see how much her body could affect his, even as he stood two feet away. A light scent of jasmine drifted in the air...her scent. She was more beautiful than anyone in his kingdom. He was the ruler of all Maldovia after all. Why shouldn't he have such a prize to call his own?

"So you're going to ransom me." Tashama looked down at the floor.

He wanted to pull her from the chair and hold her close, to feel her warm breath against his neck. "You want to go home. We'll help you return there."

"Good." Tashama ran her hands over her satin skirts. "Sooner, than later, I would hope."

"As would I." Aleron turned to leave. How could he say such a thing, when he meant just the opposite? She brought out the worst in him without even trying.

He walked out of the room as Listra walked in and closed the door. "Did he scold you much?"

"Of course not. He loves me. That's why he gets so perturbed with me. I don't share his sentiments," Tashama said, then, seeing the strange look on Listra's face, she added, "I don't have the same feelings for him that he has for me. It angers him. His fiancée won't like that he feels this way for me, I'm certain."

"Fiancée?"

"The woman he's to marry."

"He hasn't decided on one yet, though Carissian has urged him on several different occasions to make a choice."

"And the lady he was walking with in the gardens?"

"Lady Daveal." Listra nodded.

"Devil. So who is this woman?"

Listra hooked the drapes to the wall. "If you're not interested in the prince, why are you interested in knowing about Daveal?"

"I'm sick of not being able to get around. A little court gossip would be welcome."

Listra sat down and lifted her needlework to her lap, but said nothing further.

"She's a member of a royal family, I take it?"

Listra still said not a word as she concentrated on her work.

A blue fabric caught Tashama's eye as she turned to look through the window. A young man crouched next to four-foot-high shrubs. *Jaran, the youngest thief from the prison tower.* He motioned for her to come to him, but she shook her head as she pointed to her feet.

Tilting his head down, he showed he understood. He held his hands together and rested his cheek on them as he closed his eyes. She nodded. He waved, then darted down the path.

Tashama turned to Listra. "So what are you embroidering?"

Listra smiled as she showed her the tapestry. Tashama touched the green shimmering-scaled tail of the mermaid reclining on a moss-covered boulder while the surf splashed spray into the air. "It's lovely. Where will you display this?"

"The tapestry is for the prince's coronation. He will be crowned king of Maldovia in two days. I'll make it into a pillow to add to the rest of his collection."

"Oh." Tashama turned her attention back to the window. "He's already so full of himself, he'll never be able to fit into his crown, unless it's as big as the circumference of his lake."

"You say the oddest things."

"Yes, but they're true." Tashama ran her fingers through her silky hair.

Listra set her needle in a pincushion. "They say you're quite taken with the appearance of the prince."

"He's different than my kind. That's all."

"There are many who are intrigued by your fair coloring. I heard one of the guards say he couldn't get enough of that blond hair. That's why you must wear a veil."

Tashama reached back to braid her hair. "Do you have something to tie this with? A ribbon or some such thing?"

Listra reached her hand into the pouch tied at her waist, then handed a blue ribbon to Tashama.

"Thank you. I hope that I haven't been too much of a bother to you."

"I've been given the task of being your lady-in-waiting for the remainder of the time you'll be here. Many are anxious to serve you."

"Why?"

Listra ran her hands over her skirt. "Because of your confrontations with the prince. There's been quite a bit of conversation in the ladies' chambers concerning this when we turn in for the night. Because of my assignment, my position has been somewhat elevated."

Tashama laughed. "Well, at least someone appreciates I'm here." She finished braiding her hair, then set the tail of the braid in her lap. "I heard one of the men call you a princess, though."

"I'm the prince's first cousin. My mother was the king's sister."

"I would think your position is already quite elevated."

"There are twenty-two princesses. We are all cousins of Prince Aleron."

"I see. Then, as one of many of the prince's first cousins, who would you like to see the prince marry?"

"A woman who will satisfy the prince's desires so he will be happy in his reign over Maldovia."

"The prince should please his wife, and in doing so, she will find favor with him."

Listra smiled. "The ladies find you amusing. You twist our concepts so. It's difficult to imagine you can be a Karthlander and the ruler of your people with such strange notions."

"Will you help me with something?"

Listra tied Tashama's braid. "If I can."

"I would like to sit in the gazebo."

"With veils covering your hair."

Tashama studied the gardens, then finally nodded.

"I'll have the guards carry you and will sit with you before the meal."

～

AFTER LISTRA APPLIED veils to Tashama's hair, she opened the door and made her request known to the guards. Soon Tashama sat with Listra in the lacy white gazebo overlooking a pond she hadn't noticed before. Orange-scaled fish swam under the hogwort pads. Tashama leaned forward to get a closer look. Suddenly, a water sprite flew into her face, and she sat back, startled.

"Tashama," the sprite whispered on the breeze as she fluttered about Tashama's head. "Tashama, they've got you again."

"Go away, you pesky sprite."

The blue-winged creature giggled and dove into the water as Tashama shook her head. Listra's mouth dropped open.

"What's the matter?"

"Did you understand what she said? Could you hear her words?"

"Certainly. They're annoying, aren't they?"

Listra's eyes widened.

"Do not tell me that you cannot understand them."

"Nobody I know can, my lady. They make strange tinkling noises, and like the birds or other animals of the wild, we cannot understand their speech. What did she say?"

"Nothing important. They are like gnats, annoying! By the way, please call me Tashama."

"But you are..."

"A princess and so are you."

"But you will be queen of Karthland."

"Not if your prince has his way."

Listra cleared her throat and changed the subject. "Our people say you have the gift of future sight. Can you tell me what you see for me?"

Tashama shook her head. "I cannot tell for everyone."

"Will you try?"

"I don't want to see anything ill."

"Please?"

Tashama nodded. "All right." She reached out for Listra's hand as a lady's laughter peeled through the quiet. "Devil?"

Listra corrected her, "Daveal."

"Well," the prince said as he and Daveal walked into Tashama's view, "I had not expected to see *you* here."

Listra stood up and curtsied. "Her hair is veiled."

"Good, then she can sup with me." He turned to the raven-haired lady who still clung to his arm. "Later, my lady." The woman cast a scowl in Tashama's direction, then turned and hurried away. The prince motioned to one of his guards. "Carry her to my quarters."

Aleron walked in front of his guards, and Tashama whispered to Listra, "Will you stay with me the whole time we dine?"

Aleron looked back at Tashama and raised a brow. "Are we afraid, my lady?"

"Of course not, but I've been told I've been too agreeable in your presence before."

"Hardly." Aleron sighed deeply, then shook his head as he made a face.

They arrived at his chambers, and he turned to Listra. "You may have the rest of the evening off."

"Am I not to attend to the lady tonight, Your Highness, after she has retired to bed? Should she need something to drink or another pillow or some company or some such thing?"

"No, dear cousin, you have earned the evening off."

Tashama frowned at Aleron.

Listra curtsied deeply. "As you wish, sire." She hastened out of the room.

The guards laid Tashama on the pillows, then Aleron gestured for the servants to bring the feast. He sat beside her as she fiddled with the ribbon tied in a bow at the end of her braid. "You can remove your veils now, my lady."

"They feel good where they are now, thank you very much, sire."

He smiled. *You are afraid of me, though you deny it.* Aleron waved for the lobster to be brought forth.

Tashama smiled at the red-shelled creatures garnished in parsley-type leaves. A servant leaned over to pull the meat from the shell for her, and she slipped her fingers around the sweet meat.

"You seem to like lobster best of all of the meals we've had here."

"Oh, yes." She ate the tender meat.

After she finished her lobster, she turned to him. "I'm afraid to say this as you may think me rather piggish, but could I have another?"

Aleron smiled. He waved to his servant who bowed then hurried away. *I cannot give her to Loran no matter how much Carissian advises me to do so.* "I think you must be like the mermaid who relishes such delicacies of the sea."

"Oh, yes. Living in the heart of Texas like I did, lobsters were so expensive and brought in from such a distance, I rarely had the opportunity to enjoy them."

"Tell me about this Texas." Aleron took a drink of his wine.

"It's a big place with rolling hills, lakes, rivers, prairies, semi-tropical areas, palm trees, pine forests, canyons, beaches, the Gulf of Mexico. You can just about see anything you'd want to see without ever leaving the state."

"Like here."

Aleron studied the veils on Tashama's hair, then turned to a servant. "Leave the trays of food here. We'll serve ourselves. You may withdraw now."

Aleron handed a bowl of cherries to Tashama. She examined the purple fruit. "Does it have a pit?"

"A pit?"

"A seed?"

Aleron smiled. "You say the oddest things."

She bit gently into the fruit to ensure she didn't bite into a seed, then, finding none, she smiled. "No seeds."

"Do the cherries in Texas have seeds?"

"We remove them before they're served, usually."

"This Texas sounds like a peculiar place. I've given it much thought. I cannot fathom where it would be located in connection with Maldovia, Karthland, and the land of Inherian."

"Far away from here. You couldn't imagine how different it is from your, well, our world."

A servant walked into the chambers with another lobster as Aleron considered her gown. "You don't think me too..."

"Go right ahead, Princess. Eat to your heart's content. If you wish, you may have another after this."

She dug the tender, pink-veined meat out of its shell. "I believe this will satisfy me."

Aleron finished his wine, then ate a bowl of rice while Tashama finished off her lobster. After she wiped her hands on a linen napkin, she sipped her wine while he lay down on his side to observe her. "Why did you not wish to wear the veils?"

"The pins poke into my scalp, and the veils weigh down my hair. They feel cumbersome and unnatural to me, just as wearing them would be for you, I would imagine."

Aleron smiled as he touched Tashama's braid, which curled on the pillow beside him. "I have not the lovely tresses to attach such a thing to as you do." He took a deep breath. "I do not believe your wearing sheer veils will be a sufficient deterrent to interested admirers. The glimpse of beauty screened beneath the cloth tantalizes the viewer even further, rather than discouraging interest in the sight. Therefore, you may remove your veils."

She ran her finger over her full lips, indicating the vaguest of smiles as she considered Aleron. "All right."

She reached up to pull the pins from her hair while Aleron

poured another goblet of wine for himself. She folded the veils onto the floor beside the pillows, then sipped his wine as she lay back on the cushions.

"Better?" he asked.

"Much." She knew she would get her way eventually. But for other things, she would have to be the one to make it happen.

15

Aleron set his goblet on the floor, then moved closer to her. As he lay on his back, he placed his arms behind his head and stared up at the mural. He smiled as she scooted closer to him, her shoulder touching his.

"If you look carefully, you'll see a mermaid catching a lobster near the rocks under the surface of the foam just to the right of that outcropping of pink coral." He pointed to the location.

"Where? Oh, yes, and a merman nearby who's watching her. Do you think he'll snatch it away from her?"

Aleron laughed. "Why would he do such a thing?" His hand groped around the pillows until he held the end of her braid.

"It looks as though he cannot decide which he would rather have—the mermaid or the lobster."

"And the mermaid?" He untied the ribbon from her hair.

"Why, she has chosen the lobster, of course." Aleron unraveled her braid. "What *are* you doing?"

"Seeing your hair wound so tightly gives me a headache."

"My hair gets in the way when it's undone." She wriggled to get comfortable on the pillows. "Why have you dismissed the servants?"

"They talk."

"Will they not talk concerning you having dismissed them?"

"The stories are greater this way." He smiled as she frowned at him. "You have said I'm full of myself. What does this mean?"

She shook her head. Aleron touched his fingertips to her cheek.

"Your skin is as soft as the newborn peach in springtime." He rubbed his chin and furrowed his brow. "While mine has a fine stubble, always by late evening."

She touched his face and smiled. "It tickles."

He kissed her hand, then leaned over her. Her heart beat beneath his chest, and he smiled as she closed her eyes and puckered her lips slightly in anticipation of his kiss.

"Sire!" Carissian said, before Aleron could touch his lips to Tashama's.

"Carissian!" Aleron exclaimed as he sat upright.

"May I have a word with you, Your Highness, alone?"

"No."

"Sire."

"This is not a good time, Carissian." Aleron jumped to his feet. Grabbing his sorcerer's arm, he yanked him into his bedchambers.

"What are you thinking, sire? You cannot get tangled up with the Karthlander princess."

"I only wish a kiss from her lips, Carissian."

"One thing leads to another. You must send her back to her room."

Aleron's face turned dark. "You forget your place, Carissian. You advise me, you do not make demands of me."

"Forgive me, Your Highness." Carissian bowed deeply. "I'm only concerned that the woman has truly bewitched you. The word throughout the palace is how several wish the lady would be theirs, and now the gossip is that the prince has fallen in love with the prisoner. Sire, consider this. She's the ruler of the realm that has warred with us for years. She *is* the enemy."

"She's the ruler of naught, Carissian. She's in exile, remember?"

"Exile is it now? What if Loran wants her back? Are we to refuse to send her to him if he agrees to the hefty ransom we've asked for?"

"He will kill her, of that I'm sure."

"What difference does this make to you? She cannot be your wife."

The prince stared at his advisor, then, as his brow knitted tightly, he scowled, "What's the matter with you? I have no intention of marrying such a creature. She intrigues me, nothing more. Still, I wouldn't wish to sacrifice her for some paltry sum of money."

"The sum *is* substantial."

The prince waved his hand at his advisor for his silence, then walked back into the room. He considered Tashama as she slept soundly now. He shook his head. "You were to report concerning activities on the battle front, not come barging in here to give me grief."

"General Karam has taken Chrisholm Island. Word is he'll stop at nothing to free the princess from Banff."

The prince sat at his desk. "She truly is an inspiration to her men. But if General Karam serves Loran..."

Carissian shook his head. "Apparently, his allegiance is to the princess, once he learned she lived."

"Then their forces are splitting over the woman." The prince smiled. "Is this not a good thing?"

"Possibly."

"Then if we keep her here, the troops loyal to the princess's family will turn on Loran's troops if they try to take her?"

"But *we still* have her, sire. They will band together nevertheless to fight us—perhaps with a divided cause—but with the same number of forces."

The prince rubbed his chin. "Then we must somehow provoke

General Karam's forces to fight Loran instead. Once both sides weaken, we can take the whole region over." He turned to observe Tashama. "You will deliver your people to me, Princess. You have been sent to me by the gods."

"You must...," Carissian said, then changed his wording, "wouldn't it be more prudent to return the princess to her chambers tonight, sire?"

The prince stood up from his desk, then walked back into his bedchambers. He pulled a blanket from his bed, then walked back into the room where Tashama slept. After covering her with the blanket, he stood up straight. "I'll see you in the morning, Carissian."

BEFORE THE SUNLIGHT was even streaming into the prince's bedchambers, a lantern light shone into Tashama's eyes as she blinked them in annoyance. The healer crouched near her feet, and she covered her head with a pillow. "I'm removing your bandages, my lady." He unwrapped her left foot.

"Couldn't you do it later?" she mumbled under the satin pillow.

"Is she as obstinate as usual?" Aleron leaned down to get a look at the sole of her foot.

She pulled the pillow from her face and frowned. "I should've known you would be the reason for this vexation. Do you not know my sleep is not to be disturbed unless I want it?" She covered her face with the pillow again.

"What do you think?"

The healer touched her skin. "How does it feel, my lady?"

"It tingles like my foot has gone to sleep."

"Good, then you should be able to walk on them without too much discomfort. By tomorrow, they'll feel almost as good as new."

"Good." She rolled onto her stomach.

The healer reached down to unwrap her right foot. He touched the wounds. "Your injuries were less severe on this foot, my lady." When she said nothing in response, the healer said, "My lady?"

"Go away," she said under her breath.

"It's time for your swim," Aleron said.

She shook her head, and the pillow wiggled with the movement.

"Now, Tashama. I want to see you swim."

"Later."

"You cannot swim."

"You are right. Leave me be. I was dreaming about a handsome prince who swept me off my feet and had taken me to a lovely restaurant in Dallas..."

"My sorcerer says this is not so."

She pulled the pillow from her head and rolled onto her side. "Is everyone in here?"

"Only those who count. I want to see how your feet feel when you walk."

"Later."

"Now. Do I need to have my guards help you to stand?"

She clasped her arms together. "Can you not sleep, Your Highness, as you desire to see me so?"

"See you swim, you mean." Aleron motioned to his guards.

They helped Tashama to stand, and she teetered on her tiptoes.

"Do they still hurt?" Aleron took her arm and waved for his guards to step away.

"I'm afraid to touch them to the floor."

Aleron smiled. "Why do you not tell me what bothers you instead of behaving as though you intend to undermine my authority?"

"I wanted to sleep longer. My dreams were disturbed last night."

"By?" Carissian asked.

Aleron said to the healer, "Is there a risk that her feet are still too tender to walk on?"

"A dream," Tashama said in reply to Carissian.

"Of course, but we won't know unless the princess takes her first step," the healer said to Aleron.

"A dream." Carissian's gaze caught Aleron's.

"I will help you." Aleron encouraged her to take a step with him. She walked on the tips of her toes, and he smiled. "You cannot walk like that forever."

"Certainly, I can. It feels very comfortable up here."

"All right, then. Perhaps after you show me you can swim, you can walk."

"Can you tell me about this dream?" Carissian asked.

She shook her head. "I cannot remember what it was about. Just that it woke me last night and I couldn't get back to sleep for a while."

Aleron led Tashama to his bath with a quickened step.

"Are we in a hurry, sire?" she asked.

He glared at Carissian. "Quit reading my mind."

They entered Aleron's bedchambers as servants lit the sconces on the walls. The room was filled with a soft light shimmering off the marble bath.

Tashama stared at the onyx marble with white streaks swirling onto the tile as it covered the pool. Candles floating at intervals in the still water cast faint light on the sparkling surface. She turned her face up to Aleron. "I may drown because I'm not yet awake."

"I will rescue you if you fall asleep."

"What will Devil think of your making me swim in your bath like this?"

"Daveal? What I do is none of her concern, nor anyone else's for that matter."

They reached the edge of the bath, and Tashama raised her

arms above her head. He frowned. "What are you doing, Tashama?"

"I need to have the sheer overdress removed. Do you want me to drown in your pool because of the weight of my wet gowns?"

"You wore them in the lake."

"In desperation."

Carissian shrugged as the healer and his guards waited in breathless anticipation, to Tashama's amusement.

"If you insist." Aleron struggled to slip the sheer fabric over her arms. She continued to stretch her arms in the air. Aleron stared at her. "You cannot be serious."

"If I'm to take a bath, I always remove my clothes."

"You're not to take a bath, just swim for me."

"Very well." The tips of his ears had reddened slightly. Good, she had embarrassed him for a change, instead of him doing so to her. She slipped to sit down at the edge of the pool, then poked her feet into the water and took a deep breath.

"Are they all right?" the healer asked.

"They feel hot, but I'm sure they'll be all right, thank you, healer." She slid into the pool and touched her toes to the slippery floor. Six men watched her. "Do we have to have such an audience?"

Aleron waved to his guards to leave the room. When they had left his chamber, Tashama waved her hand at the healer. "And your healer?"

"He'll stay in case your feet hurt."

"And your sorcerer?"

Aleron shook his head. "Swim."

"Really, it would be better for me to swim in the lake. It's not deep enough here."

"Swim."

"All right." Tashama pushed forward with her toes, then floated on the surface of the bathwater for a moment. Taking a deep breath, she made a shallow dive underneath the water and swam like a mermaid boxed into a narrow channel.

Her golden hair flowed around her like the delicate tentacles of a jellyfish. "She's swimming," Aleron whispered.

Carissian shook his head as he stared into the pool. "I wouldn't have truly believed it if I hadn't seen it for myself."

"Is she part mermaid, do you think?"

"No, the maids said she had all of the features of a human when they helped her with her bath."

"But how can she swim?"

Tashama surfaced at the other end of the bath. "Have you seen enough?"

"No, let me see you do it again."

"Oh, honestly. If you'll be nice, I can teach you to swim, too."

"Mortals cannot swim." Aleron folded his arms across his chest. She could truly swim. He couldn't believe his eyes. And Listra had informed him Tashama knew the language of the water nymphs. What other powers did she possess?

"Right." Tashama slipped beneath the surface of the water and swam to the other end of the long bath. Bubbles forming around a built-in seat pulled her like a magnet. She scooted into the marble chair and leaned against the flow of churning water. "Now what?" She leaned her head against the pillow and closed her eyes.

Aleron studied her gowns as the wet fabric accentuated her curves, then, as Carissian cleared his throat to get his attention, he turned to him. "What?"

"The lady has swum for you, sire. Do you not think it prudent to allow her to return to her chambers to change into dry gowns?"

Aleron motioned for his healer to leave. The man gathered his bandages and basket of salves and hurried out of the room. Aleron considered Tashama further. "Have her maids dress her here. It would not do for her to drip water all the way back to her chambers."

"And you, sire?"

"Me what?"

"Surely you have other business to attend to."

"I'll see you momentarily, Tashama, to see how you fare with walking once you've changed."

Aleron grabbed the sorcerer's arm and led him out of his bedchambers. "You can really be quite annoying at times, Carissian."

"Yes, sire."

Tashama slumped deeper into the bubbles. Aleron took a deep breath, then pulled Carissian from the room.

LATER THAT AFTERNOON Tashama sat in her chair by the window while Listra embroidered the mermaid's golden strands of hair on Aleron's tapestry pillow. "Is it nearly finished?"

"Yes, it is—and not too soon either."

Tashama saw the young thief in his shabby, blueberry-colored tunic crouching by a dark, green-leafed shrub dotted in blue flowers the same shade as his garments. He nodded to her as she caught his eye. After placing his hands together, he rested his head on them as he closed his eyes. He opened his eyes and shrugged.

Tashama indicated that she had slept, using the same gesture of her hands, and then pointed toward the other wing of the castle. He nodded. He displayed a slip of blue paper to her, then stuck it between the delicate leaves of the shrub. She bowed her head.

He dove out of sight, and a guard shouted, "Stop that boy!"

16

Listra dropped her tapestry to the marble floor and ran to the window. "Did you see who it was?"

"Not a sign of anyone." Tashama frowned when the head of the guards hurried to her window.

"Did he...did the boy threaten you in any way?" The guard huffed and puffed as he tried to catch his breath.

Listra shook her head. "We didn't see him."

"But he was on this very path. He had to have come right by here."

Tashama sighed deeply. "I must have been distracted as I watched Listra embroider."

The guard turned to Listra. "A guard will be posted in the gardens, in the future." He bowed and rushed off.

"He'll tell the prince." Listra straightened her back. "Were you protecting the young man?"

"If I did not see him, how could I be protecting him?"

Listra shook her head. "I cannot see what you can with these special gifts of yours, my lady, but your cheeks darkened when the guard questioned us."

"I blush easily, if that is what you're referring to."

The folded blue sheet of paper fluttered slightly in the breeze.

She took a deep breath as she hoped Listra wouldn't catch sight of it. "The guard is one of the ones who watched as the prince removed my sheer overdress. Having him watch me like that, then seeing him here before me once again, embarrassed me, nothing more."

Listra's lower lip dropped as her eyes widened. "I'm sorry. I had no idea," she said quickly, then hurried back to her chair. She drew her tapestry off the floor. "I've been afraid to ask you what you saw about my future. I saw your eyes widen as I touched your hand while helping you earlier this morning. I know you don't want to tell me what you saw, but I can't shake the notion from my mind. My imagination is very vivid, and I think I must be going to die soon or..."

"You will betray the prince's trust in you." Tashama considered how she'd get the thief's message waving back at her.

"Surely you do not see me do this. I would be exiled and lose the love of my family and everything I believe in. Maybe you are wrong."

"Yes," Tashama said softly. She truly liked the woman. Had she been blessed with a sister, she would've wanted her to be just like Listra.

"You are never wrong, are you, my lady?"

Tashama shook her head.

"But how could I do such a thing?"

Tashama ran her hands over her golden skirts.

Listra put her tapestry aside. "What happens?"

"You'll find you have no choice in the matter, Listra. The tidings are not entirely bad, however. You will fall in love too. This is all that I know."

"But I'm to marry Duke Coryn at the end of the month. He is extremely loyal to the prince."

Tashama shook her head. "The marriage will never come to pass."

The door was thrown open. Tashama and Listra turned as Daveal rushed into the room. "Leave us," she said to Listra.

"You forget I'm the prince's first cousin," Listra said.

Daveal turned to Tashama and sputtered, "You...you..."

"Does the lady have a speech impediment?" Tashama asked.

"If you think the prince has any more interest in you than just to use you as a pawn..."

"You're right about that." Tashama touched her gold braid. "I'm just a pawn in the scheme of things, though he did enjoy watching me swim in his bath this morning."

Tashama smiled as Daveal's cheeks grew red. "Now, she's the one to blush," Tashama said to Listra, then she turned to Daveal. "You know, Devil, I've offered to teach the prince to swim even. I believe he'll soon take me up on the offer. Of course, I'll have to hold his bare chest as he floats on his stomach in the water while he gets used to..."

"The name is pronounced *Daveal* for your information." Daveal faced Listra. "And as for *you*, when the prince marries me, you'll find little protection for you concerning your position here."

"Ah, but the lady will be more powerful than you can ever imagine." Tashama winked at Listra.

"*You*, Karthlander, won't be the prince's plaything for long."

"I should say not." She tilted her head to the side. "Why, he intends to marry me, haven't you heard? By marrying me, I will be the greatest pawn he can have." Daveal's eyes narrowed. Tashama waved her finger at the woman's face. "You know, with that pointed little chin and that high forehead, bangs and a haircut could really improve your appearance in a big way."

"You think you're very clever."

"I know so, Devil. I can tell you right now, the prince is on his way to see me this very minute and will not be happy to find you here."

The guard opened the door a speck. "The prince is on his way."

Daveal glared at Tashama. "This isn't the last you'll hear from me."

She hurried out of the room, and the prince exclaimed, "Lady Daveal!"

"Sire."

Listra turned to Tashama. "Why did you say I would be more powerful?"

"Shhh." Tashama held her finger to her lips and whispered, "Because it's true."

The prince walked into the room and nodded to Listra. She curtsied to him, and Tashama bowed her head to him as she remained seated.

"Your feet still bother you?"

"Yes, sire."

"I was made aware a young thief, one who'd been locked in the tower with you specifically, was near your window a short while ago."

Tashama smiled. "Yes, I invited him in for tea, Your Highness, but he had already enjoyed teatime earlier in the day, so it would seem."

"Leave us," the prince said to his cousin.

"Of course, Your Highness." Listra hurried out of the room.

The prince walked back and forth in front of Tashama. "The gardens are to be always guarded. If I have to, I'll chain you to your bed at night."

Her lips turned up slightly as she ran her fingers over her braid. "You mean I won't be sleeping on the pillows in your chambers any longer? Last night's dreams seemed most vivid only..."

"Only?"

She frowned. "When I woke, I could not recall them."

The prince studied her as his brows furrowed, then he folded his arms across his chest. "Was the thief to rendezvous with you last night?"

"Of course, Your Highness. It was awfully inconsiderate of me to have stayed with you last night instead."

The door opened, and Carissian walked into the room. "I've been informed about the thief."

"Cannot keep any secrets around a court, I always say." Tashama leaned into the sumptuous pillows of her chair.

"Do you think, Carissian," the prince asked, "he had planned to ferret the prisoner away, but by her staying in my chambers last night, he was thwarted?"

Tashama faced the window. "Quit trying to read my thoughts."

Carissian rubbed his chin, then, as his eyes followed her gaze, he hurried out of the room through the window.

"What is it?" The prince watched Carissian lean over the blue-flowered shrub.

"A piece of paper caught here in the branches." He pulled the paper from the branch, then unfolded it.

Tashama jaw dropped.

Carissian refolded the paper. "The guards' concern was warranted, Your Highness."

The prince nodded, then as Carissian walked back into the guest chambers, Tashama stared at the note he still grasped in his hand. The sorcerer handed the message to the prince. His brow wrinkled while he read the message. He handed the paper to Tashama. "Seems the communique was for you, Princess."

17

Tashama stared at the strange symbols, then smiled. "Possibly, but I cannot read what it says."

The prince turned to Carissian, who nodded. "She sees unrecognizable symbols she cannot seem to decipher."

"But we all use the same language. If she is Tashama..."

"She has been living in Texas these past ten years, Your Highness. Our written language was consolidated after she left the region."

"I see." The prince smiled at her. "Seems you couldn't have followed these instructions, nor could you have left a message for this band of thieves after all."

"Now why would I do that, sire?" She laid her hands in her lap. The prince shook his head. "We'll leave a decoy in her place tonight, and when the thieves come to steal her away, our guards can catch them in the act. As for the lady, she would be safer in my chambers. There she'll remain for the night."

"Devil won't like it, Your Highness," she said. "She already is pretty incensed that I promised to teach you to swim. She didn't like the idea that I would have to have you stripped," she added, then paused her speech. Both he and his sorcerer hung on her words, and she continued, "...to the waist so I could float you on my hands until you got used to the feeling of floating in the water."

"You said this to the lady?".

"Why? Did I do the wrong thing?"

Carissian shook his head. "She's still dangerous."

"Devil?" Her brows arched with the question.

"*Daveal*," the prince corrected her. "Why can you not pronounce her name right?"

"Devil," Tashama said. "It just slips out that way."

"Does it mean something to you?"

"Devil? Doesn't it to you?"

"Not a thing—just an annoying mispronunciation of her name is all."

"Well, that's something." Tashama smiled.

"I thought you said I was her savior," the prince said to Carissian.

"Devil?" Tashama asked.

The men ignored her as Carissian shook his head. "She is wily, sire. She's attempting a rift between Lady Daveal and you."

"Nonsense," Tashama said. "Why the rift already existed well before I ever arrived. Is that not so, my prince? If this was not so, he would have married the lady already by now."

"He couldn't have until after the coronation," Carissian said.

"But he would have made a firm...," Tashama said, then glanced down at the lower half of the prince's tunic, "commitment by now."

The prince studied Tashama, then noticed the sorcerer watching him, as if trying to decide if what she had alleged was truly the case. "She is wily. You're right about that, Carissian. What should we do with her?"

"I've thought of tying her to a rock in the Prathaen Sea. There, she could do no more harm."

"So who is the decoy to be?" Tashama looked out the window.

"Who has blond hair like me?" Carissian shook his head. "Seems, there's no one who would look right for the job."

"If we use the lady herself, would we be able to ensure the thieves are unable to abscond with her?" the prince asked Carissian.

"Chain her to the bed, sire, as well as have our guards posted. That should do the trick, do you not think?"

"You mean I will not get to sleep on your pillows tonight?" She stretched her arms above her head.

"You will get to please me in a different way tonight." The prince waved for Carissian to come with him.

The prince and his sorcerer left the room, and Listra hurried back in. "I don't know why he dismisses me like he does." She sat on her chair. "He knows you should have a chaperone at all times, and besides that, you'll tell me what he said anyway, will you not?"

"I'm to be used as bait for the thieves tonight."

"You—yourself?" Listra shook her head. "What if they are successful?"

"I'll be chained to my bed." Tashama stood up on her toes, then rested her feet gently on her soles.

"Are you all right?" Listra jumped up from her seat.

"Yes, they feel like they are asleep still and prickle with the touch, but I want to stroll in the gardens. Would you mind terribly?"

"I would love to take a walk with you, as long as you feel you're able."

"Yes, I've been lying around way too much." *And I must find a way to leave this place at once. I have not forgotten my quest, dear Karth-land. I will lead my people to victory.*

The ladies walked through the exit, and Tashama took the path she'd seen the prince take before. Listra said, "You do not know anything more about my...future?"

"No, I'm sorry, Listra. Maybe later I'll see something further. I didn't want to upset you."

They neared a pool of water winding through islands of ferns. Lantana-like flowers hung on vines that dripped into the still waters, making Tashama smile. "Is it very deep?"

"Yes, my lady. Above our heads."

"Much?"

"I'm not certain. Only you cannot walk along the bottom and keep your head afloat."

"I want to swim."

"In your golden gowns?"

"I swam in the others earlier today."

Tashama studied Listra. The princess wanted to see her swim more than anything else in the world, but feared the repercussions. "I don't think it's such a good idea."

The pool meandered out of sight behind palm-tree-like plants, and Tashama studied them. *Where does the pool end? Possibly it's a means of escape.* She sat down at the edge of the pool, then slipped her feet in. "Just a little swim? Maybe I could even teach you how to swim also."

"Oh, no, my lady. Mortals cannot swim."

"Sure, they can." She dove into the pool, splashing water onto the peach tile.

Listra cried out. "Oh, please, my lady. Come out of there at once. The water is too deep. You'll drown for certain."

Tashama paddled the water with her hands and feet. "The water is just right. Do you see how I keep myself afloat? There is nothing so mysterious about swimming. Follow me as I take a little swim." Tashama dove beneath the surface of the water. As she resurfaced, Listra ran to keep up with her along the pool edge.

When the foliage blocked Listra's path, she darted around the planted island. Tashama smiled. *I do not want to get you into trouble, dear Listra, but this is the freest I've felt since my last swim.* After swim-

ming several yards, the prince's voice caught her ear, and she
stopped to listen.

"What would the thieves have intended to have done with her?"
the prince asked.

"Ransomed her to Loran? I don't know for certain," Carissian
said.

"And there's still no word from Loran?"

"None. I would have thought..."

"Shhh," the prince said. "I heard splashing from the pool."

"Princess!" Listra said in as loud a whisper as she could manage.
"The prince and Carissian are nearby. They heard you."

"Get in," Tashama pleaded. "Get in and I'll show you how to
float, but do hurry."

"I'm afraid," Listra said.

"Come, you can do it, and I will not let you drown."

Listra slipped into the pool and held onto the edge as Tashama
took her hand and pulled her gently away. "Lean back and relax."

Listra flailed her arms about.

"Relax," Tashama repeated, and as Listra grew quiet, Tashama
rested her hands beneath her back. "Do you see the sailing ship up
there?" Tashama nodded in the direction of a cottony-white cloud
that drifted overhead.

"Yes, yes, and a man's face and big nose jutting out from it over
there."

"Yes." Tashama looked in the direction of the footsteps. She
smiled as the prince and Carissian approached. "I'm teaching Listra
to swim, Your Highness. You may be next if you do not chain me to
my bed tonight."

"Whosoever said you could do such a thing?" The prince placed
his hands on his hips.

"Why, I didn't think there would be anything wrong in teaching
the lady to swim, Your Highness. I'm sorry." Tashama helped Listra
back to the side of the pool, and as Carissian and the prince pulled

the lady from the water, Tashama swam beneath the water and headed in the direction she hadn't explored yet.

The three took chase after her as the prince hollered for the guards. "The woman is a menace," the prince said to Carissian. "And what were you thinking, Listra?" He couldn't believe she was swimming in the garden pools.

"She wished to swim, and I said I didn't think..."

"With Tashama, you must say no, with no room for her to wheedle her way through to getting what she wishes." He sighed heavily. She was a handful. Could he ever tame her free spirit?

"Yes, Your Highness."

He glanced down at her wet gowns. "Go get dry gowns on before the whole of Banff sees you fairly naked."

"Yes, sire." Listra ran back to the guest chambers.

"The pool splits into three different directions from here, sire. One leads to the pond where the fish are kept, one heads toward the west end of the gardens ending abruptly where the waterfall dumps into it from 50 feet above, and the other..."

"At my chambers."

"Yes, sire."

"Which way?" The prince studied the blue waters.

TASHAMA SURFACED for air and smiled at the tropical surroundings where no one could spy her from the path. She caught her breath. The blue fabric of the thief boy hiding in the leaves of a palm caught her attention. He stared at her with his mouth agape, and she hastened to his side.

"Warn the others, they lie in wait for you tonight. They found your note to me." Guards shouted orders nearby. Tashama waved her hand at the boy. "Leave here, quickly."

"You're swimming," the boy said.

"Yes, yes, but do hurry and leave."

He nodded, then slipped away from the edge of the pool and disappeared into the lush foliage. Tashama dove under the water and swam. Hearing shouts as she resurfaced, she found the pool had neared the path for the viewer's pleasure. She smiled at the guard who motioned to the others, then she dove under and continued on her way.

She rose again. Vegetation hid the path. There was no sign of her captors, but voices shouting drifted over the shrubbery. She swam along the water's surface. Spying a bridge ahead spanning the narrowing pool, she frowned as several guards poised on the stone walkway with a fishing net readied. She studied the net and the depth of the water as the prince and Carissian hurried to join the men on the bridge.

After calculating the risk, Tashama dove down to the blue-tiled floor and pulled herself through the warm waters. The sparkle of brilliant blue flittered ahead in the water. A water nymph waved for her to advance, but Tashama, still beneath the waters, studied the wavering forms of the men above her as they held the black net over the water.

The nymph fluttered about Tashama's head and yanked at her hair in the direction of the bridge. Tashama swam for the bridge as she pulled the water behind her while the nymph swam beside her. The black mesh dropped into the pool, but instead of ensnaring her like she had feared, the water swirled with the blue wings of water sprites of varying sizes as they pulled the net up and away. Tashama surfaced below the bridge as her lungs gave out.

"The net didn't catch her."

"She hasn't passed this way!"

"She's under the bridge!"

"Ready the net for the other side!"

Tashama dove under and headed for the other side of the bridge before the men had a chance to move the net. She resurfaced some distance beyond. Several still leaned over the railing as they stood on the bridge, while they shook their heads at her. But along the path, the prince and several others took chase again.

Disappearing beneath the silky water, she swam until bubbles foamed about her. She rose to the surface of the pool to investigate their source and smiled at the waterfall spilling from the pink rock formation above. The prince, Carissian, and the guards ran to the edge of the pool, sixty feet from where she floated in the bubbling surf. She ducked under the waterfall. Running her hands through her hair, she smiled as the prince folded his arms across his chest.

"How do we get her out of there?" the prince asked Carissian.

"Some of the men can fetch a raft, sire."

The prince glanced back at one of the men who had handled the net. "What happened back there? It looked as though you couldn't have missed."

"Yes, sire. The net was in perfect condition when we threw it into the water. When we pulled it out, there was a hole big enough to allow a mermaid to slip through. That one, in fact." The guard pointed at Tashama.

Tashama explored the formation of the waterfall while several of the men hurried a raft to the site of the pool. They launched the makeshift boat, and three of the strongest boarded it.

The prince shook his head as Tashama waited until the raft neared the waterfall, then she dove underneath and headed back the way she had come.

"Hurry!" the prince shouted.

"She dives too low." The guard reached for her, but then, as he felt her hair slip into his grasp, he pulled taut. The prince smiled as the guard pulled her golden strands into the sunlight. She surfaced and grabbed hold of her hair as she tried to free it from the guard's firm grasp while the men paddled the raft next to her.

"Let go of my hair!" she scowled, but one of the men grabbed for her wrist while another leaned over and grabbed her other arm. Within seconds, they pulled her from the water.

She lay on the raft in resignation as one held her wrist in a tight grip while the other two paddled to shore. When they arrived at the edge of the pool, two more guards pulled her to her feet. Listra hurried to cover her with a blanket as the men all gaped at her. She turned to the prince, who motioned for her to take Tashama back to her chambers.

"What was that all about?" the prince asked Carissian as the guards escorted Tashama back to her bedchambers.

"She's stretching her wings as the water nymphs do to see how much she can get away with while you hold her captive, I do believe, sire."

"I GUESS the prince isn't too angry with you this time, or I fear he'd throw you in the tower again, my lady," Listra said as they entered the bedchambers. "Why do you disobey him so?"

Listra helped her off with her wet gowns. "I will not be anyone's prisoner, Listra. Not Prince Aleron's, nor Loran's, not anyone's."

"There are rumors you do such things to attract the prince's attention."

"If in doing so he realizes he cannot keep me in line, then so be it."

Listra pulled a velvety-green cloth, glittering with sparkles of gold, over Tashama's head. "He was supposed to have practiced his coronation ceremony this morning. I doubt he'll be pleased you have interrupted his busy schedule."

"Busy schedule?" Tashama ran her hands over the soft fabric. "He plagues me to no end. When does he have time to schedule important matters of state? Besides, *he's* the one who wanted me to swim."

"It seems your antics have rather distracted him. He was to hold court yesterday concerning the disposition of several criminal cases. The court was cancelled. He was to have attended one of his baron's weddings. He never made it to the ceremony. Instead, he was roaming the sewers for you. His portrait was to have been completed several days ago, but the royal painter let it slip that the prince hasn't been able to sit still since you arrived here."

Tashama smiled. "Good."

Listra hurried to dry Tashama's hair as voices approached. "The prince," Tashama said. "What does he miss this afternoon that was so important?"

The prince entered her chambers. "Weapons instruction."

She glared at him. "Do you never knock?"

His eyes roved over her forest green gowns. "You had time to dress."

"And had I not?"

His lips curled up in mischief as he reached out to touch her sleeve. He ran his hand down her arm. "Where did you think that you were going to this afternoon? Another underground lake?"

"The water was just too inviting. I had to take a swim."

"And attempted to drown my cousin in the process?"

"Not I." Tashama patted Listra's arm as the lady pulled a comb through her hair.

"If my guard had not caught your hair, where would you have gone?"

"I wanted to explore the gardens via the pool. I found the experience most exhilarating."

"How did you cut the net?"

"I had help."

"You had no daggers."

"Of course not, Your Highness. I might have cut myself with such a weapon."

The prince reached into the pouch tied at his waist and handed the two gold bracelets back to Tashama. "You may have these back."

"Why, I thank you, sire." Tashama hurried to fasten the bracelets as Listra stopped to watch.

The guards pulled the door open for Carissian's entrance. Tashama shook her head. "I would think a gentleman would knock first before entering a lady's chambers."

"You are a prisoner," Aleron reminded Tashama, "and as such are afforded what luxuries that I wish to bestow upon you." The prince turned to hear what Carissian had to say as the expression on his face indicated his concern.

"Sire, Prince Loran states the princess is not who she claims to be."

18

"The princess is not the princess?" The prince raised his eyebrows in amusement. "He says this, does he now?"

"Yes, sire."

"And?"

"No ransom will be paid for the prisoner."

"Why would Loran say she's not of the royal house?"

"To discredit her claim to the throne, sire. As long as she has no following, she won't be a threat to him."

The prince watched as Tashama sat on her cushioned chair. "What of General Karam and his men?"

"He is but one bee in a hive of bees. Unless he can get the swarm to follow him, he won't leave much of a sting."

"Says you, Carissian." Tashama ran her finger over the velvet fabric of the arm of her chair, causing the fabric to darken. She looked up at the prince. "What do you intend to do with me now?"

Footsteps ran toward the guest chambers, and everyone turned as a messenger ran into the room. "Does no one have to knock when they come into my room?"

"Sire." The messenger paused to catch his breath. "Prince Loran wants another prisoner exchange."

"For?"

The messenger glanced over at Tashama. "The lady, Your Highness."

The prince laughed. "When she is not even Tashama?"

"He states, Your Highness, taking a woman prisoner is not an acceptable practice for either of our peoples."

"Does he?"

"Yes, sire. He says even though the woman is deluded, she should be returned to the Karthlanders."

"Deluded?" the prince said as a familiar smile presented itself. Her lips mirrored his. "And she would be exchanged for?"

"One of your men. He didn't say which he'd offer in return."

"Do you have the list of names of all of my officers?"

"Yes, sire. Prince Oshon is at the top of the list."

"What do you think, Carissian?" the prince asked.

"I think," Tashama inserted, "you should ask for all the prisoners in exchange for me. Do so, and I will go willingly."

The prince laughed. "You will go whether you wish to or not if I so desire."

"Loran will kill her," Listra said. "You cannot be serious about handing her over to him."

The prince frowned at his cousin. "Did I want your opinion in this regard?"

"I'm sorry, Your Highness." Listra stepped back into the background as Tashama took a deep breath.

"Thank you for your concern, Listra." Tashama stood, then walked over to her. She unfastened the diamond and emerald bracelet from her wrist. "I want you to have this—in memory of me when I am gone."

"But it is too extravagant a gift..."

"It will do me no good where I am to go."

Carissian examined the list of prisoners' names. "The exchange would certainly benefit us."

"I will escape from here anyway, Prince Aleron. Why not give me up freely, and you will gain much more that way?"

"Why would you propose such a plan, Princess?" the prince asked. When she wouldn't say, the prince turned to his sorcerer. "Why would she propose such a notion, Carissian?"

Carissian rested his chin in his hand as he considered her impish expression. "I cannot fathom what she's thinking. She's a woman, and they think not rationally."

"She's cunning, you say."

"Yes," Carissian agreed.

"Yes," Tashama said.

"Come, Carissian. We will discuss this matter further in my chambers while we allow the lady to get her sleep."

"Do let me know what you decide, Prince Aleron." Tashama walked over to the bed. She frowned as the guard entered the chambers, carrying a chain covered in velvet cloth.

"To protect your soft skin, Princess." The prince waited for the guard to chain Tashama to the bed.

"I will never teach you how to swim." Tashama lay on the bed. "But, Listra, if I'm still here tomorrow, I'll give you another lesson if you would like."

"Unless I wish it otherwise," the prince said, motioning for the guard to secure the chains, "you won't leave your bed until my guards return in the morning to set you free."

The guards examined the chains to ensure the lady could not free herself during the night. The prince said to Listra, "Be sure the lady is given what she needs to help make her comfortable during the night."

∼

THE PRINCE WALKED BACK to his chambers with his advisor. "So what do you think, Carissian?"

"The lady will not be able to wiggle out of his constraints this evening."

"No—about the prisoner exchange?"

"I don't believe it would be in the lady's best interests if we were to hand her over to Loran, but if we could get all of our men released..."

"Loran wouldn't agree to such a thing."

"I would rather like to propose such a notion to him, wouldn't you, Your Highness?"

"Not that we would take him up on such a thing."

"Because?" The prince frowned at his advisor, who shook his head in return. "Sire, you mustn't feel anything for this woman. She must be treated as a prisoner, nothing more."

"All right. Make our wishes known to Loran."

"And if he agrees?"

"He won't agree."

"But if he does?"

The prince walked into his chambers, then unfastened his belt and dropped it to the floor. "The lady brought it on herself. Tomorrow, Carissian." A knot formed in the pit of Aleron's stomach. The notion of giving up his mermaid was intolerable. *No,* he shook his head. He wasn't giving her up. Not ever for any price.

TASHAMA SQUIRMED against the chains as she tried to get comfortable while Listra stood nearby and watched. "Can I get you anything, my lady?"

"A key to undo the padlock? For heaven's sakes, there are guards outside my window and stationed by the front door. How could I hope ever to escape?"

"You have escaped three times already. And now with a member of the thieves' guild trying to help you to break out of here, the prince is justified in taking more extreme measures to make you stay put."

"Until he turns me over to Loran, you know." Tashama rolled onto her side, then yanked the chain as it twisted around her shoulder.

"He cannot. I know he cares for you. He wouldn't turn you over to Prince Loran. He knows what the Karthlander prince will do to you if he can get a hold of you."

Tashama sighed deeply. "He will do what his advisor advises him to do, Listra. Nothing else matters."

LATER THAT MORNING, Tashama felt a hand tug at her wrist. She opened her eyes and saw the young thief working with a tool to unlock the chain that bound her. She smiled at the tousled hair of the youth. After he freed her hands, he took her arm and led her into the gardens. To her surprise, two guards slept beside her window. Jaran ran with her down the path toward the prince's chambers, then, as they neared his door, the man turned onto another path. This one soon led to the Bachava Temple.

Tashama stared at the golden dome, then the thief waved at a figure skulking in the shadows of the building. The man there hurried to Tashama and pulled a black gown over her head. While she adjusted her skirts, he attached black veils to her hair and face. "We have an escort for you beyond the gates as soon as they're opened for morning commerce. Until then, you'll have to bide your time in the chapel."

Tashama nodded, then was escorted into the middle of the pews. "We'll come for you in two hours."

"Thank you." Tashama squeezed the man and boy's hands.

"Thank you, miss, for freeing us from the tower."

Tashama slipped into one of the pews, and the thieves

vanished. She turned her attention to the vaulted, gold ceiling as it shimmered high above her. A golden statue stood on an altar before her. He smiled as his eyes watched her while his hands stretched out in a gesture of welcome. His golden robes swept the ground, and his golden sandals were visible beneath them. A crown of golden leaves rested on his short, curly hair.

The scamper of footsteps caught her attention, and she dropped to the floor between a row of seats.

"Oh!" she heard a young woman exclaim. "Please, stop, you'll offend Bachava."

"Bachava," the man sneered. "Why do you save yourself for such a deity when you could be married to me?"

"Oshon, tell me how you managed to escape from the Karth-landers."

"Word has reached Prince Loran that our prince finds favor with Princess Tashama. Loran is concerned our prince won't hand the woman over to him."

"But I don't understand what this has to do with you."

"If the prince doesn't turn her over to Loran to obtain the release of our men, I'm supposed to rendezvous with them and turn over the woman secretly."

"You speak of treason, Oshon."

"The Karthlander woman spellbinds our prince."

"Oh, Oshon, I fear you'll be caught."

"I gained my freedom on a promise. I won't break my word."

"To the Karthlanders."

"You seem to be upset with me, my love."

"My father finally agreed I could leave the order to marry you if the Karthlanders released you, but if he learns of this..."

"The release of my men was all I was concerned about. This woman blinds the prince."

Their footsteps drew nearer Tashama. She lay still, but the dust on the floor tickled her nose. Twice she rubbed it. Her eyes watered and her nose wrinkled. She closed her eyes and cringed as her sneeze reverberated throughout the temple.

The heavy footsteps of Oshon's metal-edged boots ran toward her, causing her to jump from her location and run down the aisle parallel to him. He dashed down the aisle she'd been in, and she ran as fast as she could to the doors of the temple.

She pulled the door open just as Oshon grabbed her arm.

She cried out, and a temple priest standing at the entrance jumped back. "Good gracious." The priest held his chest. "What are you doing with one of my women, Oshon?"

Oshon released his hold on Tashama, took a step back, and bowed his head to the priest slightly. "I thought she was a thief."

The priest shook his head. "I understand by the grace of Bachava the Karthlanders freed you." He motioned for Tashama to leave them. She hurried outside.

Oshon said to the priest, "Yes, and I must speak to the prince concerning the matter."

"I take it you were leaving a substantial offering for your providential release from your captivity." Rattling of coins caught her ear, then the priest said, "Bachava will shine on you."

"Yes." Oshon scowled; his footsteps drew in her direction again.

Tashama disappeared into the gardens. She hurried to pull off the black garments as she slipped onto a planted island next to the meandering pool hidden from prying eyes. After folding the clothes into a neat stack under one of the ferns, she hurried back to the path and toward her chambers. Seeing Oshon headed that way, she hesitated.

Once he had run past, she darted toward the prince's chambers and the path that passed his apartments, leading to the temple. She approached the temple, but saw the priest speaking with another, and she turned back toward the prince's chambers. The warning bells rang out, and she knew her absence had been discovered. With a heavy heart, she ducked into the prince's quarters.

Before the prince could rouse himself from his sleep, Tashama dove for the pillows piled high in his outer room. She fought the urge to smile as she kept her eyes closed while boots tromped into the room. She knew they stood staring at her, wondering how she ever ended up there.

Acholuria said, "What..."

One of the men interrupted him in a whispered voice. "We thought she'd escaped from her chambers. We had no idea the prince had brought her back here in the middle of the night."

Aleron, still bare-chested, walked into the room. "What is the problem? Why are the bells ringing?"

His chief guard pointed at Tashama as she curled up like a kitten in its pillow nest. "What is *she* doing here?" the prince asked. He couldn't believe his eyes. Dressed in satin nightclothes revealing her curves more than any other garment she'd worn, he motioned to one of his men. "Get a blanket at once."

Carissian appeared. "Sire, the lady managed..."

The prince pointed to Tashama. "How did she get here?"

"The padlock was pick-locked. Our guards were drugged. What she is doing *here,* I have *no* idea."

The guard hurried into the room with the blanket. The prince motioned to Tashama with a nod of his head. The man straightened the blanket over her body, and she sighed.

Aleron folded his arms, but before he could speak, Oshon walked into the chambers. "How did you..."

"I managed to escape, sire, when they had the changing of the guard." Oshon looked down at Tashama. "Why are the bells being rung?"

"The lady slipped out of her room, but she didn't go very far," the guard said.

The prince raised his brows as Tashama opened her eyes. "Have them stop ringing those annoying bells."

She smiled, then yawned. "Your Highness." She stretched. "I had the most wonderful of dreams. How about you?"

The prince motioned for all but his sorcerer to leave them. "I suppose you do not wish to tell me what happened?"

"I just couldn't get comfortable last night. The chains kept getting in my way. Then I realized if I returned to your chambers, nobody would bother me, and I could have the most pleasant of dreams."

"Did she, Carissian?"

Carissian shook his head.

"My sorcerer says this is not so."

"I can see that. I do have a question to pose to you, however."

The prince nodded.

"Do you not think it odd Oshon escaped from his captors as he did? Surely you don't think he could have done such a thing on his own."

"You were listening then. You weren't asleep at all." He took a deep breath. *She is as cunning as Carissian says.* "You infer Oshon was allowed to do such a thing."

"Certainly."

"For what purpose?"

"Should you not hand me over to Loran, he has made a promise to the prince that he will be the one to do the deed."

The prince straightened. "You say this just as you try to create friction between Daveal and me. You're very clever, Tashama. Carissian is right about you."

"Devil." Tashama pushed a blond curl behind her ear. She turned to Carissian. "Do I not speak the truth?"

"I cannot tell. I can see you're trying to deliver something to me, but you're fearful the surroundings and people involved may somehow reveal something you do not wish me to see." Carissian's eyes bored into Tashama's for several seconds, then he shook his head. "You fight me every step of the way."

"She's fabricating this, Carissian."

"Yes, sire. I would have to say so, unless she'll allow me to see what she has seen or heard."

"Do you know, Prince Aleron, when your sorcerer tries to read my thoughts, he touches me where he ought not?"

The prince glanced over at Carissian, whose face revealed the slightest hint of amusement. "She is dangerous, this one, is all I will say."

Carissian vanished. Tashama's eyes widened. "You did not dismiss him, my prince. Why is that? Have I touched on the truth of the matter?"

"When he reads my thoughts, all I notice is a gentle tugging in my forehead, nothing more."

Tashama smiled. "Ah, yes—but he cannot read my thoughts easily. He employs other methods with me to try to distract me. But do not take my word for it. Your sorcerer's actions speak for themselves." She could tell the prince was still considering the notion when she proposed another question. "If Oshon were to find out I knew the truth about his escape and feared I could convince you of his traitorous plans, what do you think he would do to me?"

"He will not disobey me."

"You do not know much about this leader of your cavalry, then, Prince Aleron. He has made this promise to Loran and has vowed to keep it."

"He wouldn't have told you such a plan, should he have planned to do such a deed."

"You are right, of course. I overheard him speaking to a woman."

"Who?"

"I wouldn't know—just Devil and Listra are the only two ladies of your court I know by name."

"If you saw her again?"

Tashama shook her head. "She loves Oshon and he...she, but her parents will not permit her marriage to him."

The prince rubbed his chin, then hollered, "Carissian!"

The sorcerer appeared before him. "Yes, Your Highness?"

"Who do we know that Oshon has taken a fancy to?"

"None that I know of, sire."

"They meet in secret," Tashama said.

"Where?" Carissian smiled. "The temple. You think you can keep up this charade, but you cannot."

"The temple?" the prince said. "Does she speak the truth then?"

Carissian furrowed his brow. "She was hiding in the temple when Oshon spoke with one of the women of the order—the princess speaks the truth."

"We cannot have him detained unless there is proof." The prince turned to Tashama. "And the thieves? What does she tell us about them? Any clues?"

"Not a one, sire."

"Sire," a messenger said as he rushed into the room,

"Prince Loran states he will exchange one of your highest-ranking officers—or some other who pleases you—for the girl."

19

"Not good enough." Tashama played with her braid.

The prince stared at her for a moment, then turned his attention to the messenger. "All or none."

"Yes, sire." The messenger hurried out of the room as the prince faced Tashama. "Tell me what your reasoning is."

"I'm only a woman, sire. I have no reasoning."

"If he agrees to my demand, I will have to turn you over to him."

"Honor requires such a sacrifice."

"He will kill you."

"We all must die, Your Highness."

"You are not afraid?"

"I will be free."

The prince shook his head. "I don't understand you."

"Have you no knowledge of our prophecy?"

Carissian shook his head as the prince looked to him for acknowledgment.

"My people believe I will lead them to victory. If I must die to do so, then so be it. I don't know what fate awaits me. Perhaps this is what the gods have decided."

"We rule our own destiny," the prince said.

"In part, yes. We cannot just lie down and expect the gods to live our lives for us. This is true. I will lead my people one way or another. If not in the flesh, my spirit will do the deed."

Carissian rubbed his chin. "She believes this to be true, Your Highness."

"She is deluded," the prince said. "How can I hand over such a creature to Loran?"

"You'll have no choice." Tashama stood.

"Return her to her room," the prince said.

Tashama was led away, and he turned to Carissian. "I want the lady to sleep in my bed tonight. We'll have one of my guards sleep in the lady's place."

"And you, sire?"

"That is none of your concern."

"You cannot sleep with the princess."

"I will not touch her."

"Sire, she's an unmarried maid of the highest royal rank. You cannot lie with her."

"You won't dictate to me, Carissian. You're to advise me, nothing more."

"Forgive me, sire." Carissian bowed. "I'll make the arrangements at once."

LATER THAT EVENING, Tashama was led back to the prince's chambers, cloaked in darkness. As the black veils were removed from her face, she stared at the bed, clothed in pale blue, trimmed in gold. "This is the prince's bedchambers," she said to the guard.

"Yes, my lady," the guard said.

"Where is the prince to stay?"

"I wouldn't know, Princess."

"Will Listra not attend to my needs tonight?"

"No one is to know you are here, my lady."

"He's trying to catch the thieves again."

The guard smiled. "And he'll be successful tonight, rest assured."

"What am I to do?"

"My lady?"

"I'm tired, but I cannot sleep in the prince's chambers."

"His wish was for you to do so."

The guard left the room, but two more stood nearby. She walked toward the pillow room, but one of the guards blocked her path. "You're to stay in the prince's bedchambers tonight, my lady."

"I was going to sleep on the pillows."

The guard stood firm.

"Very well." Tashama returned to the prince's bed, then pulled a blanket and two pillows from the mattress. She made a bed on the floor on the other side of the expansive room. After lying down, she soon fell asleep.

The prince smiled as he stared at his curtained bed, then walked over to it with a firm stride. Pulling aside the curtains, he furrowed his brow with concern as he found no sign of Tashama. "Guard!"

Two of the men rushed into the room while the prince waved at his bed.

"Over here," one of the men said as he spied her sleeping across the room on the floor.

"Return her to my bed."

The guard lifted her and laid her on the prince's bed. She sank into the feather mattress. The prince whispered, "Leave us." And the room was silent.

For over an hour, the prince studied her sleeping soundly as he sat in a chair nearby. The moonlight cast a shimmering light across her face, and her dark lashes fluttered with her dreams.

Finally, he took a deep breath and strode to the other side of the bed.

He pulled off his tunic, then climbed onto the mattress, and the motion made Tashama roll over to face him. He paused. Her chest rose with a gentle breath as he slipped closer to her. He reached out to touch the silky strands of golden curls, beckoning for his caress. She puckered her lips slightly. He leaned over to plant his lips against her mouth when armored boots clanked as they rushed into his room.

"Sire," the man said, making the prince bolt from the bed.

He grabbed the knight's arm so as not to rouse the princess and pulled him into the outer chambers. "Have you caught the thieves?"

"No, sire, the guard was nearly killed."

"What?"

"Whosoever came for the princess intended to kill her, not steal her away."

The prince rubbed his smooth chin. "I want Oshon arrested."

"He still sleeps in his quarters, sire. He's being watched as you commanded."

"He ordered to have the job done. What about our guards?"

"Both were unconscious. Your healer is seeing to them now, but he says that on the previous night, they had been drugged—tonight, both had been struck with such a blow, they were lucky to be alive."

"The thieves wouldn't have done such a thing. Oshon must have ordered…"

Carissian appeared. "I've been told of the circumstances concerning the guards. Oshon must be caught in the act of treason before he can be arrested for such a thing. We cannot just accuse him without evidence."

The prince considered his bed. "Must we wait until the princess is murdered under my own roof? And then what? Do you think General Karam and his forces will not seek revenge? Loran will use this, too, as a means to further his cause against us. Though in reality, he will applaud the deed."

"They will not try again tonight. Should we not return the lady to her own quarters?" Carissian asked.

"She is safe where she's at for the moment." The prince motioned for everyone to leave. "We will discuss this further in the morning." He knew she would be safe with him. Whoever wanted to harm her certainly wouldn't want to do the same to him.

The men left to guard the outer room, and the prince returned to his bedchambers, then stared out the window. The streaks of light from the moon sparkled on the white stone walk as a diminutive, gowned figure caught his eye—merely a shadow in the dark. The prince glanced back at the bed, then looked out the window. The figure had vanished.

The prince strode to the bed, then stared at the empty mattress still imprinted with Tashama's form. "Guards!" The men rushed into the room, and he pointed out the window. "The princess has escaped. Sound the alarm! Find her!"

The prince ran to retrieve his tunic as one of the guards hurried to the bell tower. The others rushed across the moon-streaked square. While he fastened the ties of his garment, Carissian appeared. "Sire, there is further grave news."

The bells resounded, causing the prince to shake his head. "Yes, yes, the lady has disappeared once again."

"Princess Listra has also vanished."

"What?"

"One of the ladies informed me she never turned in for the night. I haven't been able to find any sign of her."

"Has she been to see Lord Coryn?"

"He has been away for the last several days on a trading expedition, Your Highness."

The prince grabbed up his sword, then hurried into the square with Carissian at his heels. "Would he have returned late, and the lady was welcoming him home?"

"He has not returned, Your Highness."

"What next?" The prince strode across the square now filled with soldiers as the word spread that the search was on for the princess.

"Sire!" one of his men shouted. "The guards at the gates said two women and several men left through them only moments ago."

"The gates were closed..."

"They had just opened for commerce, Your Highness."

"Was it the princess, do they think?" The prince hurried to the gate.

"The women were dressed in the order of the Bachava. Their business is never questioned."

"And the men they rode with?"

"Dressed as monks of the order. No one had any doubt they were who they appeared to be."

"Has the High Priest been questioned?"

"He's being roused as we speak, sire."

"Have my horse saddled in the meantime. Ready the others to ride."

"Yes, sire."

The prince turned to his advisor. "Listra, do you think?"

"I fear so, Your Highness."

"The Karthlander woman is undoing my realm."

The prince stormed with Carissian to the gate, where the guards both bowed quickly to their sovereign. "We would have stopped them had the bells been rung before we let them go, Your Highness, beg your forgiveness."

"Was there any indication that the one lady was Princess Tashama?"

"The black veils of the order do not permit the viewer to see much of the woman, Your Highness."

"Sire!" a monk called out as he ran toward the prince. "None of our monks are missing from the abbey. Whosoever wore such habits was not some of our own."

"And the women of your order?"

"All have been accounted for."

The prince's horse was brought to him. "Then we must ride and bring them back here at once."

FOR TWO HOURS, the prince and his soldiers searched for the women as they followed a trail through the woods that led directly to the mountains. A heavy fog blanketed the forest as sparks of light flared up from time to time while woodland sprites entertained the men. The howling of a wolf set off the rest of its pack, and the prince paused his horse as he looked up from the hoof prints imprinted in the soil he'd been studying.

He frowned as there was no sign of his men. A blanket of white mist as thick as any blizzard encircled him. His fingers gripped his leather reins tighter as his blood pumped through his veins as if in a race. His breath quickened as he fought the panic in his heart.

To be in the woods alone was a dangerous venture, even for the stoutest of warriors. And now with Loran's men encroaching on the forest with increasing boldness, Aleron knew he had to find the women and his men soon, or they could all perish.

20

"Carissian!" Aleron called out. There was no further sound than the snorting of his horse and no other sight than the fog mixed with his horse's breath. "Carissian!"

"Shh," a feminine voice hushed him, and as he peered into the low-hanging cloud, he saw not a soul stirring.

"Carissian!"

"You'll get us both killed," the voice whispered. "Bestill your heart and come seek shelter with me."

The prince pulled his sword from his sheath. "Show yourself."

"So you may slash at me with the razor-sharp edge of your blade? Find your own way then."

The prince nudged his horse into the cool, wet air toward the whispery voice, but still not seeing the creature who had spoken to him, he sheathed his sword. "All right. Show yourself."

"I stand before you, oh prince. Do you not see me in the mist?"

The prince stared at the fog in front of him, where he could barely see the twitching ears of his very own steed. "I cannot." He leaned forward in his saddle.

"The woodland sprites warn me they come for us."

"Who?"

"Why, my enemy and yours."

The prince kneed his horse to step closer to the voice. "Are you not afraid of me?"

"I am Tashama, and I am not afraid."

"Tashama."

"Lower your voice, Prince, or they will find us."

"Tashama." Aleron's heart surged. He urged his steed forward. "Where is your escort?"

"We've become separated in the mist, and the woodland sprites have led me to you."

A hand touched his leg, and he looked down at Tashama, clothed in white lace. "Where is your horse?"

"He knocked me from my saddle," she whispered. "He was not supposed to have done such a thing."

Aleron reached for her arm, but she stepped back. She blended with the mist, and he pleaded, "Come with me, Tashama. Ride with me."

"No, we must escape to the mountains. There is a way, but the horse cannot follow the way we must go."

"I won't leave my steed."

"He'll return home on his own."

"My people will think me dead."

"You will be so, if you don't come with me. Do you not feel the shaking of the earth beneath your horses' hooves? Do you not feel the air warm with the breath of their horses as they surround us even now? They have not freed your men yet, Prince. Without me to use as a bargaining tool, Loran will not free them. I will not go with him willingly."

Aleron stared at the mist. He couldn't go with her, but he couldn't leave her alone. She was his prisoner. No, she was the one he loved. "Tashama."

"Goodbye, my prince."

"Tashama, wait." He jumped from his saddle, grabbed a pack,

then slapped the horse's rump. "Wait for me." His voice was dark and hushed this time.

"Over here," she urged him. He ran to her side, and she handed him a tunic and breeches of white. "Wear these. They'll help to cloak you from their view."

"Where did you..."

"The thieves."

"Was Listra with you?" The prince fumbled with his ties. Her hand reached over to help. Her fingers deftly untied the leather ties as he pulled his tunic off. She smiled at the sight of his bare chest. Warmed inside, he fought the urge to pull her close so she could feel his smooth chest against her breast. He grabbed the white tunic. She tucked his own into his bag while he changed into white breeches. Once done, he grabbed her arm. "Where do we go now?"

Tashama hesitated as a woodland sprite dropped from an elm. "We follow the stream winding its way through the forest near here. Come." Tashama hurried along the unmarked path toward the water flowing nearby as the prince still gripped her arm.

Horses' hooves filled the air behind them as they navigated through the twisted tree branches, grabbing at her hair. One caught hold, and the prince hurried to untangle the branch. She grabbed his hand. "Boost me up!"

"What?"

"Into the tree. Boost me toward that branch."

The prince grasped her by the waist and hoisted her toward the branch. She climbed onto the limb, and he joined her.

They rose higher into the safety of the tree, and as they drew close to the trunk, horses' snorting filled the air.

"What do you see, Valmor?" a gruff voice said.

"She has been here, Prince Loran, but I've lost track of her."

"Continue the search!"

The horses rode south, while Tashama took a deep breath.

"Pudgy still from the overindulgence of being of the second royal house."

"Could his sorcerer not see you?"

"I have no idea what powers the old fellow possesses. I only wish Balthazar were here."

"Or Carissian."

"I would not want him to be here." She climbed back down through the maze of branches. Before she could drop from the tree, the prince landed on his feet then held his hands up to catch her. "Oh," she said as she made the drop. "Thank you."

"Thank you for saving me back there."

"I want to make peace with your people and mine, Prince Aleron, do you not realize this?" She hastened toward the creek.

"I couldn't have turned you over to Loran for any amount of prisoners in exchange, you know."

"Your honor..."

"I wouldn't have, Tashama."

She ran as light-footed as the cheetaur as she hopped over exposed tree roots and ducked beneath low-hanging branches, all the while barely making a sound. *He shook his head. You'll be mine, Tashama. I will not give you up to any other.*

The prince followed her lead. When they arrived at the creek, she stopped at the edge of the water as it tickled the tips of her ivory leather shoes. A water sprite darted out of the water. "They come for you, Tashama! Hurry! They're headed this way. Valmor leads them!"

"What can he see?"

"He doesn't see what we have in store for him. Quickly cross, royal cousin of the water nymphs. Cross now!"

Tashama grabbed the prince's arm and splashed across the stream as her long skirts dragged in the water. Midway across, men shouting reverberated from the woods. They turned. Valmor, leading Prince Loran and several of his men, waved his hand at them.

"Stay, Tashama." The nymph fluttered about her head. "Stay and welcome them."

"He will kill me," Tashama whispered back. "He will kill Prince Aleron."

"Hold still," the water nymph entreated. The river began to rise inappreciably at first, but as the water flow tugged harder at their legs, Tashama obeyed the nymph.

"We must go," the prince pleaded as he pulled at Tashama's arm.

"No, we will be safe here." She placed her feet farther apart to keep her balance in the swelling stream.

"Wait, Tashama," the nymph implored. "Wait until we say."

Loran's teeth peeled into a wicked grin as he observed the two waiting for him in the stream. "How were we ever so lucky to have come across the two of you like this? Prince Aleron, I see you're handing over the princess to me after all."

"She is not Tashama, so you have said."

"My mistake. Unfortunately, I did not bring your men for an exchange. In fact, I do believe having you as a pawn will be a better deal. Bring them!" he shouted to his men.

"Wait, Tashama." The nymph wavered with flapping wings just above her head.

Horses' hooves pounded the water, as the roaring of a mighty waterfall filled the air. Everyone turned as a wall of water descended upon them.

"Cross now," the nymph urged.

Tashama and Aleron slogged through the river and collapsed on the eastern shore. Before the mounted soldiers reached the halfway mark, the water pulled them under, carrying them without mercy to their watery grave.

"Come." Tashama glared at Valmor, while Prince Loran pulled

his horse back from the torrent overflowing the banks. "I don't know his powers. It wouldn't be safe for us to dally here."

The prince grabbed her arm, then hurried her through the woods as wood nymphs fluttered about. "He looks for a way to catch you, Tashama," one of the sprites said.

"Loran?" Tashama stopped to wring the water out of her gowns.

"Valmor."

"What powers does he have? Do you know?"

"He studies you and now knows you have the power of the water world. He will not try again to cross your path in that manner."

"What do they say to you?" The prince squeezed the water from his tunic.

"They warn us Valmor is trying to learn my secrets."

The prince studied her as she pressed the water from her hair. "You're not immortal." The prince frowned at her.

She smiled. "No, I've already told you that I am not."

"They won't be able to gather reinforcements until tomorrow at noon. And they'll still have to figure a way to cross the swollen river," the nymph said. "The glade you'll find safe for the night."

"To the glade." Tashama clasped her fingers around the prince's. "The nymph said we won't have to worry about Loran and his men for the time being."

"What other secrets do you have, Tashama?" The prince squeezed her hand slightly as he walked with her through the woods.

"Tell him you love him, Tashama." The nymph flew about Tashama's head. She flew backwards as Tashama waved her hand at the nymph as she would a pesky gnat. "Tell him, Tashama," the nymph repeated as she flew about the prince's head. "Or I will."

"He will not understand you." Tashama furrowed her brow.

"I will make him understand."

"What is being said?" the prince asked as Tashama felt her cheeks grow hot.

"They can be annoying. That is all."

"Tashama loves you. Tashama loves you!" The nymph darted in front of them.

LATER THAT EVENING, Aleron and Tashama made their way to the glade, and as she spied a lake, she headed straight for it. The prince smiled as he hurried to catch up to her. "The water draws you as if you were a mermaid seeking the sea, Princess."

"I'm a cousin to the water nymph. So they claim."

"And the woodland nymphs?"

"They make no such claims."

"But you understand them."

"Yes, I was born with certain gifts."

"But you are not a sorceress."

"No. Only those of the first royal house had any such gifts. Loran has none. This is not to say he is not powerful, however. Still, I wonder what his sorcerer, Valmor, can do. Sorcerers are formidable adversaries. I've always feared them."

"Like Carissian."

Tashama sat down by the water's edge, then pulled off her shoes.

The prince pulled off his boots and set them aside. "Carissian can shake mountains, but he says you can move men like no one else can. You are more powerful than he."

"He says this?"

The prince nodded. "Do you think it would be safe to build a fire? We need to dry our clothes. The night air will soon grow cold."

"Yes, Loran and his men will be no more trouble tonight."

The two grabbed their shoes and then moved them to the location the prince determined suitable for building a fire. They built a fire ring with stones, then returned to the forest.

They entered the woods, and the prince gathered a couple of rotting logs for a fire, while Tashama grabbed branches littering the forest floor. "You shouldn't do such work," he said.

She smiled. "You're taking too long. I want to be warm."

He laughed. "I've never known anyone like you before."

"And you'll never know another like me again." She dumped the twigs onto the growing stack of firewood.

"Of that, I'm certain," he said under his breath.

After lighting the dry timber, they watched as the tiny flame licked at the tower of branches, then, as the fire caught hold, the prince pulled at his ties as he attempted to unfasten his tunic. Tashama reached over to help him as the wet ties fought to be undone, then smiled as she observed his muscles tighten in his waist as he stood taller. "Do you approve?"

"What is there not to like?" She pulled the white veil off her hair. He stared at her dripping wet gowns, then, as she noticed his concern, she pointed at his pack. "You wouldn't have something in there like a blanket or a bite to eat, would you?"

He opened the pack, then poured the contents onto the grass.

She pulled at her outer gown, but the wetness made it cling to her like a second skin. Halfway situated over her waist with the skirt above her head, his hands touched the hem, making her gasp. "I'll help you." His warm voice washed over her like bath water as he struggled to slip the garment over her head. He smiled as her cheeks warmed. "Like peeling a butterfly from its cocoon."

He turned to observe his pack. "A blanket." He motioned to the items from his bag. "Only rather as wet as we are."

"Nothing to eat." She rubbed her bare arms and leaned over to get a better look at the objects, her sleeveless shift clinging to her body.

"I'm afraid the biscuits dissolved in the water."

Tashama nodded, then headed back to the lake.

"Where are you going?" He jogged after her.

"I'm hungry, Prince, and if you will not feed me, *I* will have to feed us."

"Oh, you will, will you?"

"Certainly." Reaching the edge of the lake, Tashama knelt. "Water nymphs, we're hungry. Have you anything for us to eat?"

A sprite bolted out of the water. "You love him, Tashama. Tell him so, and you will eat."

"We are not that hungry." Tashama sat back on her skirts.

"What do they wish from you?" the prince asked.

"Tell him, Tashama, and you will eat."

"No." Tashama stood.

The nymph laughed, then dove back into the water with a resounding splash.

21

"What did they wish of you?" Aleron asked Tashama.

"Nothing I wanted to do for them," Tashama said.

"Could I have done something for them? We are hungry. What do they wish?"

"They are pesky." Tashama turned toward the fire.

They walked off the pebble beach, and a thud from behind made the prince turn. He laughed. "Thank you, water spites." He grabbed up the fish and hastened after Tashama. "What did they wish of you?"

"I won't tell, so quit asking." Red peppers dangling on stalks nearby caught her attention. "You have chili peppers here."

Aleron shook his head. "We cannot eat those."

She pulled one from its stem, then bit into it as Aleron held his breath. Smiling, she coughed. "Great stuff." Her voice was hoarse from the burning juices of the pepper. She cleared her throat, then walked beside the prince's pack and grabbed up the wet blanket. She shook it out and stretched it over the fire.

Aleron carved the end of a stick, then stuck it through the center of the fish. Afterwards, he hung it on the makeshift spit over the fire. "Nobody ever eats those things. We thought they were poisonous."

Tashama smiled. "Great Texas food." Then she grew serious. "The sun grows low in the fall sky. The air has already turned cooler by several degrees. Our clothes will not have time to dry properly before nightfall." Her arms were already covered with bumps from the cold as the slight breeze whisked about her.

The breeze carried the smoke in her direction, and she moved to the opposite side of the fire. The prince rubbed her arms to warm them as they stood before the flames.

"Your shift is still so wet," the prince said softly.

"Yes, and your breeches, too, but we will not remove them."

"Modesty aside..."

"No, unless you want me to leave you here alone. Then you may remove the rest of your garments to your heart's content. I'm certain the water sprites would be intrigued."

The prince leaned down and pulled her wet hair aside. "Even your hair is still so wet, Tashama. You're bound to catch a chill."

"Then it is the gods' will."

"You said once you must do what you can, that the gods cannot live your life for you."

"You left me to fend for myself, oh prince, with men who had not the luxury of being with a woman of their choice for several months. Maybe longer. I was able to carry myself with dignity and respect while living among them. Do not think I'll succumb to your charming ways, for the sake of staying warm and dry."

"I'm sorry, Tashama. I cannot take back the terrible way I've treated you, but I am sorry. I was wrong to have dealt with you in the manner in which I did."

She nodded as she wrapped her arms around herself in an attempt to quit shivering. He walked over and touched the blanket. "The blanket is dry now. Will you not cover yourself in it? I will turn from your view, and you can remove your shift. Then we can dry your garment over the fire. Your hair will still be wet, but you should be warmer."

He offered the blanket to her.

"Will you look away?"

"I promise. I don't want you to become ill."

She took a deep breath. "Then look away, Prince, and do not turn this way again until I tell you to do so."

"Of course." He handed her the blanket, then turned his back to her.

TASHAMA DROPPED the blanket to the ground, then pulled the shift over her head as quickly as she was able, as her hair caught it half-way. As she struggled to loosen the hair from the fabric, the prince folded his arms across his waist. When he felt she'd had enough time to remove the gown, he said, "Are you ready yet, Princess?"

"No!" The panic in her voice made him smile.

"What seems to be the trouble?" He rubbed his chin.

"My hair."

"Do you need my assistance?"

"No, and do not turn this way."

She dropped her wet shift on the ground. The prince said, "Ready?"

"No!" Tashama grabbed up the blanket and pulled it over her shoulders. "All right." She held the blanket tightly closed with her clenched hands.

"Much better." He picked her gown up and hung it over the fire. "Our food is done. Have a seat, my lady." Tashama continued to stand as the prince pulled the fish from the fire, then cut it up for them to eat.

"Do I have to hand-feed you?" He handed her a portion, but she wouldn't give up her hold on her blanket.

"I'm not hungry any longer." She stood in the warmth of the fire.

"You have to eat to keep up your strength, if we're to evade Loran and his men tomorrow."

Tashama released her blanket with her right hand and reached for the fish he offered her. She nibbled on the meat, and he sat and stared up at her. "Why do you not sit and rest?"

She shook her head.

"You cannot stand there all night." He ate his filet.

"When I'm done with my meal, I will lie down."

He returned to the fire to turn their garments. "They are dry on one side. I'll gather some more wood. Would you like to help?"

"No, thank you."

The prince chuckled. "I'll be back in a moment then."

The prince headed for the woods, and Tashama hurried after him. Hearing her light step behind him on the fallen leaves, he smiled. "You will have a time carrying any sticks, Princess."

"I only wanted to supervise you." She tilted her head to the side.

"I see." He watched the knuckles of her hands turn white with the grip she had on the blanket. They reached the woods, and he gathered a larger log. Then, as he walked back to their primitive camp, he studied her concerned expression. "You are not afraid, are you?"

"I haven't slept alone under the stars before, without a strip of clothes on and with a strange man to keep me company."

The prince laughed. "Well, I do not believe anyone has called me strange before. And I must say," he said as he pushed the log into the fire, "I have never slept with a naked woman before under the stars at night, either."

Tashama touched her garment and still feeling it wet, she frowned. "Why does that notion not comfort me?"

He shook his head. "You have nothing to fear from me, Princess." He touched her hair. "Your hair is still so wet."

"Yes, well, I cannot remove it either."

"Nor would I wish for you to do such a thing."

"Turn away," Tashama said.

The prince folded his arms across his chest. "I'm not used to a woman telling me what to do, my lady."

"I want to lie down, but I'm afraid I might expose something I wouldn't want to."

"Ah, when you give me reasons for your concern, I'm more apt to consider your request more favorably." He turned his back. After waiting for a minute, he said, "Are you all right, Tashama?"

"Wait, I'm trying to get comfortable."

A rock hit another on the grass nearby.

Another clunked some distance in the glade, making the prince chuckle. "Would you like for me to make your bed?"

"No!"

The prince tapped his foot on the ground. "My backside is quite warm, but I want to warm my bare chest with the fire. Are you sure you're not..."

"Okay."

The prince watched her as she closed her eyes, and the flickering flame cast a warm light over her ivory face. She licked her lips, then twisted slightly to get comfortable, making the prince sigh deeply. *You are sight more wondrous than I've ever known.*

EARLY THE NEXT MORNING, Tashama shivered as the fire had long been extinguished. Her back was warm, and she smiled as the prince snuggled close to her.

She closed her eyes, but then voices without words caught her attention, and she sat up suddenly. Seven men and three women sitting on white horses with their blond manes stirred by the light breeze as the party watched her from a few feet away.

She rose to her feet and woke Aleron. He jumped up and pulled his sword from his sheath. She grabbed his hand and shook her head, then turned to consider the blond-haired people with fine features and pointed ears. "Elorian Elves," she whispered. "They won't harm us."

The leader of the group motioned for his women to dismount, then waved at his men in the same manner while he continued to sit on his horse. "What do they want?" Aleron whispered back.

"I don't know."

Aleron and Tashama watched as the men hurried to construct a square tent while the women pulled bundles off their saddles. "The woodland nymphs called them to come to our aid," Tashama whispered.

A male voice spoke to her, and she turned her attention to the leader. "He says we must change our clothes. The forest colors of the elven garments will help to camouflage us." She hesitated as Aleron shook his head. *He'll learn my language before long.* "They'll cloak us while we travel with them."

"I must return to Banff." Aleron sheathed his sword. "I cannot leave my kingdom."

Tashama turned to the leader and listened to his words spoken without body. "He says you do not have to come with us. You may stay." She faced Aleron. "You cannot stay, Aleron. Loran will kill you if he finds you."

The ladies said to Tashama in their silent way, "We are ready for you, my lady."

"I need to change," Tashama said to Aleron. "You would do well to do so."

Tashama walked into the tent. Aleron grabbed the garments offered to him, then yanked his tunic from his chest.

"Why will they not speak to me?" He pulled the green and tan tunic over his shoulders, then hurried to fasten it across his chest.

"Oh, you are tickling me," Tashama giggled as the ladies helped her on with the gowns. Giggles erupted from the elven maids. "Because, Aleron, they feel you have perpetuated this war between our peoples and in so doing their own people have suffered as a direct result of the continued conflict—disruption of commerce, thievery on the part of the soldiers who forage into their lands for foods, and so on."

"Loran is the one who keeps waging war. We only defend ourselves."

"Ah, it is not that you want to take over my kingdom too?" Tashama walked out of the tent.

Tashama smiled as Aleron stared at her gowns. She touched the green ribbons cris-crossed between her breasts, accentuating her feminine form, then ran her hand over the overskirts of blended tans and green sheers cut sharply up the length of the garment in triangular form, allowing the viewer a glimpse of her shapely legs. He took a deep breath as he finished pulling on his boots.

"You could be an elven maiden." He hurried to repack his satchel.

She pulled her blond hair back over her shoulders. "Only I do not have the correct shape of ears." Tashama turned back to listen to the leader of the elves. "They have brought only one horse for us to ride, as the woodland nymphs carried only word of me on the wind. They suggest I ride with one of the other maidens, while you take the steed."

"I will ride with you, as I would not want to become separated from you." Aleron mounted the horse, then reached down to pull her into the saddle with him. "Since they seem to be rather at odds with me, I would not desire to be traveling without you."

Tashama smiled. "They only fear we'll slow them down this way. They say it'll be many hours before Loran can find a way to cross the swollen stream. He has already gathered another army of men, however, to accomplish the task." Tashama glanced over at one of the maidens who spoke to her, and she nodded and smiled.

"What did the lady say?"

"She says you are very handsome for a human."

"And you agreed with her?" He pulled Tashama closer. She rested her head against his chest and nodded. "And what do the elven men say about you?"

"They are careful not to speak concerning me."

"Oh?"

"I am Tashama and will bring peace to the region. I am the key to prosperity for the entire population. You say I cannot lead my people without a husband to do the task for me, but this is not so. Certainly, I will wed soon, but it is not my husband who will quell our difficult times. Indeed, this husband of mine *will be* important as he will desire to please me, so he can win my favors."

The prince took her message and smiled. She smiled and rested her head against his elven tunic. "I'm sure your husband will do everything in his power to please you, Tashama." Aleron leaned over to kiss her head. The elven maidens giggled.

THE BRILLIANT BALL of flame settled in the west as the party of elves and their human counterparts arrived in Ramoria.

Everyone dismounted from the horses as Aleron helped Tashama down from his steed. One of the ladies waved her hand to her. Tashama took Aleron's hand as they walked along a green moss-covered stone path. Columns of green marble suddenly appeared, blending into the vegetation as pink-flowered vines wound their way up the striated pillars. She touched one of the flowers, and the blossom wiggled slightly. "Have you ever been here before?" she asked him.

"No, and you?"

"When I was little, my father brought me here to trade with the elves. One of the maidens gave me a sapphire—not in trade, but as a gift. I've found them to be the most generous of people."

"The jewel was not a part of your possessions when you were brought to Banff."

"No." Tashama shook her head. "During the terror that followed when my father and mother collapsed in the great hall during supper, I left the jewel in my room as Balthazar ferreted me away."

"To Texas," Aleron said.

"Yes." Tashama nodded at one of the maidens.

"What does she say?"

"We must follow her to the place where we will sleep the night. The queen of the elves will meet with us tomorrow. She and her husband have retired for the evening."

Tashama and the prince followed the maiden up winding stone stairs surrounded by ferns and drooping palms. "Only the queen will meet us? Why not the king? My coronation!" Aleron stopped in his footsteps. "I cannot believe I've forgotten about the most important moment in my life."

22

"You can schedule another coronation." Tashama tugged at his arm to continue the long flight with her.

The prince shook his head. "I cannot believe you can beguile me so as to make me forget about such a thing."

They finally arrived at a Greek-like structure with marble columns and goose-down mattresses surrounded by pillows; all set amidst plants to obscure the view of the next sleeping couple. Tashama smiled at the maiden. "No, he will sleep alone tonight."

Tashama nodded to the elf, then turned to Aleron. "She wants to know if you have angered me in some way as we lay together so compatibly early this morning. Since I do not want to lie with you, she desires to know if she could do so instead."

"Where will you sleep?" The prince folded his arms across his chest.

"I will sleep with some of the single maidens."

"Are you angry with me?"

Tashama smiled. "When I choose a mate, I will sleep with him. Goodnight, Prince Aleron, soon-to-be king of the Maldovians."

She waited. Would he select one of the maidens? The elven maids giggled in anticipation. Aleron smiled wickedly at Tashama.

She followed another to the end of the expansive building. Here, she found thirty ladies of various ages.

One of them motioned for Tashama to take a place on one of the mattresses. Tashama lay down. One of the maidens soon joined her. "He did not select one of the single maids to lie with, this love of yours. He has met the test. Did you want to return to his bed?"

Tashama shook her head. "He has already met a test by coming with me in the first place, but he must meet many more before he can be the one for me."

The maid smiled as she lay down beside her. "He is very handsome and has a commanding presence. He will make a good husband and father to your offspring and will rule wisely beside you."

"Yes, well, he will need more training before he is the right one for me."

EARLY THE NEXT MORNING, Tashama met with the queen of the Elorians. When the prince woke, Tashama greeted him in an arbor covered in wisteria. The purple, grape-like flowers hung in bundles all across the arbor, shedding their sweet scent into the air.

"Why did you not wake me?" The prince frowned at her.

"You would not have understood the queen's words. Your coronation is important to you, Prince Aleron. The Elorians have offered to escort you safely back to Banff."

"And you?"

"I must continue on my way."

"I won't leave you."

"I must leave here as the queen fears repercussions from Loran if he should find the Elorian has given me refuge."

"You cannot travel alone, Tashama."

She smiled. "A group of the Elorian will take me as far as the mountain pass."

"You're still attempting to return to Karthland."

"I must get word to General Karam that I'm free and ready to lead my people."

"Against me," the prince said.

Tashama touched the wrinkle in his brow. "Against Prince Loran. Return to Banff. Be king of the Maldovians. When I have ousted Loran from his despotic rule, I will make peace with you."

"I cannot let you go alone." The prince attempted to follow her. Several elves readied arrows in his direction to dissuade him, but he persisted. "I want to go with you, Tashama. You should not be alone."

Tashama smiled as he pleaded with her.

"All right, but General Karam and my people may not be happy to see you, Prince Aleron." As she could see he wouldn't be discouraged, she said, "We must change our garments again because this will put the Elorians at further risk if Loran's men find us wearing elven clothes ."

Tashama was led to a tent to change, where one of the maidens said, "He has passed another test."

"Yes, he has." Tashama pulled the sparkling, emerald-green gowns over her head.

"You will blend into the emerald-blanketed walls of the mines, should Loran and his men discover your route. The dwarven miners will not bother you."

"As long as they don't feel we're there to steal from them."

"Prince Aleron pays them well to excavate gems for him. He can aid you somewhat until you clear the mountain ring. The journey for you will be more dangerous when you return to your homeland."

TASHAMA AND ALERON entered the valley with their elf escort, but soon after, the leader of the elves pointed at the sky. A hawk soaring high above caught her eye, and she nodded. Before the prince could ask about the matter, five of the elves had pulled arrows from their quivers and centered them on the string of their bows. The five feather-guided arrows flew, and the hawk vanished back into the forest.

"What was that all about?" the prince asked as the party continued on a path to the mountains.

"Valmor can see through the eyes of his familiar–the hawk, apparently. The Elorians couldn't hope to hit the bird because he soared so high above us, but he would shy away if they attempted to shoot him with their arrows."

"He knows, then, where we're headed."

Tashama nodded. "The Elorians have a diversionary plan, however."

The party rode deeper into the mountain pass. The leader of the party waved at a couple who hid in one of the folds of the jagged moss-covered rocks. The lady and the man walked forward, then Tashama said to the prince, "We must dismount. This couple will take our places. They'll continue to the pass where the dragon lies in wait. The Elorians have no trouble with the dragon, but Valmor will not attempt to cross his path."

"And he will think we've gone that way?" Aleron helped her off the horse.

"Yes, my prince. The pass would have led us to the western edge of Sorenson. He will seek us there."

"But this will lead us to?"

"The elves say Napolia, where my castle lies in wait."

Tashama slipped the gold bracelet off her wrist, then fastened it to her decoy's arm. They kissed each other's cheeks in friendship, then Tashama turned and inclined her head to the leader of the men. He answered her in the same manner, then turned his horse to lead his people back along the path they'd come.

"What did they say to you, Tashama?"

They entered the caves, and Tashama shivered. "They wished me success in my quest."

"And me?"

"If I am successful, we all will win."

Their footsteps crunched on green stone, and Tashama observed the crushed emeralds lining their way. "Who would have ever thought it could be just lying there for the picking?"

"Who goes there?!" a gruff voice shouted, but before either could say a word, they were surrounded by dwarven guards.

"Prince Aleron and this is Princess Tashama, royal heir to the Karthlanders' throne."

The one guard stared at the two, then grunted. "What would you be doing with the likes of the Karthlander woman?"

"Trying to keep her safe." The prince frowned at the dwarf. "We must pass through here and quickly."

"You buy our emeralds at a fair price, Prince Aleron, and you are welcome here. But the Karthlanders are forbidden to come to this place. They have stolen too many of our gems."

"She is with me. "We must go through here. It's most urgent."

The dwarf shook his head. "We've had some difficulty in the pass leading to Karthland if that is where you're bound. Yesterday afternoon, the walls shook, blocking the tunnel. My men are still attempting to clear the cave-in."

"Is there another way?"

"To the west through the dragon's lair."

"No," Tashama said. "The elves go that way to throw Loran off our track."

"You're running from Prince Loran?" The dwarf's bushy burgundy brows furrowed as he tugged at his long beard. "Well, there's another way, though I don't see how you'll make it." He pointed to a cart on wheels. "Climb inside the cart, and I'll send you as far as I can. After that, it'll be up to you to find your way."

Aleron hurried to help Tashama into the cart. He climbed in with her and said to the dwarf, "I'll be back to make some more purchases soon."

"Should you live, Prince Aleron." The dwarf pulled a lever. "Should you live."

The creaking of the metal wheels against the iron track echoed off the sparkling emerald-encrusted walls as lanterns cast fluttering lights against the glittering surface. A slight cool, damp breeze stirred up by the motion of the cart surrounded them. Aleron drew close to Tashama and wrapped his arms around her.

"Do you trust them?" Tashama looked up at him.

"I've had no problems with the dwarves in the past."

"Would they sell us out?"

"You said Valmor would follow the elves to the dragon's lair."

"But if he does not? Sorcerers are a tricky lot. Sometimes—not often, but sometimes, they can trick me up."

"Like Carissian?"

"And Balthazar!"

Aleron shook his head. "The dwarves do not like the Karth-landers."

"When my dad ruled, we had no problems with them. It must be Loran's doing."

"You shiver. Are you afraid?"

"Yes," Tashama said softly.

"Of Valmor?"

"Of closed-in spaces. It's like a tomb down here in the bowels of the earth. I cannot leave this place any too soon."

He kissed her forehead, then rested her head against his chest. "Close your eyes then. What you cannot see, cannot harm you."

They rode in silence for some time as the cart chugged up steep inclines, then dropped sharply down into deep chasms while the air grew laden with the smell of seeping groundwater and freshly-stirred earth. For several minutes, the cart twisted right, then suddenly turned left and stopped. Tashama opened her eyes and frowned. "It dead ends."

"There is a narrow passage over there," the prince said.

"But no more ride, I'm afraid."

After jumping out of the cart, Aleron lifted Tashama out.

Then he hurried to a lantern hanging from a wall. Tashama rubbed her arms as she stared at the dark passage. He hurried to her side. Terror filled her eyes, and he pulled her close and embraced her warmly. "Come, Tashama." He took her arm and led her through the single-file passageway.

"Oh," she whispered, "if I could only close my eyes now."

"The floor is too uneven." He started down slippery steps, dropping several feet below. He stopped at a narrow landing. The cave walls had given way to a black emptiness, and he grabbed Tashama's hand as he examined a place in the rock where there was a low, narrow opening with only enough room for an average-sized man to crawl on his belly.

"I cannot." Tashama balked.

"I won't leave you behind, Tashama." He lifted her chin. Her eyes moistened with tears. Her lips quavered, and he pressed his mouth to hers and kissed her hard. Squeezing the breath from her chest, he wrapped his arms around her. "Come, I'll go first, but you must follow close behind."

She nodded as a tear cascaded down her cheek. He kissed her hand, then knelt before the opening. Then he shoved the lantern in front of him and began the arduous crawl through the low passage-way. After he had made it some distance, he called to her, "Are you all right?"

"My gowns." She choked on the words.

The fear in her voice disheartened him as he longed to comfort her, but his only hope was in getting through to the other side, where they would be able to stand together. "Your gowns?" he asked.

"I can barely maneuver in them."

He'd never considered the trek Tashama would have had to make dressed as she was. "Can you pull them up a bit?"

"There's not enough room for me to twist even one of my arms back to do anything with them. My shoes keep hanging up on the hem of my skirts as I try to push forward."

"Can you go back?"

"No!" The anguish in her voice indicated she was ready to break.

"Tashama," Aleron coaxed, "we'll continue as slowly as it takes us. I won't leave you behind." She lay her head on her arms as she sobbed aloud. "Tashama." Her sobs drowned out his voice, and he waited until her sobs had quieted.

"Tashama, let us try some more."

"I cannot," she whispered.

"Reach out and touch my foot." The tips of her fingers touched his felt boot. His heart was warmed by the feel of her hand clutching his foot. "Listen. I will crawl a little farther, then you'll do the same. I want you to touch my foot when you have reached me, then when you're ready, we'll begin again. "Tashama?"

"Yes," she whispered.

He moved several inches down the path and took a deep breath as he felt her hand slip from his boot. When he felt he had gone far enough, he said, "All right, Tashama."

Her skirts rustled as she tried to follow him, and then after several minutes had passed, she touched his foot.

"We're doing just fine, Tashama." He waited while she caught her breath. Her slender fingers touched the softness of the top of his suede shoes, and he hated to pull away from her, knowing she drew comfort from making contact with him in the tomblike passage.

"Are you ready?"

"Yes."

He inched his way farther.

For over an hour, they crawled in this manner, and then she sniffled. He tensed. "It shouldn't be much longer."

"I cannot go much farther. I cannot. What if it dead ends? We cannot crawl backwards. Oh, Aleron, I cannot do it."

"It won't dead-end. There's fresh air ahead. My flame flickered."

"I cannot smell the fresh air." Her tone of voice suggested the notion had lifted her spirits slightly.

"We can do it, Tashama." He continued to crawl. Only a few feet away, he discovered an opening, no more than a quarter-sized round, leading up through the caves, and through this, a tiny ray of light filtered. He took a deep breath as he grew concerned about how Tashama would view the finding when she reached his location. He moved forward again.

When he paused some distance from the shaft of light, he waited for her to catch up, but when she didn't touch his foot in the time he had calculated she should have reached him, he called out to her, "Tashama, are you nearly to me?"

She whispered back as she held her hand to the light, "The breath of fresh air."

"Yes, but my flame flickered again." Though he hated to deceive her, he feared he might lose her to the shaft of light. "There must be more fresh air in front of us. Come to me, Tashama. I feel better when you're able to touch me."

"The light feels good on my fingers." She examined the way it bounced off her fingertips as she wiggled them through the light.

"Tashama," he said in desperation as he watched her, "I heard the tinkling of a water sprite. There must be water ahead."

She turned her small face toward him. "What did she say?"

"I cannot understand them. You must come this way and tell me what they say."

"They'll know the way out."

After several tense moments, she touched his boot.

He sighed deeply. "You don't know how much it means to me to be able to feel your touch again, Tashama."

"I don't hear the water sprite." She cocked her head to the side. "Are you sure that is what you heard?"

"Yes, just like at the lake. Are you ready?"

"Yes." This time her voice showed resolve.

He moved much farther ahead this time as he could hear her struggling to keep up with him. He smiled as he felt her touch his boot much more quickly this time, and after allowing her a shorter rest, he continued again.

For nearly another hour, he made the crawl with encouraging words concerning the sounds the water sprites had made, while she, so desirous of finding them, followed him in earnest. Then, as the narrow opening spilled out into a cavernous structure, he stared into the cave. "We're here, Tashama." He looked for a way to get to the floor of the cave, some 60 feet below them.

"And the water sprites?"

Her hand wiggled his foot. He smiled. "I hear running water nearby and can smell the fresh water flowing from above ground into the cave."

"Let me see." She pushed the sole of his foot to get him to move.

"The climb down looks awfully dangerous. Let me find a way out of here, then I'll guide you."

She waited while he pulled himself from the narrow passage that widened at the mouth, then she crawled forward. When she arrived at the opening, she took a deep breath. Aleron clung with his fingernails, gripping the moss-covered rock below her, the tips of his boots poked into willow footholds.

She stared in disbelief. "Oh, Aleron," she whispered. "However did you manage to climb out of here?" A rock jutted out from the passageway, and she reached up and touched it. He, meanwhile, contemplated how to bring her out of the passage safely.

"I don't have much to hold onto here." He climbed toward her. "I've contemplated having you climb onto my back, but I'm afraid you might pull me from my meager holds. I'm not sure you'll be strong enough to pull yourself up by the handhold above your head. That's how I came out in the first place."

"I will have to try, will I not?" She sat at the edge of the opening. She dangled her feet over the edge, then turned slightly to grab hold of the rock. Placing her weight on her arms, she dangled precariously against the wall.

"Your toes will not reach the next step. Try to reach for the next handhold to the right of your shoulder."

She looked at the rock, then reached down as her toes slipped against the rough surface, and her arms wearied. "I cannot hold on much longer." Her breath came quickly.

"To your left now. There's a place for your left hand just beneath your left shoulder."

She looked down, then reached for the next rock, but nearly lost her grip with her right hand as she scrambled to get her footing. He pushed her left foot into a stirrup-like formation. "We must keep going, Tashama. You do not have the strength in your arms to make such a climb, and you're already shaking quite a lot. I will guide you."

"Okay." She waited for him to find the next best move. Then, as he found it, he reached for her leg and tugged in his direction.

She crouched to relocate her foot to the new location as he sighed deeply. "And your right foot, just a little below that."

For twenty minutes, they made the climb down, then as they neared a curtain of emeralds, Tashama sensed the arrival of the elves. She turned her head in their direction as they entered from across the cavernous room. "The Elorians say the dragon wasn't at home for the first time in a hundred years at this time of day. He was chasing a female when they arrived. And the passage through to Karthland was blocked."

"Blocked?" the prince said.

"Yes, they found the passage that led into this cavern, but they say Valmor and Loran are not far behind. The Elorians will follow the path we have taken and return to Ramoria. They don't fear small spaces like I do."

"And us?"

Tashama inclined her head to the elven leader. "He senses there is a waterfall and an underground lake nearby. I must see this water sprite that has spoken to you so often."

The prince and she continued along the curtain. The elves crossed the cavern to where they had been and began the climb up the cliff. Their fine agile bodies maneuvered the cliff like spiders clinging to their web. She nodded to the leader and then ducked into a smaller room. Dripping water made her smile. She ran across the moss-covered stone and knelt beside the bubbling water. "Water nymph, what word have you for me?"

The nymph darted from the water. "He comes for you." She fluttered about the prince's head. "And for him. Loran is angry that you have made him take chase for so long."

"How can we escape him?"

"There is no escape to Karthland from here, if that is what you seek."

Tashama sat on her skirts. "What do you mean?"

"You will have to go the way you came."

"We cannot."

"Or face Loran, who follows close behind."

Tashama shook her head.

"Or come for a swim with me."

"But the prince cannot swim."

"Then teach him. It is in your power to do so."

Tashama slipped into the water. "Come, Prince, you guided me through the passageway and down the side of the cliffs. Come with me now, and I will assist you through the water."

"Is there no other way?" Aleron crouched at the water's edge.

"Loran will be here soon. Valmor has no power over water. We'll be safe going this way."

The prince shook his head. "This goes against all that I know, but I will trust you, royal cousin of the water sprites."

"Slip into the water and hold onto the ledge."

The prince did as he was told, then Tashama drew close to him. "Someday I will teach you to swim, but today, I will use a lifeguard maneuver I learned in Girl Scouts."

"In Texas?"

"Yes, now lean back and relax. I'll keep your head afloat and will swim with you to the other side of the lake beyond the waterfall."

"And then?"

"And then, I will instruct you further."

Tashama pulled Aleron toward the waterfall, and as the water splashed over his head, his posture stiffened. "We are almost there," Tashama whispered in his ear. "And they are almost here," she added as she saw Valmor stalk into view. She smiled.

"He cannot see us beyond the waterfall, and he would never think we could swim across the lake." Then she frowned. "But he can sense we've been here."

She pointed to a light area in the water beneath the rock wall. "We must dive below and swim to the other side. It is the only way."

"I cannot swim under the water."

"You can, my prince. If I can crawl through a pipe-like tunnel for nearly two hours, you can swim beneath the surface of the water for a minute or two. Take a deep breath, and I will pull you along. One..., two..., three." She dove beneath the surface as she pulled him with her.

She smiled as the water nymphs clustered about the prince as they tugged at his clothes and hair while they helped her to get him to the air. They finally made it past the wall of rock. Tashama pulled the prince to the surface, then held his head above the water while they both gasped for air.

Then, she swam across to the other side of the lake and held onto the rock as he climbed out of the water. He turned to help her out when he caught sight of white gowns shimmering in the corner of the cave.

When the lady recognized the prince and Tashama, she ran forward. "Sire." She curtsied low to him.

"Listra," he scowled at her.

"Forgive me." She turned to Tashama. "We have failed, my lady."

"I cannot believe you of all people," the prince said.

"What is wrong?" Tashama touched Listra's tear-soaked cheek.

"Carissian blocked all the passageways to Karthland. He shook the mountains while we were lost in the mists. He has come for the prince, and he has come for you and me now."

"Where are the thieves?" Tashama squeezed the water from her hair.

"They have hidden. I couldn't let them get caught because of me."

"I cannot believe you would have aided the princess's escape as you did, Listra." Aleron wrung out his tunic.

"Oshon and his men were going to murder her, sire. You know that as well as I. I couldn't let that happen."

"No one will murder her," The prince glanced over at the passageway that led into the cavernous room. He smiled to hear Carissian's welcome voice as Tashama rolled her eyes.

"Carissian," the prince said in greeting. "Seems your quick thinking has saved us all."

"You, maybe," Tashama said. "Not me."

The guards rushed into the room, and the prince said, "The

women are to be guarded all the way back to Banff. Take them to the horses."

"Will they be shackled, sire?"

"No. Carissian and I will be along shortly, then we will ride together."

"I should have left you behind in Ramoria," Tashama said.

"You wouldn't have made it without me." The prince couldn't conceal the delight he felt in being with his people. He knew he had a good chance of losing Tashama should she have made it to Karthland.

"And you, without me." Tashama shook her wet hair at him.

"Swimming with you was indeed an exhilarating experience. I will take you up on your offer to teach me to swim." He considered Tashama's green gowns, which clung to her figure.

"I retract my offer."

The prince waved for Tashama and Listra to be removed from the cavern. They left the room, and the prince grabbed Carissian's arm. "So tell me, Carissian, what has gone on while I've been away?"

"Your people are waiting for the crowning of their king."

"Good, I'm ready to do my duty."

"And the princesses?"

The prince shook his head. "Listra is right in worrying that someone, if not Oshon, wants Tashama dead. We cannot dismiss this lightly. The princess must always be safeguarded."

"What of Loran?"

"He still searches for us in the mountains. Come, let us go. I want to change into Maldovian garments."

The two men exited the caves. Aleron mounted his horse, and he smiled at Tashama. She glowered at him. "Cheer up, Princess. You would have returned to captivity on the other side of the mountains when Loran caught hold of you in your own homeland.

Your accommodations would not have been half as grand as they are at Banff, I would venture to say."

"Captivity is captivity, wherever it is." She tilted her head up while she looked straight ahead.

EARLY THAT EVENING, when they arrived at Banff, Tashama and Listra were returned to the guest chambers while the prince headed to his apartments to schedule his coronation.

Tashama yanked off her outer gown while the guards still stood in the room, and Listra hurried to push them out the door.

"My lady," she said as she helped Tashama with her next gown. "I know how distressed you must be."

"No, Listra. You don't know the sorrow I feel." Tashama sighed deeply. "And when he was passing the tests so well." She walked into the bath chamber, then pulled her sheer gown over her shoulders. The emerald cloth slipped to the floor, and Tashama jumped into the bath. She dove under the water, then surfaced at the other end of the pool. "There are no roses." She swirled her hand over the surface of the water.

"No, as we were not expected back here this evening. I will ensure we have some tomorrow, however." Listra sat at the edge of the bath. "Can you teach me to swim?"

Tashama nodded.

"He's angry with me." Listra removed her gowns. "He wouldn't look at me the whole time we rode back to Banff."

"I'm sorry, Listra. I hadn't meant for you to get into trouble over me."

"The fault was not your own. Oshon intends to murder you. I couldn't allow that to happen. But it seems odd that this is the way I've betrayed the prince's trust. I haven't found anyone to love."

"This will too, come to pass." Tashama motioned to Listra to join her. Then she helped Listra swim in the water. As Listra paddled her hands and kicked her feet, Tashama released her. Listra sank. Tashama laughed. Listra touched her feet to the floor, then surfaced. "Oh, I do not think I have your ability yet."

Again, Tashama helped Listra to float, then she scooted her across the water to the edge of the bath. "Kick with your feet."

Listra kicked with her feet while she held onto the edge of the bath, and Tashama smiled. "I will have you swimming with me in Karthland before you know it."

"You should not joke about such a thing, my lady. We are already in big enough trouble as it is."

"I'll be in bigger trouble should I stay here." Tashama grabbed a vial of soap sitting at the edge of the bath and squirted the silky pink shampoo onto her hand. She ran it through her hair, then the door creaked open to their chambers.

"Are you decent?" a man's voice called out.

"No!" both of the women screamed.

"The prince asked me to see that you were both all right."

"We are both all right!" Tashama yelled. "Go away! I am teaching Listra to swim, and you are interfering with her lessons."

"Yes, my lady."

Hurried footsteps led back to the door, then it shut.

Tashama turned to Listra. "The healer?"

"Yes." Listra took a deep breath. "The prince cannot be too angry with us if he wanted his healer to check on our health."

"Nonsense." Tashama dipped her head underwater to rinse the soap from it. "He only wanted to know what we were up to."

"Do you think so?" Listra picked up the vial of soap and applied some of the sweet-smelling fragrance to her hair.

"Of course." Tashama climbed out of the bath, then grabbed a towel stacked with others nearby. She ran the soft violet cloth over her body as the door opened. She quickly pulled her towel taut, then listened for some word from the intruder.

A woman walked into the room and curtsied. "Your meal is served. I will return for the platter in a little while."

The woman left, and Listra rinsed her hair. "That is not a good sign."

"What?"

"The prince doesn't want to eat with you this evening."

"We have been together alone long enough." Tashama wrapped a towel around her hair.

"Robes are hanging on the pegs over there for our use." Listra pointed her dripping wet finger at the wall. "We haven't had the time to use them before, but tonight, I believe, would be the perfect time for their use."

Tashama pulled one of the velvet robes off the peg and touched her finger to the rose-pink fabric. "Pink or green?"

"Either is fine for me." Listra climbed out of the bath, then pulled the towel over her skin.

"Are you hungry?" Tashama walked into the room wearing a pink robe, then observed the lobsters, prepared in their shells, on platters covered with grapes and apples.

Listra joined Tashama. "No, I was fed well."

Tashama fingered the grapes as she eyed them with suspicion.

"What's wrong?" Listra tied her robe around her petite frame.

"Would it not be easy to rid themselves of two nuisances with just a dab of poison?"

23

L istra stared at the food, then frowned. "Some poisons are impossible to detect. Odorless, colorless. We would only know if the food was tainted if we were to partake of it."

"I have not eaten for a long while, but if I eat of this, I may never eat again." Tashama lifted the tray, then carried it to the window. The guards turned to observe her, and she threw the food onto the walkway. "Poisoned," she said, then carried the tray back into the room.

Servants hurried to clean up the mess, a grape escaped the others' fate, and she picked it up. The knocking on the door caused the two women to turn and face it.

"Yes?" Listra called out.

A guard opened the door. "The prince desires your presence at the meal."

"Another meal, Listra. But I presume this one will be safe." A smile crossed her face. "Should we go dressed like this?"

"The prince might like to see you attired thus, but he would surely frown on seeing me dressed this way."

"I will wait for you to clothe yourselves properly." The guard closed the door behind him.

Tashama hurried to pull golden gowns over her head, while Listra pulled pink ones over her own. Then, the women took turns drying their hair. By the time Tashama had attached veils to Listra's hair, the women were already late in attending the prince's supper.

When they arrived at the great hall, everyone had already taken their seats at long white-clothed tables, and the princesses were directed to one of the lower tables. Tashama observed Daveal sitting beside the prince at the elevated head table while Carissian sat on the other side of his sovereign. Tashama took her seat beside Listra.

Tashama asked the lady who sat next to her to pass the bread, but the lady ignored her. Tashama turned instead to Listra and smiled. "I guess she doesn't like my company."

Listra shook her head. "We are being treated in such a manner because we took the prince away from them when he was due to be crowned. Within a week or two, he selects his bride from among the single ladies. There was much fear that he was lost, and Oshon might have ruled in his place. He is my cousin as well. Oshon would not have led the Maldovians as well as Aleron."

"I do not believe either is that well-suited for the job."

Tashama turned to the disagreeable lady. "I have returned the prince to you, but believe me, he snores at night something fierce when he sleeps with a lady. He has no manners either. Why, I had quite a time getting him to turn away from me while I stripped my wet garments from my skin."

The lady's mouth dropped open as her eyes widened, then she picked up her plate and hurried to another table.

Tashama laughed out loud, then reached over for the bread.

"Bread, Listra?" She cut a slice from the loaf.

"Butter?" Listra handed the butter to Tashama.

The prince studied her, and she leaned down and whispered in Listra's ear, "I believe I am unnerving the prince. I wonder what else I can do to annoy him."

"You mustn't do anything further." Listra sipped her wine.

Tashama ate her slice of bread and then sat back in her chair.

"I believe I will make him aware that his staff is trying to poison us."

"But we don't know that for certain."

"Let him decide for himself."

Tashama stood. The voice-filled room died to a hush. She walked toward the head table, sure every eye in the great hall watched her. While her eyes remained fixed on the prince's, his gaze studied her gowns instead, but as she walked in front of the table, his eyes met hers.

"I want to make you aware that Listra and I already had supper served in our room this evening." She paused for effect. "I assumed the food might make us ill, so I disposed of it—or I should say some servants hurried to dispose of it. I want to thank you for the generosity of offering me lobster, as I love such cuisine so much. I didn't want you to think me ungrateful."

Tashama turned back toward her table, stopped, then pulled the grape from her bodice and placed it beside the prince's plate. "I forgot. This is all that remained from the first supper." The prince eyed the grape, but Daveal swept it off the table with her hand as she reached for her cup. Then she crushed the grape under the heel of her shoe. "Oh, I tried to stop it from rolling away, Your Highness."

Tashama tilted her chin up slightly as she considered the woman before her, then nodded. She returned to her table, while the conversation began to build slowly like a stream growing in strength, until the words grew as loud as a river gushing over rapids.

"What did you say to the prince?" Listra whispered to Tashama as she retook her seat.

"The food was poisoned. Simple as that."

"We have no proof."

"One little grape, but Devil managed to squish it all over the floor with her shoe. However, I've implanted the seed of doubt where she is concerned. She helped very well with the endeavor." Tashama considered the first supper they'd been served. "Of course, the grapes might not have contained any poison. Most likely, the lobster would have though. I'm certain the word was spread about how much I like the food."

"Yes, and I do too." Listra cut off a slice of roast and handed it to Tashama. "What did you mean earlier by, 'he was passing the tests so well'?"

"Nothing." Tashama sipped her wine. "Nothing at all."

"Does he really snore?"

"No." Tashama smiled. "But the word will soon get all over court that he does, don't you think?"

"And did he watch you…"

"He helped me to remove some of my wet gowns, but he was a gentleman, always."

A servant wiped up the grape from the floor.

Listra shook her head. "I wonder if the prince will have it tested on anyone."

"He ought to test it on Devil."

The two continued to eat their meal, then Listra cleared her throat. "I believe Oshon is quite angry with you too."

"Yes, well, he shouldn't have made plans to turn me over to Loran. Such a notion is traitorous, and it certainly wasn't my fault that the man bought his freedom in such a way. And to top that off, he is seeing a woman of the Bachava order."

"No." Listra's eyes grew round.

"Certainly. How else do you think I overheard his conversation? I was hiding in the temple when they were speaking. He tried to kiss her, and she wouldn't allow him to."

"No," Listra repeated and Tashama laughed.

"Certainly. Only the dust in the temple made me sneeze. You would think they would keep the place dusted better than that."

"The incense is what probably made you sneeze."

"Oh, well, the incense then."

Listra glanced over at the head table. "Carissian is watching you."

"Yes, he's trying to read my thoughts. I give them to him freely now, and this puzzles him."

"Can you read his thoughts? Some say you cannot."

"Certainly." Tashama licked the peppermint flavor off her fingers. "Um, I'm glad we were able to eat tonight. I really was quite hungry."

"The prince hasn't eaten much." Listra tilted her wine cup to her lips. "He cannot seem to take his eyes off you, though Daveal has tried to get his attention several times. Her face is three shades darker than I have ever seen it as a result of his ignoring her."

Tashama smiled, then took her drink, stood up, and toasted it to the prince. "To your successful coronation, Prince Aleron!"

Everyone raised a toast to the prince, and Tashama sipped her drink. "And to mermaids and the like," Tashama said under her breath as she sat down. "Did you finish your pillow for the prince's coronation?"

"Yes, but now I'm not certain he will want it."

"Will you attend the ceremony, tomorrow?"

"If I will be allowed."

"I won't."

"You will not be allowed?"

"No, I won't attend."

Listra shook her head. "I do not see why you wish to aggravate the prince so."

"It is he who aggravates me. He promised to stay with me while I returned to Karthland, and then what does he do? He returns me to prison."

"To keep you safe from Loran."

"And who is going to keep me safe from the Maldovians?" Tashama finished her wine, then waved for a refill. "I don't know, Listra. I felt it my duty to my people to return here and lead them to victory. Now, I'm not certain I should have ever been brought back."

"Why would your sorcerer have brought you here and not to Karthland?"

"He made a mistake. There was a tornado." Tashama's eyes filled with tears. She looked over at Listra. "I was angry with him for making the mistake and not coming to rescue me afterwards. If he's not here, then maybe he's dead." She stood slowly as the conversation dropped off in the great hall.

"He must be all right." Listra reached out her hand to Tashama's.

"He has been like my father." Tashama walked away from the table. "For these past ten years, I...I would not be able to rule without him by my side." She turned and ran for the door as the prince motioned for the guard. "Let me go!" she screamed as two of the guards grabbed her arms and made her stop. "Let me go!" she repeated as she tried to wrench her arms free from their tight grip.

Then she collapsed amidst sobs as the prince stood at his table. He motioned for Tashama to be removed from the hall, then hurried to conclude the feast.

THE PRINCE HURRIED out of the hall with Carissian. "What was the matter?"

"She was thinking about Balthazar when she had visions he might have died in the tornado."

"Tornado?"

"I believe it was the black funnel-like object dropped down out of their clouds. I've seen her envision this image several times. The image is life-threatening. I believe now her injuries when we first discovered her were due to this. If so, Balthazar may no longer live."

The prince rubbed his chin, then shook his head as he stopped in his footsteps. "She cannot rule without a royal sorcerer by her side."

"Nor without a husband."

"I want the grape analyzed for poison."

"The princess believes the grapes were not poisoned, only the lobster."

"Then I want to have the lobster analyzed as well."

"Yes, sire."

The prince quickened his pace down the long hall. "You seemed to have been concentrating on the princess quite a bit tonight."

"She was very talkative this evening. She revealed how she was discovered in the temple by Oshon. The incense made her sneeze."

The prince smiled. "A spy, she is not."

They arrived at the guest chambers, and the prince said to the guard, "Have my healer come at once."

"Yes, Your Highness." The guard hurried off as the prince walked into the room with Carissian.

"You are tired." The prince stood next to the bed where Tashama hugged a pillow against her chest while she stared at the wall with her back to him. "We've had an arduous day, and you must rest."

"I shouldn't have returned here," Tashama whispered as she shook her head slowly from side to side. "Nothing matters anymore. I shouldn't have returned here."

Carissian rubbed his beard with concern. "She's distraught, Your Highness. I'm not sure what to make of her like this. I would rather deal with her when she's obstinate or cunning or anything, but like this."

"She needs to sleep. I know I'm exhausted. Have my healer give her something to aid her sleep. I'm retiring early myself. Busy day tomorrow." He slapped Carissian on the shoulder. "What with the coronation and all, it will be an early morning."

The prince walked into the hall. Listra was brought to the room by her guards. The prince ignored her and hurried on his way while Listra hastened into the room. As the healer soon followed her, he asked Listra, "What was the matter?"

"She fears her sorcerer has died."

The healer nodded, then bowed to Carissian. "The prince wishes her sedated," Carissian said.

"Of course." The healer pulled a goblet from his robes. After mixing a blue liquid and a pink one from two separate vials, he leaned over the bed to speak to Tashama. "Drink this."

"Is it poisoned?" she asked.

"No, my lady. It is safe for you to drink."

"Then I don't wish it." She waved her hand to him to take it away.

"The prince wants you to have the most pleasant of dreams."

"I don't wish it." Tashama pulled the pillow over her head.

Carissian chuckled. "She is being stubborn again. This is a good sign."

The pillow was pulled away from her face, then the guards held her arms as the healer raised her head and poured the liquid down her throat after parting her pursed lips.

The mixture dribbled down her cheek, and he wiped the excess away with his sleeve. He turned to Carissian. "Enough of the mixture made it down her throat. In a few minutes, she will sleep."

Tashama frowned at them. "No."

Carissian cast a scowl in Listra's direction. "Stay with her until she sleeps." He headed out of the room.

Listra sat on the bed and held Tashama's hand as a tear trickled down her own cheek. "Tashama, you mustn't fear so about your sorcerer. They are hardy souls, and Balthazar was known to have been more cunning than the rest."

Tashama fought to keep her eyelids open as she saw another tear slip down Listra's face. She reached her hand up to touch Listra's cheek and shook her head. "Do not be sad, dear Listra," she whispered.

"My own people reject me. All I have is your friendship now. I cannot lose you too."

"You'll find one who'll win your heart." Tashama touched Listra's hand. She squeezed her hand lightly as her eyelids shut closed. "You'll always be my friend."

"Who is the one whom I am to love?" Listra implored as she rubbed Tashama's hand. "Tashama, who is the one I am to love?"

24

"She cannot hear you as she is in the world of dreams," the healer said to Listra.

Says you. Tashama took a deep breath. *These drugs will not make me sleep. I forbid it.*

"You must get your sleep as well, Princess Listra. Everything will look better in the morning."

"Thank you, healer."

He left the women alone, and Listra removed her hair veil and gowns, then slipped into bed beside Tashama. "At least you can have pleasant dreams while I am struck with the truth."

How can I have pleasant dreams, to think...to think...oh, Balthazar.

Later that night, Tashama ran from the black funnel spitting glass as it whirled in front of her. Balthazar flew past her, his white beard and hair suspended midair, while his steady blue eyes studied her.

"Balthazar," Tashama said.

A hand shaking her shoulder stirred her from her sleep, and she stared groggily at the black-hooded woman standing before her in the shadows of the night. "Have you come for me?" Tashama's glazed eyes tried to discern the woman's eyes behind the black veil. "You have no eyes." Tashama attempted to push the woman away.

"You must tell the prince Oshon has done nothing to cause you harm. He is innocent of the charges you have preferred against him."

"Oshon?" Tashama said, confused. "No, Balthazar. Where is Balthazar?" She slipped from the bed and fell with a thump to the floor.

"You must tell the prince." The woman leaned over Tashama. "You must tell him Oshon has done nothing of what you say. That you have lied. If you do this, he will leave you be."

Tashama stared at the woman's black shoes, then reached out to touch them. "Balthazar," she whispered.

The woman slapped her hand away. "Oshon and I will be married if you free him from the ostracism he now bears. Only you can set this right."

"Balthazar is gone." Tashama sobbed as she grabbed for the lady's skirts.

The woman backed away in annoyance. "If you will not right this wrong, Oshon will do what he set out to do, you stupid woman."

"If he is gone, nothing else matters." Tashama stood up and then walked toward the bath.

"What are you doing?" The woman grabbed Tashama's arm.

Tashama shook her loose. "I will find Balthazar."

The woman watched for a moment, then as Tashama walked into the bath, the woman ran for the guards. Tashama listened for a moment. Metal-edged boots ran toward the bath, then she slipped beneath the water.

"TASHAMA!" Listra cried out.

Hands tugged at Tashama's arms. Tashama coughed for a second as her skin touched the cold tile.

A man's hefty fingers wrapped around her wrist. "She is fine."

She saw Listra grabbing a robe and tying it around her waist as she ran to her.

"What happened?" Listra dropped to her knees, then cradled Tashama's head in her lap.

"Apparently, she tried to go for a swim in her dreams. The drug the healer gave her has not worn off."

No, I didn't, did I? I was trying to find Balthazar.

"Tashama." Listra rubbed her cheeks and called to her. "Tashama."

"Balthazar." Tashama tried to roll onto her side. *Why do you bother me so? Where's Balthazar?*

"You must leave," Listra said to the guard, "so I can get these wet gowns off her."

"When the healer gets here."

The healer hurried into the room and shone a light into their faces. "What is going on in here? Why have we no lights?"

"The princess must have been sleeping when she tried to take a swim," the guard said.

The healer frowned at Tashama and said to the guard, "You may leave us."

"What must we do?" Listra groaned. "She's clearly not capable of being safe in here."

"She's only sleeping now." He took a deep breath. "I imagine tying her to the bed would help, but I could not do such a thing without prior authorization."

"What is going on here?" Carissian asked as he appeared at their side.

"The guard said the princess was asleep when she took a swim, only she nearly drowned." Carissian studied Tashama's face for some time, then frowned as Tashama considered his. "A woman from the Bachavin order was in the room a short time ago."

Go away, you meddling sorcerer.

Listra's eyes widened as her hand touched her lips. "She's not safe here, Carissian. You must warn the prince. She's not safe."

Tashama stared at Listra through the haze. *The prince? He doesn't believe there's any danger here. No, Texas, the tornado.*

"We've had the grape analyzed. There was no poison in the food."

"And the lobster?"

Carissian shook his head.

"That's good." Listra sighed deeply.

Carissian studied Tashama further, then rubbed his forehead. "She dreams of Balthazar. Remove her gowns and put her to bed."

"Should we tie her to the..."

Carissian waved his hand to silence the healer. "I'll stay the rest of the night." Carissian shook his head. "I'll be back in a little while."

Listra struggled to remove Tashama's wet gowns. *Leave me be, Listra.* Then Listra dried her and after slipping the robe over her shoulders, she belted it at the waist. "Come help me with Princess Tashama," she called to the guards standing outside their window.

Tashama wrinkled her forehead. *Quit shouting, so. I can hear you. Just quit shouting.*

Once Listra had covered Tashama with her blankets, Carissian appeared, then took his seat in one of the velvet chairs. "Return to bed, Princess Listra. There will be no more disturbances tonight." But almost immediately after he said this, the prince barged into the room. "Your Highness." Carissian jumped from the chair. "She's sleeping comfortably, sire. All is well."

The prince walked to the bed. He touched Tashama's cheek and whispered, "What nightmares do you have, dear Tashama?"

"My sorcerer is gone," she whispered back in a voice nearly inaudible, "and so are you."

"I am here, my princess. I will not forsake you."

"They are all gone. She has no eyes—blackness all around—Balthazar."

"Who has no eyes?"

"One of the order of the Bachava, sire." Carissian drew close to the bed. "What did the woman want?"

"She came here?" the prince asked.

"Yes, sire," Carissian said.

"She struck at me—stupid, stupid, stupid woman, she called me." Tashama balled her hands into fists and struck the feather mattress.

Carissian rubbed his forehead. "This doesn't sound good, Your Highness."

"Oshon killed Bachava...no, no, Balthazar is dead, oh, Balthazar." Tears ran down Tashama's cheeks, and she groaned with grief.

"She's confused. The drug has confused her."

The prince touched Tashama's hand and then squeezed it gently. "What did the Bachavin woman want, Tashama?"

Tashama shook her head. "He'll marry her, but who will marry me? He won't marry me, he won't."

"Oshon?" The prince's voice rose in disbelief as Carissian touched his shoulder.

"She's confused. Some of what she says, she repeats as truth. Some, she confuses in her mind."

"Oshon will marry the Bachavin woman he met in the temple?"

"No, here." She wrinkled her face in disgust. "She, she, she, no, Balthazar," Tashama sobbed.

"She sees images of Balthazar as he flies through the air due to the circulation of an unbelievable force, such as that of a wind elemental gone awry, and then the sorcerer vanishes from her sight. The hooded woman haunts her, and she believes the woman is taking her away."

"Did she try to drown Tashama?" The prince touched her still-wet hair as it fell over her shoulder.

"Tashama," Carissian said, "did the Bachavin woman push you into the water?"

"Tell a lie, lie, she said, tell a lie, Oshon," Tashama whispered, then shook her head. "I cannot tell a lie...I won't...no...I cannot... Oshon said, he said..."

"Oshon was going to turn you over to Loran if..."

"Oh, Valmor," Tashama said.

"Oshon, Tashama. Oshon was going to turn..."

"Lies, no." Tashama squirmed on the mattress. "Marry him, okay, marry him, no lies."

"She wanted you to tell lies about Oshon?"

"Balthazar." Tashama raised her hands to her face and sobbed aloud.

"Can my healer give her something to calm her?"

"I'll be right back, sire." Carissian vanished.

The prince caressed Tashama's arm, then turned to Listra. "Leave us."

"But I am not properly dressed, Your Highness. Where would you have me go?"

"Step into the hall for a moment."

Listra frowned at the prince as she held her robe tightly, then hurried out of the room.

"Tashama." Aleron pulled her hands away from her face. He kissed her lips softly, and as her breathing calmed, he pressed her harder. She kissed him back this time, and he stopped, then stared at her. "Tashama?"

"She'll tattle on me. Tashama loves him, Tashama loves him. Tattle, tattle, pesky sprites."

The prince smiled, then kissed her mouth again with determination. She wrapped her arms around his shoulders as Carissian cleared his throat. The prince stood up quickly.

"Where is my healer?" the prince asked, vexed.

"He is preparing a stronger mix, but it appears you have something that calms the lady just as well. Where is Princess Listra?"

"She wanted a breath of fresh air."

The healer walked back into the room. "Sire, Princess Listra wishes to know if she can return to her room."

"Yes, of course. The lady, herself, wished to leave for a moment after all. The choice was hers as far as when she wanted to return."

Listra hurried back to bed, and Tashama shook her head. "Lies, all lies."

Carissian chuckled.

The healer gave a new potion to Tashama, and she licked her lips. "Mint julep. Kiss me again, oh lover of mermaids. Kiss me again." Tashama reached out her hand for the prince, though her eyes never opened, and he kissed her hand in response.

"Well, I would imagine none of you would do," the prince said to his healer and Carissian as he saw the expression of amusement on their faces. "You are staying for the rest of the night?" he asked Carissian.

"Yes, sire."

"All right, well, I have a very early appointment with destiny. Good night, my lady." He kissed her cheek, then turned on his heels and left the room.

Tashama opened her eyes and stared at the healer who had turned to speak with Carissian. "Let me know if you need me for anything further." Then he hurried out of the room too.

Carissian extinguished the lights, then folded himself into the soft-cushioned seat. His gray eyes studied her as she felt his gentle probes touching her thoughts.

EARLY THE NEXT MORNING, the prince's chest swelled as he watched his people file into the great hall to observe his coronation.

Carissian stood by his side as Aleron tapped his foot on the red carpet covering the marble floor for the special event. "I do not see my favorite princesses."

"I was informed Princess Tashama is still sleeping. The second potion she was given was a little stronger than the healer anticipated."

"Then have him give her something to wake her up. Everyone in my kingdom is to witness my coronation today."

"Yes, sire." Carissian disappeared.

Twenty minutes later, Carissian reappeared before the prince. "Your healer has tried two potions to wake her. He said it may be another half hour before they do the trick. Even so, she probably won't be quite herself."

"We will wait, Carissian."

"Yes, sire." Carissian raised his brows as Listra held Tashama's right arm while the healer held her left, and the guards walked on either side of the party as they entered the great hall.

"Let's get on with it, shall we?" The prince smiled as Tashama arrived.

The Bachavin priest began to chant, and Tashama said, "What language does he speak?"

"Shh," Listra said.

Tashama took a step closer toward the prince, who stood forty feet away. "Is that the prince down there?"

"Shh," Listra said again. "Yes," she whispered. "Soon to be king."

"His crown has got to be as big as a lake..."

"Shh," one of the men standing along the side of the hall said. "Keep the Karthlander prisoner quiet."

"I am no prisoner!" Tashama raised her voice while she pulled Listra and the healer with her as she walked over to the man. She poked her finger at his chest. "Take that back!"

"Shh," a woman said. "Is nothing sacred to you, Karthlander? The prince is soon to be crowned. Mind your tongue."

"Mind your tongue!" Tashama said. "Mind your tongue!"

"Tashama," Listra whispered, "do be quiet or the prince will have us removed."

"To Karthland?" Tashama's eyes widened. "Good! I want to be removed!"

There was a hush of voices as Carissian appeared at her side. "The prince wants her to see his coronation, but keep her quiet for heaven's sakes."

"Is it big enough?" Tashama touched the dagger at Carissian's waist.

"The dagger is only ceremonial."

"His crown, I mean."

"Keep her still," he said to the healer, then vanished and reappeared at the prince's side.

"Poof!" she mused. "Poof, poof, poof." She studied the gold crown the priest blessed, and then she shook her head. "He needs a bigger one!"

"Shut her up," one of the men growled.

"Make me!" Tashama glared back at the man.

25

The man took a menacing step toward Tashama, and she stood her ground while one of her guards pushed the man back. "You touch her, and it'll be all of our heads," the guard said to the man.

"How long is this going to go on?" Tashama sat down on the red carpet.

"No, my lady." The healer lifted her to her feet. "You must stand during the ceremony."

She leaned her head against his shoulder and closed her eyes.

"Are you still tired?" Listra whispered to Tashama.

"I cannot stay awake and yet." Tashama opened her eyes, then yanked her arms free from her captors and skipped down the long red carpet before Listra and the healer took her arms and made her step aside. "I feel I'm on a caffeine high."

The women of the Bachavin order watched the prince in silence, and Tashama pointed at the group. "I know you came to see me last night. I remember."

"Tashama—shh," Listra said.

"She did," Tashama persisted as she glared at the black-veiled women.

Carissian studied her, and she shook her head at him. "Quit trying to read my mind."

The prince received his crown, and cheers erupted. Carissian appeared before Tashama. "You'll come with me."

"No, I must congratulate the prince."

"King."

"Yes, him too."

"Later. You will tell me which of the women of the order came to your room last night."

Tashama glanced around the hall and saw Oshon glowering at her. "She was veiled. She had no eyes."

"You have other ways of knowing, Princess Tashama. You'll point her out to me now."

"Here, in front of all of the gods and everybody?"

"In the temple."

"I must congratulate the prince."

"Later." Carissian took her arm.

"Congratulations, Prince!" Tashama shouted over her shoulder as Carissian led her away.

"King, you little fool," a man said to her.

"King, you little fool!" Tashama shouted back to the prince, then she turned to the man. "My mistake." She patted Carissian's hand, gripping her arm. "Is this to be our first date?"

Carissian shook his head. "The king is in such good spirits today, he has ignored your little antics and not had you removed from the proceedings as I would have done."

"That is because he wants to kiss me." Tashama quickened her pace toward the temple.

"You were the one who asked for him to kiss you."

Tashama stared at Carissian for a moment, then smiled. "You only say this, but it is not so."

"You cannot read my thoughts truly, can you?"

"What makes you think that?"

"Just a hunch."

"If I cannot read thoughts, how will I know which of the women came to my room last night?"

"You have other gifts."

They walked into the temple where one of the priests greeted them. "This is highly irregular." He twisted his belt between his fingers.

"The procedure will only take a few moments," Carissian said to the priest, then turned to Tashama. "Begin."

Tashama stood before one of the women, then touched her wrist. She moved to the next. As she made it halfway through the line of women, the king walked into the temple. "Has she identified the woman yet, Carissian?"

"Not yet, sire."

Tashama touched the correct woman's wrist, squeezed her wrist tightly, then moved onto the next. Carissian frowned.

"What?"

"The princess showed no recognition, but the woman she just passed up feared having Tashama touch her."

Tashama finished with the women and turned to Carissian. "None of these visited me in my chambers. The woman must have been an imposter."

The king said, "Carissian will speak with the woman the tenth from the right on the first row. I wish her name, as well. That'll be all."

"I said nothing about the woman, Your Highness," Tashama said in front of the women before they disbanded from the temple.

"No, the woman told on herself to Carissian."

"Oh, then I cannot be held at fault."

"Are you feeling better?" Aleron led her out of the temple.

"I'm feeling much better. Did I have too much wine to drink last night? I cannot remember much about the evening, except for the woman invading my sleep."

"And you took a swim."

"No."

"I'm afraid so."

Tashama frowned as she tried to recollect, then she shook her head. "I don't remember. But something had upset me—Balthazar." She walked in silence for a few minutes, then nodded. "If he is gone, I will have to live without him, though it won't be easy." She saw Oshon as he stood near the king's quarters, and her eyes grew big. "I believe I have the solution to this problem, however."

She hurried over to Oshon and grabbed his wrist, but he jerked his arm away from her and stepped back as the king watched. "If you will permit me this, I will prove you mean to do me no ill will, and you and your bride-to-be will have been absolved of any wrongdoing."

Oshon glanced over at the king, who, with a single nod of his head, consented to the impromptu trial. Tashama took the cavalry officer's wrist and held it for some time. A slight smile appeared on her lips as Oshon's wrist grew sweaty.

Her smile widened. "King Aleron, you have nothing further to fear from this officer. He intends to do nothing for Loran's cause. But he wishes for you to attend his wedding as he intends to wed the woman Carissian is now questioning."

Her eyebrows arched as he contemplated the matter. "I tell the truth, Your Highness."

"But I wonder if I should not have had Carissian studying you as you used your gift. Somehow, I feel there's more to the situation than you will reveal to me."

"Is he free from further ostracism, sire?" Tashama folded her arms as Oshon waited to be released from the nightmare he had created for himself.

Aleron shook his head. "I believe I will live to regret this. I do not normally make such lofty decisions without my advisor at my side."

"You are king now, so be king and decide."

Carissian appeared next to Aleron. "Have I missed something?"

"The princess used her powers to find Oshon not capable of treason."

Carissian took the same posture as Tashama, crossing his arms over his chest. "She did, did she? I would have liked to have listened in on this one, Your Highness."

"Do you call me a liar?" Tashama asked.

"No," Carissian said. "But sometimes you omit things you do not wish for me to see."

"That was my very thought on the subject," the king said.

Carissian studied Oshon. "It is up to you, sire."

"He is exonerated then. Having a royal member of the household accused of committing treason reflects badly on all of us. Spread the word at once. Oshon is cleared of any wrongdoing."

The look Oshon gave Tashama was as harsh as any before. She tilted her head to the side. "You're welcome, Oshon." Turning to Aleron, she took his arm and led him toward the gardens as his lips turned up in amusement. "So sire, now you must make a selection for a bride, I'm to understand."

"I have a list of fourteen names."

"And Devil is on this list?"

"First name on the list, actually."

"I want Listra absolved of her involvement with helping me leave here before. She only tried to keep me from being harmed." The king shook his head. Tashama frowned. "How can you win my favor if you will do nothing to satisfy me?"

"My kisses satisfied you last evening." A smile stretched across his face.

Tashama glanced back at Carissian, who followed them a short distance behind. She frowned as he smiled broadly. She turned to Aleron. "I don't remember. It must have been the drugs that made me do it if I did any such thing at all."

"Does she speak the truth, Carissian?"

Tashama faced Carissian. "Must you follow us everywhere? We were having a private conversation."

"She remembers, sire, and with much satisfaction, I might add."

"Feeble he grows." Tashama pulled Aleron along the path.

"Our stroll is becoming a race, Tashama." He tugged at her to walk more slowly.

Tashama waved her hand at Carissian. "How can I concentrate on a walk with you if you have *him* with us?"

"You may reveal something in your conversation to me that Carissian..."

"I will tell him nothing and you either if you insist on having him walk with us."

"Is it the drug that makes her this way?" he asked Carissian.

"This place called Texas has made her so unruly. Though the drugs the healer used to counteract the others may have made her a bit more unstable."

Tashama smiled, then she took a deep breath. "Please treat Listra with some kindness, sire. She is your cousin after all and wants nothing but the best for you."

"Her pillow sits on my bed. It is the only one I allow to rest in such a place of honor."

"You won't look at her or speak to her. And because of this, everyone else takes this as meaning they should not either."

"She is with the other ladies at this moment. You need not fret about her so."

Tashama relaxed her tense posture. When she did, Aleron leaned over and kissed her cheek. She shook her head. "You should not do that to me, as you will soon be marrying."

"It is customary to show an expression of affection between royal families."

"Amongst Maldovians, you mean. I imagine Devil will not be

too happy should you continue to treat me in this manner when you marry her."

"What makes you think I will choose her?"

"She is the only one I ever see you with." Tashama touched the gold belt at her waist. "Was the grape poisoned?"

"What made you think of that?"

"Devil crushing it beneath her foot."

"It was not."

"And the lobster?"

The prince hesitated to answer her, and she studied Carissian. Though he showed no indication of the answer to her question, she nodded in response. "The lobsters were disposed of before you could test them, so I thought."

Carissian smiled slightly. "You are guessing."

"No." Tashama looked at the path beneath her feet. "I know it to be so."

"Well, without the so-called evidence, we cannot be sure your fears were truly warranted or not. The food would have been discarded after all when it was thrown so wastefully to the pavement."

Tashama took a deep breath. "But I imagine the food would not have gone to waste." She glanced back at Carissian. "Would it have?" He wouldn't say, and Tashama added, "To the pigs, perhaps?" Carissian still remained silent. "Why do you not tell me, Carissian?"

"I'm thinking about what has been done, but you cannot see this, can you?"

Tashama turned away from him. Aleron laughed. "She cannot tell what we are thinking. Knowing this to be true, I feel much relieved."

"Why? Do you have secrets you want to hide from me?" Tashama asked him.

"Some things even Carissian shouldn't know, but I'm afraid I can't keep him from probing my thoughts like you do. But you still cannot see what my future holds?"

"No, I cannot see what the future has in store for you."

"She sees something, but she fights allowing me to see what she observes," Carissian interrupted.

The prince squeezed Tashama's arm more tightly. "You must let me know what you see, Tashama. I can be quite hard to live with when I want to know what gifts my courtiers want to bestow upon me, and they want to keep them secret from me until the appointed day."

"All right." Tashama looked back at Carissian. "Ask your sorcerer."

Aleron turned to Carissian, who smiled back at him. "You wouldn't wish for me to say, Your Highness."

"What?" the king said.

"You are kissing the lady, and she finds the experience most pleasurable."

"You didn't have to let him see this." Aleron pulled Tashama along at a quicker pace.

"Now you are pulling me along as if we were in a race." Tashama laughed.

"So, where do I get to enjoy such a pleasurable experience with you?"

"That I don't know." Tashama's eyes studied his dark brown ones. "Maybe it's just a figment of my imagination."

Aleron shook his head. "No, and not just wishful thinking either."

"Sire, this continued delay to select a bride from one of the eligible women of our realm confounds me." Carissian sat in the king's anteroom. Aleron leaned back in his chair as it was situated behind his desk while he observed the mermaids in his mural. Carissian added, "She's been so demure of late, I thought perhaps she was settling down to the notion she would just live with us, but something is brewing in that crafty mind of hers."

Aleron glanced over at Carissian. "What?"

"I knew I could get your attention."

"What is she planning to do now?"

"I've considered how we could turn her over to General Karam's forces. He will keep her as safe as he can, and she will undoubtedly encourage him to remove Loran from his throne. We couldn't hope to do better than this."

"No." He resumed considering his mural.

"You cannot marry the Karthlander princess, sire."

The king frowned at him. "I am king now, yet you still insist on telling me what I must and must not do from time to time. Remember, you advise me, you do not command me."

"Yes, sire."

"Besides, who says I was interested? And if I were interested in marrying her, what makes it so wrong for me to do such a thing?"

Carissian groaned.

"What?"

"We have been at war with the Karthlanders for ten long years, isn't that enough? Your people would revolt if you took one of theirs for your wife."

"What word have we concerning General Karam's forces?"

"They haven't moved from Chrisholm Island, sire. Seems the bountiful food, pleasant weather, and willing women have given them other options than continuing the war with us."

"And we've made no progress at liberating the island?"

"The natives seem content with the presence of the Karthlanders. What's the difference if one people rules in place of another anyway?"

Aleron nodded as his thoughts returned to Tashama. "What is she planning now?"

26

"Escape, sire, is what Princess Tashama is planning now. I know she's scheming somehow, but I cannot find out how. She suspects someone still wishes to murder her and Princess Listra."

"But we don't know for certain whether the lobster was poisoned or not. Oshon has married now and doesn't seem to mind that the Karthlander woman continues to reside here. So what makes Tashama think someone intends to murder her, and my cousin as well, for heaven's sake?"

"Lady Daveal confronted her and Princess Listra in their guest chambers earlier in a threatening manner. She doesn't trust the woman."

"Why did you not tell me this before?"

"Princess Tashama does trifle with Lady Daveal, sire, like a cat toying with a mouse. Lady Daveal is often a tigress herself, so I didn't believe the women would behave any more than the usual sort of advisories would who were after the same thing."

"Whatever does Tashama have that Daveal would want? She's a Karthlander after all and came here with little possessions of her own."

"I cannot think of a thing." A slight smile appeared on Carissian's face. Then he grew serious. "You only have a week and a half to decide between a wife, sire."

"And if I wait two weeks? Where does it say I have to make a decision within that time frame?"

"Our laws, sire, as passed down from generation to generation. This is to prevent a king from waiting too long and not producing an heir in a reasonable amount of time. Within two weeks of the coronation, you must wed. If not, you could be forced to abdicate the throne, and the next royal figure in line would be eligible to become king."

"Oshon."

"Yes, and from what I understand, he has taken off much time from leading the cavalry of late, as he sees to other priorities."

"His own offspring?"

"Yes, sire. So you see, you should not delay any further."

"I will not be rushed into the matter."

"If the list is too short, we could add some lesser noblewomen to the list."

"No. You truly do not know what measures Tashama is taking to try to escape?"

Carissian shook his head. "She has been teaching Listra to swim. I wondered if perhaps she was preparing her for some venture they may wish to make."

"Where?"

"At the pool that meanders through the gardens."

"When?"

"At this hour, I would think. The activity draws quite a crowd every day. You won't see a soul in the hallways loitering as usual about this time."

The prince jumped to his feet and headed out the door before Carissian could finish his statement. "Are you going to stop the entertainment?"

"Do you not have other business to attend to?"

"No, sire. Accompanying you seems to be a more interesting business."

As they arrived at the pool, Aleron saw a crowd gathering at the bridge, then he dashed that way. He watched as one of the ladies pointed at the pool, while several others smiled and nodded.

"Oh, sire," one of the ladies said as she quickly curtsied to him. "Princess Tashama has taught Princess Listra to swim underneath the water already."

Aleron studied the women as they swam underneath the bridge. "Have none of you anything better to do?"

"It's the hour of free time, sire," Carissian said to Aleron.

"Then why does she do this during this particular time of day?" Aleron hurried to the waterfall.

"It's the only time the guards have allowed her to have free time also, sire."

"She has no regularly scheduled duties. Anytime is free time for the lady."

"Yes, sire."

They stood at the edge of the pool. Tashama and Listra poked their heads underneath the waterfall. While they ran their hands over each other's long hair as the fall ran over them in a steady stream, then laughed.

Tashama whispered to Listra, though her spoken word would not have made it to his ear just the same. Listra nodded and dove under the water, and then Tashama followed her. The two soon vanished beneath the bridge.

When they swam across to the other side, they dove under the water and swam until they came to the secretive islands of plants that hid them. Both climbed out, then covered their wet gowns with towels and hurried back to the path. Aleron caught up with them. "I wish a word with you," he said to Tashama.

"Yes, sire?"

Listra hurried back to their chambers.

"You do not find our ways too disagreeable?"

"Of course not, Your Highness."

"And yet you wish to leave still?"

"Who has said such a thing, as if I wouldn't know?"

Carissian followed a greater distance behind them this time.

"Yes, well, he believes you still wish to leave."

"As much as I cherish the thought of spending the rest of my days waiting for a royal kiss from your lips, as a gesture of friendship, mind you, I do believe my time could be better spent finding a mate of my own and running my own kingdom. Granted, I have enjoyed teaching Listra to swim."

"To what end?"

"No one in particular. She was interested, that's all."

"And should I be interested?"

"Listra can teach you. She swims as well as I do, now."

"Nobody could swim like you, royal cousin of the water nymphs and cousin to the mermaids of the sea, I do believe."

"I thank you for showing Listra a greater kindness, King Aleron." Tashama tried to change the subject. "She's much happier now."

"And because I have done this favor for you, should you not return a favor to me?"

"What is it that you desire of me?"

Carissian's arched brows told a tale Aleron didn't wish repeated. Aleron took Tashama's arm and led her back to her quarters. "Teach me to swim, tonight, by moonlight." He left her off at her chambers.

"If this is what you desire, so be it. Tonight."

When she hurried into her room, she slipped into the room containing the bath. "What did Aleron want?" Listra asked as she dried her hair.

"What every man wants of a woman. But for now, I will teach him another lesson in swimming."

"You know he is balking about choosing a wife. Many say this is because he desires you and no other, though he realizes he cannot marry you."

"Nonsense," Tashama said. "He is just a typical man who is scared to make a commitment to one woman."

"He is our king and must weigh the consequences of his decision heavily."

"He is *your* king. He is only a man to me and much the same as all the rest."

"The ladies say this isn't so."

"And what do you say, dear Listra?"

"I agree with the other ladies. Your cheeks blush when Aleron steps close to you as his breath touches your neck. I may not have your special gifts, but I can see things about you that reveal much of your nature."

"And what else do you see?" Tashama climbed into the blue gowns of silk.

"Carissian has said you are planning to leave us again. He asked me to tell him whether you should say or do anything that would indicate you planned a move in that direction."

"Dear Listra." Tashama walked into the bedchambers. "I cannot lie to you about this—as I have been just as honest with Aleron— that is to say, I must lead my people. I don't know what happened to my own mother and father, as Balthazar would never say, but I believe Loran had something to do with it."

"You think he had them murdered?" Listra sat down hard on the bed.

"I don't know for sure, but he certainly benefited from their deaths."

"But then you should have been installed in your father's place."

"Yes, with Balthazar to advise me until I came of age and wed. But he felt I would never have lived long enough to fulfill my obligation and took me away to this strange place named Texas. So you see, I must return to Karthland. It is my duty and my innermost desire."

"But Aleron won't release you."

"The choice is not his to make."

"Then you do plan to leave here."

"The guards double in strength, yet no amount will keep me here." Tashama braided her hair.

"Still, Aleron feels you are planning this move soon. Will I wake up tomorrow and find you gone?"

Tashama smiled as she touched Listra's cheek. "I would tell you all I have planned, only Carissian could read your mind and discover what I will do. I cannot have my plans forfeited like that."

"Oh, Tashama, you cannot leave me like this. Aleron will be furious again."

"He will get over it and even finally make his selection for a wife."

"You've seen whom he chooses?" Listra's eyes widened. "Do tell? The betting in the palace has gone to such great lengths."

"No." Tashama smiled. "I just meant to say, he will make a choice once I'm out of his hair."

"I do not understand this illusion you make in reference to his hair. His hair is not long enough for you to..."

"No longer here for him to think about."

"Oh, if you are gone, he will think of nothing else, rest assured. You cannot leave." She studied Tashama as she took her seat in one of the velvet chairs. "I've seen you do this a lot in the last couple of days. If I were Carissian, I could tell what you were thinking, and I would imagine you were contemplating how you would steal away."

"Then it is good you do not have Carissian's powers."

Listra wagged her foot up and down, which caught Tashama's eye. "Now you are contemplating something."

"I do not wish for you to leave, Tashama. Loran will kill you, of that, I'm certain. You have not even told me who it is I will marry. And what has happened to Lord Coryn?"

"A band of wild boar killed Lord Coryn and his party of merchants; the elves told me. Since they have not had good relations with the Maldovians, they never told Aleron of the matter."

"Why did you not tell me before? Why did you not tell Aleron?"

"I was a prisoner once again. Quite frankly, I'd forgotten. But I'm truly sorry for your loss."

"I wouldn't have wished the man the kind of death he incurred, but I wasn't happy with the notion of marrying him."

"Truly?"

"The marriage was arranged. Neither in stature nor in character did the man ennoble himself with me."

"The one you will marry will please you, I'm certain." Tashama turned away from Listra.

"Who is he?" Listra hurried over to the chair where Tashama sat.

"You do not know him, and I cannot say anything further."

"I will do anything for you if you will only tell me."

"I cannot, Listra. I beg your forgiveness, but I just cannot. If it weren't for Carissian's meddling ways..."

Listra stood. "Oh, Tashama, I cannot disobey Aleron again. You mean to say I will do such a thing again?"

"I'm sorry, Listra. Devil intends to kill us both. I didn't want to say this to you, and you must never think of this while Carissian is nearby. But she intends to kill us so Aleron will be free to wed her."

"But there are others on the list."

"She is at the top of his list. Who is it he always spends time with? Who was sitting with him at the high table in the last three days? She feels her position is secure, only if I am out of the way."

"And me?"

"She has already threatened you once. If I should die, you will undoubtedly be able to convince Aleron she was the cause of my death. You will not be allowed to live either."

"But how?"

"I'm not sure. You saw how the lady of the Bachavin order was able to slip past the guards with their consent. Perhaps they'll see fit to allow Devil or her henchmen to do the same. In any event, I believe she will make a second attempt."

"But Carissian said the lobster wasn't poisoned."

Tashama shook her head. "The lobster was never tested for the poison."

"He said…"

"Yes, well, what he said and what truly happened are two different stories." Listra stared at the floor for a moment, and Tashama took her hand. "What, Listra?"

"Thinking there was truly no threat, I've let my guard down."

"Why? Has something happened we should be concerned about?"

"A girl brought flowers into the bath, but I had not asked for them. I always use Jasmalange, roses, or the water lily. These are a different variety, and I thought since they looked stunning…"

Tashama jumped up from her chair, then hurried into the bathroom. She stared at the violet orchard-like flowers with their spotted burgundy throats tilted in her direction. "I don't know about the local floral life here. I wouldn't be able to tell if these are poisonous or not, though I have seen no sign of them in the gardens."

"Perhaps Aleron sent them to scent your bath…"

"Perhaps not. Is there a way for us to drain this water and the flowers from the bath without touching them?"

"Certainly." Listra hurried to a lever on the wall. "This will flush everything from the bath down into the sewers. But shouldn't we tell Aleron about this first?"

"Let us play a game on the party that wishes us injury. If Aleron is made aware of this before nightfall, she will know she wasn't successful and will have to come up with another plan. This way, if we should take our baths late, as is usual, no one would discover our bodies until the morning when breakfast was served.

"This way, we should be safe for another night, and at breakfast, we will wait until someone comes to check on us. Would it not be justice to walk into the great hall late and see how she takes our rather healthy appearance as we sit at our usual seats? I, for one, would enjoy such a thing."

"You mean Daveal, do you not?"

"Yes, she is the one most likely to be at the top of my list."

Listra nodded, then pulled the lever. As the water swirled out of the drain, Tashama smiled. But Listra frowned at the disappearing water. "If you see I marry someone, then how can anyone end my life."

"We must always be able to thwart them, Listra. We cannot let our guard down ever."

"Then you must leave here," Listra said softly as she saw the first of the purple flowers plummet through the drain. "You cannot stay here with me."

27

"Y̶ou and I will remain the greatest of friends, Listra. This I do foresee. And you will be more powerful than Daveal can ever hope to be."

"What will happen to her?" Listra watched the bathwater as it sank lower in the tub.

"That I do not know. I have never touched her. Quite frankly, I'm afraid of what I might see. Sometimes knowing the future can be extremely frightening."

"Do you only know the future?"

"And the past."

"Then if you touched her wrist, you could discover she had poisoned the lobster."

"Only, like in Carissian's case, if she were thinking of it."

"Then you *can* see what he is thinking."

Tashama smiled. "Certainly."

"But the word has spread across the court that you cannot. I don't know what it was you couldn't see, but…"

"I asked what had happened to the lobster when the servants removed it. He said he was thinking of what had happened, and I let on I couldn't tell. He's been suspicious of my abilities all along. He cannot believe a human could have them.

"But my family has had these abilities for centuries, the direct result of the mixture of a sorcerer in the family tree many generations ago. It caused quite a scandal at the time. In later years, the offspring had these abilities that only sorcerers had. We were able to keep the otherwise all-powerful sorcerers in their place when need be. My child will have some or all the same abilities someday."

"But then what was Carissian thinking?"

Tashama shook her head. "He had the pigs' slop pens searched for remnants of the lobster, but the pigs had already eaten everything from their troughs. Then, he had the pigs watched for signs of the poison in their systems. He felt they would die from the drug had they eaten it. The pigs are all still under quarantine. You might have noticed, no sausages for breakfast."

"Ah, the food is His Highness's favorite. I wondered why we hadn't been eating such a thing lately. But what did happen to the lobster?"

The last of the flowers disappeared down the drain, and Tashama said, "We will rinse out the bath first, then fill the tub. But no more flowers."

"I will be more cautious the next time."

"She will not try the same thing twice."

LATER THAT NIGHT, as the full moon cast a soft glow in the black velvet sky, Tashama strolled with Aleron through the gardens. He didn't seem to be in a hurry to swim. Tashama sighed deeply. "I'm being blamed for your not selecting a wife, Your Highness."

"Nonsense." Aleron walked her to the middle of the bridge. They paused to look over the railing, and he smiled as the water sprites dashed out of the water, then fluttered about their heads. "They told me your secret, Tashama," he said so softly, she had to turn to hear his words.

"What is that?" She motioned for the sprites to go away.

He smiled at Tashama, then lifted her hand to his lips and kissed it. "You said I kissed you..."

"Carissian said that."

"But he saw what you envisioned, and yet I have not kissed you once since you spoke to me of this."

"You've had more important business to attend to than kiss a royal personage in the typical form of a familial greeting."

"That is not the kind of kiss I shared with you."

"How do you know?"

"You blush quite easily, Tashama. I know this is not the kind of kiss we share."

"Tell him, Tashama." A sprite fluttered next to Tashama's head again.

"Go away!" Tashama said.

"What do they say, Tashama? Do they tell you to say how you love me?"

Tashama stared at Aleron as his eyes searched hers. She felt her cheeks grow hot. He smiled, and she looked back at the water. "You wanted to swim," Tashama responded.

"Tell him, Tashama," the sprite repeated.

"She loves you," another said as she fluttered about Aleron's ear this time. "She does. Tashama, Tashama, Tashama, tell him it is so."

"They tell me you love me." He nodded, then squeezed her hand.

She took a deep breath. "The night is already late, sire. If you desire to swim, then we should go now before it gets too much later."

"All right." He pulled her from the bridge and headed toward the waterfall. As he stood at the edge of the water, he pulled off his tunic to her surprise.

"What are you doing?" Tashama asked.

"You said you desired to touch my bare chest while you floated me on your hands. Since you told me this, I have desired nothing less." He slipped off his shoes as she stared at his breeches. A smile touched his lips as he leaned over and kissed her cheek.

After crawling into the water, he clung to the edge of the twenty-foot-deep pool. "Are you not coming? I do not believe I will be able to swim without your help, and I cannot sleep another night without feeling your slender fingers on my bare chest."

Tashama slipped into the water. "Hold onto the edge of the pool, and I will pull your legs out straight."

He did as he was told.

"Now kick the water with your feet and feel the water circulating about them."

Aleron experimented.

"Now push yourself a little way away, paddle with your hands and kick with your feet, then swim back to the edge and hang on."

He tried this. "But you have not shown me how to float on your hands."

"We needed to be in the shallower water for me to do that with you, and besides, you already know too many of the basics."

"No, you must show me this."

"The water is too deep."

"I insist."

"All right."

Aleron reached his hand out to Tashama, and she took his hand, then pulled him away from the wall. She attempted to place her hands under the prince's chest, but her own head submerged. The water sprites lifted her up. She touched the prince's chest. "Now kick your feet as if you wanted to go somewhere and pull the water behind you with your hands as you go."

After paddling for a time, she said, "Now I will let you go, and you must swim toward me. If you feel afraid, I'll come to your aid, or the water sprites will."

Aleron smiled. "You will." She moved her hands away from him, scooted away, and he paddled toward her like a new puppy just finding he could swim.

"Good. Now, you'll roll over onto your back, and I'll show you how you can float should you weary. You can stay like this and move your arms and legs and get to where you're going in this way too."

Tashama placed her hands on his back while she watched Aleron straighten his posture. "Yes, that's correct. You can even bend your legs at the knee and float like that. As long as there are no waves, you can rest for a long time like this just by moving your hands and feet periodically."

"Will you kiss me, Tashama?"

"I'm trying to teach you to swim, sire."

"If I try to move from this position, I will surely sink and drown. Will you not lean over me and kiss me just once?"

"Kiss him, Tashama!" A sprite darted from the water.

"Kiss him, kiss him," several chanted as they danced upon the water.

"They wish you to also." He touched her cheek. "I cannot select a wife, Tashama, from the fourteen other women listed, as I have fallen in love with you. Kiss me, Tashama, and show me you love me too."

"I cannot." A tear rolled down her cheek.

He reached up to wipe away the tear but sank below the surface of the water. She pulled him from the water, and he touched his lips to hers and kissed her with determination. She kissed him back as their spritely audience grew quiet. All the while, the princess and Aleron paddled their feet to keep afloat in rhythmic motion while their hands touched each other's faces as if they wanted to memorize every part before they were torn away from each other again.

Aleron wrapped his arms around her in an embrace as tight as any merman would have on his mermaid as Tashama gave into the feeling of his water-moistened lips against hers. His desire for her grew as he held her close while the nymphs giggled as they floated in her golden strands.

"He loves you too, Tashama," they chanted. "A royal baby water sprite you will make."

"No," Tashama said to the nymphs, and Aleron looked at her in surprise. "I weary. We must go in."

"All right, but I wish another lesson tomorrow night at the same time," he said as she helped him to return to the edge of the pool. "I wish to swim underneath the water as you do." After Aleron hurried to climb out of the pool, he reached for Tashama and lifted her out too.

Her gowns clung to her shapely figure. She studied his breeches as his desire for her hadn't begun to wane. He chuckled, then grabbed up his tunic and hurried her back to her chambers. When they arrived at her room, he said, "Tomorrow, I will see you at breakfast."

"Tomorrow, sire." *But not if I can help it.*

THE NEXT MORNING, Listra hurried to get out of bed. "We're late to breakfast." She slipped her robe to her feet.

Tashama sat in bed and stared out the window as she tried to consider what had gone wrong. Were her visions of being aided to escape from Banff incorrect?

Listra pulled her gown over her head. "Hurry, Tashama. We must attend the feast."

Tashama dragged herself from the bed, then selected a gown

from the peg on the wall. As she pulled the green velvet dress over her head, Listra attached veils to her own hair. "That's the gown His Highness likes best on you of all the rest."

"He told me he loved me." Tashama fastened a gold chain at her waist. Listra grew quiet as her dark brown eyes were as round as Aleron's crown. "But of course I'm sure he tells all of the ladies such a thing."

"No, my lady. He wouldn't do such a thing."

"How would you know what he says to the other ladies when he's alone with them?"

"He's always chaperoned. Though with you, it's not always been so. And the ladies do gossip, Tashama. Had he told any of them such a thing, the news would have spread like the jasmalange jelly the courtiers coat their bread with at breakfast."

"He knows it can never be between us, so he says it in mockery."

Listra shook her head. "When he said this, did he say anything else?"

"He would not choose one of the other ladies to wed, but I know this is not true."

"You have seen who he has chosen then?"

"No." Tashama slipped her shoes on. "I just know Carissian, as his advisor, will ensure Aleron does what is expected of him."

The two women walked into the hall, and the guards hurried to escort them to the great hall. When the ladies entered the room, the first course of the meal had already been served.

The room grew quiet except for a fork poking into a grape as it scraped on the pewter plate. Tashama and Listra hurried to take their seats, all the while watching the expression on Daveal's face. "Well, she's taking it very well; if she was disappointed that we're here at all, I cannot see by her emotionless face what she's thinking."

Carissian studied Tashama, and Listra said to her, "Carissian seems to be concerned about you this morning."

Tashama buttered a slice of bread. "Yes, I let it slip I was thinking of how we had to drain our bath of poisonous orchids last night."

Listra nodded. "He is speaking to a servant. Now the servant is leaving the great hall."

"Poor fellow. He'll be searching the sewers for purple orchids, no doubt."

"Princess Tashama." Carissian appeared behind her. "If you suspected someone wished to poison you again, why did you not let me in on this little secret before now?"

"You would have believed me just as much concerning the orchids as you did of the lobster."

"And now you've disposed of the evidence?"

"I got rid of the menace to Listra's and my health, don't you mean?"

Aleron watched her as Daveal studied her own plate of food. Tashama cleared her throat. "Does Aleron know of this?"

"I will tell him as soon as I get some answers from you."

"I wanted to sleep in peace last night. Had the one who wanted us dead discovered we were alive and well, she may have tried a further attempt that night. I cannot keep up my guard always after all."

"She?"

Tashama smiled. "Or he, of course. How can I know who it is?"

"You suspect Daveal."

"She is the top of the prince's list, so she is at the top of mine."

Carissian shook his head, then reappeared next to Aleron. Aleron's eyes widened, then he looked back at Carissian, who nodded. Aleron motioned to a servant, then, after speaking to him, the servant hurried to join Tashama.

"My lady, I'm Aleron's chief food tester. He has asked that I taste your foods throughout the rest of the meal to ensure they're of the freshest quality."

"Not poisoned, you mean." Tashama took a sip of her wine. "She won't try to poison us here."

"Aleron requires me to do my duty."

"Certainly." Tashama slipped a grape into her mouth and then rolled the fruit over her tongue. She bit into it as Aleron spoke to Carissian further, never taking his eyes off her.

For the rest of the meal, Tashama and Listra allowed the food tester to taste the food from each of their dishes. When they finished their breakfast, Carissian approached the women. "Princess Listra, His Highness wishes you to accompany your mutual cousin, Fatima, to Tyrone as she weds the prince of that region within the month."

"I cannot." Listra reached for Tashama's hand. "I want to stay with Princess Tashama."

"No." Carissian helped Listra from her seat. He motioned for two guards to take her away. "You'll be safer where you will go, Princess. His Highness wishes no harm to come to you."

"No!" Listra tried to pull her arms away from the royal guards. "Tashama!"

Tashama stood, then walked over to Listra and gave her a warm embrace. "We will be together again and soon, do not fear," she whispered in her ear. "Peace be with you, dear Listra."

"No," Listra sobbed as Carissian motioned for them to take her away.

Tashama folded her arms as she waited for Carissian to speak to her. He took her arm and led her out of the room. Seeing what plans he had for her, she turned to look at him with surprise. He smiled. "You do know what I'm thinking after all."

She remained quiet as she contemplated the knowledge. They walked for half an hour through the maze of corridors, then finally arrived at his quarters. He waved his fingers in an unusual pattern, making his door open, then he pulled her into his room. The door resealed, and he said, "All right, now we can speak freely here."

"I never thought you would betray your king."

"I never realized how much he'd fallen in love with you, Princess. It just cannot be."

"May I?" Tashama motioned to one of his velvet chairs.

"Certainly."

Tashama sat, then stared up at the sorcerer. "You realize if he discovers this traitorous move, you'll be banished from Maldovia?"

28

"To aid you in returning to Karthland and saving my own kingdom, the risk is worth my banishment," Carissian told Tashama.

Tashama smoothed out her skirts. "Would I be such an intolerable choice for your king?"

"Neither my people nor your own would approve such a match. The notion is folly."

"And if I gave up the idea of returning to my own beloved Karthland?"

"You could reside here under the protection of His Highness."

"As?"

"His subject."

Tashama straightened her back. "I would no more want to be King Aleron's subject than he would want to be mine. Perhaps if we resided elsewhere instead, as just a man and a woman..."

"You wish to free your people." Carissian stared out the window. "I will turn you over to General Karam, and then it'll be up to you to do what you can to bring Loran down."

"And you want *what* in return?"

"Your word that you will make peace with King Aleron once

you rule Karthland or convince the husband you choose of this at least."

"If I don't agree?"

"I know it's in your heart already, my lady. You desire more than anything else in the world to bring peace to the two lands. You'll do it if you're able."

Tashama stood. "When do I leave?"

"Soldiers will come for you tonight. Oshon will lead the force to get you to Chrisholm Island safely."

"Aleron wants me to teach him to swim further tonight. Can you dissuade him?"

"I'll attempt to, but when he has business with you, my powers of persuasion are rather limited."

"Do what you can. It'll be best for both of us if we see each other no further."

"My sentiments exactly."

"Will Listra be safe?"

"I believe you know she will be."

Tashama nodded, then walked over to the door that led to the gardens. She opened it and smiled. "Why does this not lock in some fancy way that the other does?"

"I wished for it to be unlocked so you could go that way."

"Tonight then." Tashama walked outside and glanced up at the clouds cluttering the sky. She sauntered toward her own room. Then, quickening her pace, she hurried down the path to her own bedchambers. As she entered the room, she gasped as the young thief waved to her from the canopy on her bed. He dropped to the floor. "Because you weren't here, they've posted no guards. You must come away with me now."

"But other arrangements have been made."

The boy narrowed his eyes. "By whom?"

"I cannot say, but they will take me to Chrisholm Island."

The thief shook his head. "No, no. Someone lies."

Tashama sat on the bed. "Why do you say such a thing?"

"A healer approached the leader of our guild—the one who was imprisoned with you at the compound. General Karam is paying us to steal you from here. We're to bring you to his forces nearby."

"When?"

"We were to move late tonight. But we've heard of the attempts on your life and…"

Footsteps approached her bedchambers, and the thief slipped out the window. The door was shoved open, and Daveal walked into the room, then pushed the door closed. She folded her arms and then tapped her foot on the floor as her cheeks darkened. "You've started rumors about me—ugly rumors. Not only are they not true, but you're stupid for having done such a thing."

"Oh?"

"Whosoever wishes you dead isn't being watched. So now everyone is keeping an eye on me, and when you're not expecting it, whoever plans to murder you will do so."

"Ah, so who do you think might be interested in such a thing?"

"Many do not like you, Karthlander."

"Do you mean the fourteen women on the prince's list?"

Daveal glared at Tashama. "If you think you're going to have your murder pinned on me…"

Tashama laughed. "Why, I have no intention of being murdered."

"I can arrange to have you sent away from here tonight."

"Didn't you say you were being watched?"

"No one realizes you are even back here. I was going to leave this message here for you."

Tashama stared at the strange symbols. "Sorry, I cannot read it."

"You cannot read?"

"I can read English, and some French, German, and Spanish. Maldovian is foreign to me."

Daveal stared at her for a moment. "The Karthlanders have the same language as we have."

"Yes, well, I haven't been around for the last ten years."

Daveal nodded, then read the note out loud, "At midnight, a caravan of merchants will leave the palace grounds, travel through the city of Banff, then leave you with the Elorian elves in Ramoria if you so choose, as the merchants continue on their way north."

"And if I choose otherwise?"

"Then you will die."

"But not by your hand?"

"I wouldn't wish to hurt my chances with King Aleron."

"I see. Very well. It's a deal."

Daveal took a deep breath, then nodded. "Be ready by midnight."

"And the guards?"

"Don't worry about the guards."

As the woman hurried out of the door, the thief popped his head in through the window. "You cannot trust her, miss."

"I don't. Can you come for me before then?"

"Of course." He waved his hand, then darted down the path. Before Tashama could sit, more footsteps hurried toward her room, and then the door burst open. "Tashama!" Aleron said.

"Your Highness." Tashama curtsied to him.

"You're not to be alone in here. What is Carissian thinking? Come with me at once."

"Can you not just have a guard posted, King Aleron?"

"Why?" He paused in the doorway. "Are you upset about Listra?"

"I'm certain Listra will be safe."

"Then what?"

Tashama looked down at the floor for a moment, then turned to the window. "It's just I wanted to look at the garden from my room for a while."

"I wish I could read your thoughts as Carissian can, as I can see you're troubled by something, yet will not reveal this to me." He waited for her to respond, but as Tashama continued to look out the window, he walked over to her. "Come, Tashama. It's not safe here for you without a guard." He took her arm and led her from her room. "I cannot understand what Carissian was thinking to let you back in your room without making sure you had some further protection. While you were with him, there was no threat, of course."

"You know he wanted to speak with me?" Tashama asked.

"Of course. He wanted to explain my thinking concerning Listra's attendance at our cousin's wedding. Since I must wed. Well, since I have other concerns, I'm unable to attend."

"Did she tell you Lord Coryn is dead?"

"Yes. I have not thought of who else might be a suitable groom for the princess, but it will be my next priority."

"Why did you not also send me with Listra?"

"You cannot be serious."

"If she were safer there, why would I not be also?"

"You will be safe here with me." Aleron motioned to his chambers.

"King Aleron." Tashama took no further step. "Why can't you release me? You need to marry, and so do I. We have our own king-doms to rule and..."

"I told you already, Tashama, I love you and will have no other."

"Then you will have to abdicate your throne."

"Carissian may believe this..."

"He is your advisor, sire."

"He is not all-knowing." He pulled Tashama into his pillow room, then motioned to her to have a seat.

"I cannot, sire. I must leave here soon."

Aleron grabbed Tashama's hand and pressed her fingers to his lips. "Even when your eyes were blackened like the raccoon, there was something about you I couldn't resist. Carissian feared you like no one else before this, and now I know why. You have captured my heart, and I believe he knew something like this would happen. I will not give you up, Tashama."

She sat on the pillows, and he snapped his fingers at a servant down the hall. "Bring us something to drink." He sat beside her.

She touched the satin pillows and leaned back to consider the mural. "If you were to help me to overthrow Loran..."

"And what if in so doing, your people would install you as ruler of the region, but insist you marry someone of their choice? What would become of us?"

"We will have a peace treaty, King Aleron, at least. The killing would stop."

"I wish more than that, Tashama."

"What do you want, sire?" She studied his dark eyes.

As the servant returned with a jug of wine and two goblets, Aleron waited for him to pour the wine into the cups, then said to the man, "You may leave us." Aleron handed one of the cups to Tashama, then clinked his with hers. "I wish for us to be one."

"And if I were to desire the same thing, only no one in either of our kingdoms would want such a notion?"

Aleron smiled. "I knew you wished the same as me." He drank his wine, then set his goblet down. "You can move men like no other, Tashama. You can do it. I know you can."

"I cannot deceive you because you know my secret."

"The water nymphs told me."

She frowned at him. "You do not know their language."

"No, but you managed to tell me anyway."

Tashama wriggled to get comfortable on the pillows. "Despite my loving you, I will be leaving soon. I don't know what will become of me, but I will not stay here."

"Then, my princess, I will go with you."

Her lower lip dropped slightly as she considered his sincerity.

She looked at her hands as they touched the pillows while a tear cascaded down her cheek. "You cannot be serious," she said under her breath.

He lifted her chin as her eyes glistened with tears. "I haven't wanted anything more than this ever. If you must leave, I will go with you."

"I wouldn't want anything ill to happen to you, sire."

"I insist."

Tashama nodded. "We will have to go early this evening."

"I must have another of my swimming lessons. I wish to swim underneath the water as you do."

"I'm not certain that one more practice..."

Aleron touched his finger to her lips to silence them. "One more lesson."

She nodded, then he pulled her close and held her head to his chest, and she listened to his heartbeat. He kissed her head. "We'll eat here this evening. No one will try to poison the food if they know I'll be sharing it with you. We'll swim, as several know, that is what I intended to do. I'll have provisions ready, and once we've changed into dry clothes, we'll leave."

"But how can we get beyond the gates without anyone suspecting?"

"We go with the caravan that takes Listra from here tonight. I've already spoken with the guard staff that a noble couple will be joining them. No one will suspect us."

Tashama smiled. "Then it is all falling into place."

"What?" Aleron kissed her forehead.

"I must remember to thank Bachava more often."

Aleron squeezed Tashama. "I will leave an offering for us both."

29

Carissian popped into Aleron's anteroom unexpectedly early that evening, then frowned as Aleron and Tashama napped together on the pillows as she snuggled against Aleron's chest while his arm was wrapped around her in a warm embrace.

"Sire," Carissian whispered.

Aleron opened his eyes as Carissian frowned at him. The golden-haired lady of his dreams still nestled against his chest, and he shrugged at his advisor. "Have our dinner served in here within the hour. If she eats with me, her food should be safe."

"If you wish, Your Highness." Carissian studied Tashama.

Aleron, fearing either might give their plans away to Carissian, said, "Make it lobster, her favorite dish, and quite frankly mine too."

"Certes, Your Highness." He vanished.

Aleron rubbed Tashama's arm lightly to wake her and leaned down to kiss her lips. She kissed him back, and he smiled, then kissed her further.

Carissian reappeared in the room. "Ahem."

Aleron raised his brows as Carissian wrinkled his forehead.

Aleron sat up. "She's awake." Tashama stretched her whole body, then yawned.

"Almost." She curled back up on the pillows.

"Time to eat." Aleron stood, then stretched. "I've got to take care of business. Keep the lady company, will you, Carissian?"

"Of course, Your Highness."

Aleron headed into his chambers while Carissian turned to Tashama. "Did you have pleasant dreams, my lady?"

Tashama smiled. "I will never know how it will feel to have him show me how much he loves me, but I can dream about it, cannot I? Besides, it serves you right to infiltrate my dreams while I'm sleeping."

"You knew then that I was there?"

"Of course, but you don't know how difficult it is to enjoy such a delightful fantasy and then a sightseer watches every move you make."

Carissian smiled. "I must admit, I hadn't expected to see such a thing, and it took quite a bit of strength for me to leave."

Laughing, Tashama shook her head. "Men are all alike."

"I'm a sorcerer." Carissian leaned against the desk.

"Yes, but you still have the desires of a man."

"And what makes you think thus?"

"We have one in the family tree. He became entangled with one of the royal family members. Family scandal and all that sort of thing."

"A sorcerer in the mix." Carissian's toothy grin indicated his amusement. "So that's how come you have so many sorcery skills."

"And my daughter, when she is born, will have them too."

"Not a son?"

"I suppose if it's to be a son, I would be just as content."

As the food was brought into the room, Tashama sat up. Carissian rubbed his brow. "About tonight..."

"King Aleron insists on my teaching him another lesson."

Carissian nodded. "Sometime after that then."

"Midnight?"

"It's up to Oshon." Carissian grew quiet as Aleron walked toward the anteroom.

"Well, while you're eating, Your Highness, I'll see to some other business." Carissian disappeared.

"Do." Aleron took his seat beside Tashama. "Lobster?"

"Yes." Tashama dug the meat out of the shell with relish.

Aleron laughed. "I do believe if you were a mermaid and I a merman, you would choose the lobster over me."

"Only if I were hungry for this kind of food, Your Highness." Tashama bit a piece of the succulent meat off with her teeth.

"I heard you speaking to Carissian about having a daughter." Aleron scooped up a spoonful of blueberry-covered rice. "We do have one prophecy here. My firstborn will be a son."

Tashama nodded.

"And you?"

"A daughter."

Aleron twisted his mouth. "I suppose your prophecy could be wrong."

Tashama smiled as she wiped her cheek. "Or yours."

"I heard Carissian mention Oshon's name."

"Ah, he is grateful I cleared his good name."

"Oh." Aleron finished his lobster and waved to the servant to bring another for the two of them. "It may be a while before we can have such a feast again."

After finishing the rest of their meal, Aleron nudged Tashama. "Let's take a walk in the gardens, then go for our swim."

"All right." Tashama stood and then straightened her skirts.

As the servants hurried to clean up the room, Aleron took Tashama's arm and walked her onto the garden path. "I fear we will have rain tonight as there are no stars in the night sky."

Tashama glanced up at the dark sky and nodded. "Is everything ready?" she whispered to Aleron.

"Yes, everything is prearranged. I worried Carissian was studying your dreams and would discover our plans. I've been careful not to think of them while he was about."

"I was sharing an intimate moment with my king." Tashama squeezed his hand.

"Oh? Do tell?"

"Someday, perhaps." She leaned her head against his shoulder.

"But Carissian was able to see them?"

"See us, you mean."

Aleron rubbed his chin. "He can be quite annoying at times."

"Well, it was good that this is all he saw."

After walking, then sitting in the gazebo for another half hour, Tashama reached for his hand. "Shouldn't we swim?"

"Of course." He helped her from the bench.

They arrived at the pool that meandered through the plants, and Tashama caught sight of the blue sleeve of the thief and another as they hurried into her chambers. She slipped into the water. Aleron soon followed.

She took his arms and had him hold his breath, then slip beneath the surface of the water. As he swam beside her, she smiled at him underwater. They came up for air, and she smiled at him. "You can do it!"

He kissed her deeply, then hugged her soundly, but as footsteps headed toward her room from the garden, they grew quiet. Daveal and two men hurried into Tashama's chambers. She waited for Daveal and her henchmen to discover the thieves, but no sound was heard. Then a cavalry officer rushed along the path and entered her room.

Aleron pulled Tashama from the water. "Come, we will have to get gowns for you, and you can change in my quarters. We leave now."

The two hurried to Aleron's apartments, and he gave her a towel. She wrapped the towel around her wet clothes, then used a fan to dry her hair as Aleron hurried into his bedchambers and changed into his dry clothes. As soon as he was finished, he returned to Tashama and dried her hair as she slipped out of her outer gown. Then he helped to pull off the gown under this. "I'll find some dry clothes for you and be right back."

He hurried out of his chambers while Tashama slipped out of her wet shift, then wrapped herself in the towel again. Then she shoved her wet gowns under his bed and returned to the bath to wait for his return.

Footsteps approached, and she stood next to the bath wall as she feared it would be someone other than Aleron. Listra hurried into the room, and Tashama cried, "Oh, Listra, whatever are you doing here?"

"Aleron had no one to ask but me for gowns. Hurry, put these on." She helped Tashama to apply a dry shift, then the outer gown with long sleeves, and last, the overdress with cuts down the side. "We must also apply veils. These are dark and should hide your blond hair."

After Tashama was well-disguised, Listra grabbed her hand and led her out through the window. "But Aleron?"

"He will join us, but he wishes for me to get you to the carriage. There are three. One for Fatima and her entourage, one for me and mine, and one for an anonymous well-paying noble couple...I believe this to be you and Aleron." Tashama smiled. "He loves you, you do realize?" Listra said. "For him to give up all for a woman..." She shook her head. "I only wish I could find a man to love me in that way. I'll sit with you and Aleron until you go your own way."

"His people will not abandon him."

After they loaded into the wagon, they began to head toward the gate. "I hope for his sake and all of our royal family connections that this will be the case."

"But Aleron has not joined us." She peered out through the leather flaps on the carriage.

"He said he'll come. But you know how he is. He insisted we get on our way at the top of the hour, and you were to go with us. He said there were several who were involved in some scheme concerning you, and he feared even further for your safety."

Tashama leaned against the leather seat back. She didn't want anyone to get into trouble for having offered to free her from her incarceration. On the other hand, the thieves were getting well paid, Carissian just wanted to be rid of her, and Daveal, who knew what she truly had in mind? Tashama took a deep breath.

Ten miles along their journey, the horse's hooves pounded behind them, and Tashama peeked out of the window. Aleron smiled at her as he rode his familiar stallion. She shook her head. "Not in the least bit obvious."

The entourage stopped. One of the servants tied the horse to the back of the carriage, then opened the door for Aleron. He bowed his head to Listra as she bowed hers in greeting. He took his seat next to Tashama, and she squeezed his hand. "I worried about you."

"I had to investigate what was going on in your quarters. As I peeked into the place, I saw one of Oshon's cavalry officers storm back out into the gardens, and when he departed, Daveal and two of her servants scrambled out from under the bed and hurried the same way. I was about to leave when I saw two bedraggled men, soaked to the skin, leaving your bath, then head out through the gardens too."

Tashama stifled the urge to laugh. "I guess they didn't find what they were looking for."

"Had I not been attempting to keep this rendezvous with you, I would have had them all arrested for questioning. But if I had any doubts about stealing you away from Banff, I know now it was the right thing to do."

Tashama nodded.

As they rode, two of the servants hurried back to the rear carriage, as the cavalcade was paused.

"Sire," the one said as he opened the door.

Aleron left the carriage so as not to alarm the women. "Yes, what's the difficulty?"

"Karthlander scouts were spotted beyond that bluff." The man waved his hand in the direction of the sighting.

Aleron studied the area. "We detour east then."

"But then we'll be in Alsation territory.

"Better than dealing with the Karthlanders."

"I heard that," Tashama said from inside the carriage.

"East." Aleron returned to the carriage. "Such as it is now, my lady." He kissed Tashama's cheek.

She smiled and snuggled her head against his shoulder.

"Will there be trouble with the Alsations, sire?" Listra asked.

"Not if we can help it." Aleron kissed the top of Tashama's veiled hair.

Not long after they entered Alsation territory, soldiers wearing green tunics and helmets halted the lead carriage.

Tashama peered out the window as Aleron walked out of the carriage. "They want us to turn over any Karthlander we have with us. They need one for a prisoner exchange."

"We have no Karthlanders with us."

"They say they have a mind reader who can tell where a person is from. If we've lied, it'll go bad for the rest of us."

"There are no Karthlanders amongst us," Aleron reiterated.

"They're checking out the first carriage's occupants, now, sire. Perhaps we ought to hide the lady..."

"We'll deal with this."

"Yes, sire."

As the man hurried back to the front of the train, Tashama leaned out of the coach. "I'm putting everyone at risk."

The mind reader was speaking with the princess in the lead coach.

"You can handle a mind reader with the powers you possess, Tashama." He returned to the carriage and sat beside her. They waited another twenty minutes, then, as the soldiers opened their carriage door, he motioned for the occupants to get out.

"We've had no difficulty with the Alsations." Aleron stretched his legs.

"You are King Aleron of the Maldovians, your people say."

"That is correct," Aleron replied as he stood straight and folded his arms across his chest.

"We want no trouble with the Maldovians. The Karthlanders have taken one of ours hostage, however."

"Why would they have taken one of your people?" Tashama asked.

The soldier glared at her, then walked around her in a slow circle as he studied Tashama's manner. "You are not a Maldovian."

"You are quite right about that."

He frowned as he considered her further while Aleron touched the hilt of his sword. "And yet you are not a Karthlander either."

Tashama smiled.

"But you're not an Alsation. What exactly are you?"

"A Texan, for all practical purposes. I'm sure you won't find any of those varmints around these parts."

The man turned to Aleron. "She speaks a foreign tongue."

"Often." Aleron relaxed his grip on his sword.

The soldier scratched his head. "Never heard of such a thing. What would you be doing with a caravan of Maldovians?"

"Aleron is marrying me. You see, I have special powers. I tell people's futures and see the past. I can even tell you what you're thinking."

The man smiled. "All right, tell me what I'm thinking."

"You are thinking I'm lying. Now you are wondering how I knew that."

"You could guess at such a thing."

"All right, then. Think of something else." Tashama smiled as she watched the man, whose forehead wrinkled in thought. "You bounced your baby on your knee this morning and watched him take his first step."

"Tell me what my future shows."

"Certainly." Tashama reached out for the man's wrist to his surprise, then studied him for a moment. "You will be reunited with your friend soon."

The man smiled. "We'll have a hostage exchange." He waved at his soldiers. "Allow the Maldovians and Texan to go through."

As they returned to the carriage, Aleron turned to Tashama. "About the kiss you said we were going to have..."

"We have had that kiss, Your Highness."

Listra's eyes widened.

"Perhaps we should have this discussion some other time."

"Oh, no, by all means discuss away," Listra said.

Aleron squeezed Tashama's hand. "You do know what we're thinking then."

Tashama's cheeks turned pinker. "Yes, sire."

"Then you know what I was thinking when I walked with you in the gardens the other day and..."

"Yes, sire."

Aleron pulled Tashama close as he wrapped his arm around her shoulder. She wriggled her cheek against his shoulder. "I cannot help that I have such visions of you."

"Most men have such thoughts when they look at a woman who piques their interest."

"Ahh," Aleron groaned. "I will have to have you wear the clothes of the Bachavin order to keep others from having such thoughts about you."

Tashama smiled as Listra sat on the edge of her seat, waiting to hear what thoughts these were. When Tashama said nothing further, Listra sat back against her seat. "So the Alsations will find a Karthlander to trade for the release of their comrade?"

"No."

"But you said..."

"I said the Alsations would be reunited with their compatriot."

Aleron tilted his head down. "The Karthlanders take them prisoner?"

She nodded.

"That's awful." Listra touched her cheek.

"They'll soon be free." Tashama took a deep breath.

"Even the man whom they hold now as a prisoner?"

"Yes."

"Why would he have been taken prisoner?"

"He was a spy for the Maldovians."

"Ahh." Listra looked back at Aleron who raised his eyebrows in acknowledgment.

Tashama turned her chin up to Aleron. "Teach me how to read."

His face brightened as he considered Tashama's small, upturned face, her eyes shimmering in the fading light of the carriage. "No."

Listra watched Aleron as if she were trying to determine why he said such a thing. Turning her attention to his belt, Tashama ran her fingers over the gold chain. "I taught you how to swim." As she looked up to consider his expression, she smiled as his mouth turned up at the corners.

He shook his head.

"Why not?"

"You know how to do many things I do not. This is something I will be able to do that you cannot."

"I will learn how to read your language, or I will change it to mine."

Aleron laughed. "That, you'll never be able to do. Why did it take so long just to consolidate the Karthlander and Maldovian languages into one?"

"We will see." Tashama tugged playfully at Aleron's belt.

DESPITE DETOURING THROUGH ALSATION TERRITORY, the caravan soon ran into Karthlander cavalry. As the foot soldiers searched the first of the carriages, Tashama said to Aleron as he reached for her arm, "Let me speak with them."

"What if they are Loran's men?"

"They won't let us go, no matter what, but if these are some who are loyal to General Karam, then I'll ask him to allow the rest of the party to continue on their way."

"All right, but I'm coming with you."

"What about me?" Listra asked.

"Stay put," Tashama said to Aleron's surprise.

"You stay here for now, Listra," Aleron said.

Aleron walked out of the carriage first, then offered his hand to Tashama as guards ran toward them. "Who leads you?" Tashama asked as the soldiers encircled them with spears outstretched.

"A Maldovian woman speaks for the men here?" one of the Karthlander soldiers replied.

Tashama pulled off her veils, and several of the men gasped at the sight of the Karthlander woman. "Who are you?" another of the men asked.

"I asked you first. Does General Karam lead you?" Tashama placed her hands on her hips.

The soldier grabbed her arm and twisted it back as she cried out. "Women don't speak to us like that, Woman."

Aleron was quickly disarmed as he unsheathed his sword.

"Release me at once you, you, foot soldier," Tashama growled as she attempted to twist loose from his grip. "Is General Karam here?" A mumble of voices ensued, then Tashama jerked her arm free. "I have business with General Karam!" Her voice grew with her agitation.

Horses' hooves clomped in the dark as a cavalry officer approached on horseback. "Where is General Karam?" Tashama called out to him.

The man jumped down from his horse, then walked close to her. He ran his hand through her hair. She glowered at him while Aleron's face darkened.

"You appear to be a Karthlander, and yet you ride with these Maldovians."

"They are not soldiers but a wedding party. Let them pass."

Narrowing his eyes, the officer said, "You speak with an untamed tongue that has a strange quality. Yet, you appear to be one of our women." He studied the sheath dangling at Aleron's waist. "And this one who rides with you is most assuredly a soldier."

"Do you serve General Karam?" Tashama asked in more of an appeasing tone of voice this time, then her eyes caught sight of the red sash he wore. She knew then he wore the same-colored sash of Karam's cavalry.

The officer grabbed her chin and twisted her head from side to side while she gripped his wrist as she attempted to remove his hand from her face. "Why would a Karthlander woman be interested in General Karam?"

Horses clip-clopping on the meadow floor filled the area. One of the mounted cavalry officers shouted, "What is it?"

"A Karthlander woman who presumes to speak for a caravan of Maldovians."

"Bring her here."

The officer yanked Tashama toward one of the horses.

She glared up at the rider. "I want to see..."

"Silence, Woman!"

Tashama fumed. She could see ruling Karthland would not be an easy task after all, even if she could oust Loran from his throne.

He studied her for some time as she remained silent. "What is she doing with the Maldovians?"

"They are a wedding...," Tashama said.

The cavalry officer interrupted, "If she speaks again, have her gagged."

"They appear to be a wedding party, Colonel Sorel," one of the officers said.

The colonel's eyes never left Tashama's. "But not this one."

"And the man she shared the carriage with carried a jewel-encrusted sword." The foot soldier held up the sword for the cavalry officer to see.

"He's a cavalry officer of some importance," the officer said.

"The sword was a gift for...," Tashama said, but the colonel waved his hand at a junior officer, who pulled a cloth from his belt and quickly tied it to Tashama's mouth.

As she tried to free the cloth from her mouth, two of the soldiers grabbed her arms to keep her still. The colonel said, "Release the carriages. Wait. What else is in the third?"

One of the soldiers grabbed the carriage door and jerked it open, causing Listra to scream out. "She appears to be just another female Maldovian with the wedding party, Colonel."

Listra was pulled out of the carriage to join Aleron, and the colonel considered the three of them, then shook his head. "We'll take them all with us. Release the others. Return these to their carriage and hold them."

As the soldiers hustled Aleron and Listra back to the carriage, the colonel turned to Tashama. "Is she linked?"

The junior officer grabbed her hand and examined her fingers. "No, my lord."

"With a tongue like hers, I can certainly see why not. Return her to the carriage with the others."

After Tashama was pushed into the carriage, she tried to remove the gag. Aleron reached over and untied the cloth for her. "I'm sorry, Your Highness." She threw the cloth out the window. Some of the men who rode near the carriage chuckled.

"She'll be giving the Maldovians grief now!" one of the officers shouted for all to hear.

"What were you thinking back there, Tashama?" Aleron's mouth twisted in annoyance.

"I've seen this come to pass. We could do nothing further. No matter what I said or could have done, we would have all three been taken. The red sash around the officers' waist is the same as the one General Karam wears. These are some of his officers. I wasn't sure when I first saw the foot soldiers."

Listra's eyes shimmered with tears. Tashama moved over to sit beside her and wrapped her arm around her shoulder. "Dear Listra, do not fret. No one will harm you."

"But King Aleron..."

Tashama smiled. "They will not harm him either."

"You must mind your tongue, Tashama, around these men." Aleron locked his arms together. "Soldiers, most of all, cannot abide a woman's unheedful tongue."

"They will have to get used to it." Tashama squeezed Listra with a gentle embrace. "Women can do so much for your people if you would only give them half a chance. When half of your society is kept down..."

"A third of our society is female."

"Well, there's no wonder. Being female isn't worth..."

"We treat our women with great respect."

Tashama frowned. "You would think with so few females, you would share equal status with them."

Aleron shook his head. "You have more latitude as you are a princess who's entitled to rule a country, but our women are satisfied to have us take care of them."

"And they take care of you too."

Listra considered her words, but was not sure how to take them.

"Well, I may need to go more slowly about the task, but there will be great changes I do foresee."

Tashama leaned over to the window and pulled the flap aside. Several of the officers looked in her direction, and she said, "Tell General Karam, Princess Tashama wishes to speak with him at his earliest convenience." She sat back in her seat as Aleron considered her.

He shook his head again. "You are a gem in our country, Tashama. No doubt about it."

The party rode for another twenty minutes, then the carriage was halted. Boots clomped on the ground as they approached the coach while the occupants all watched the door. Then, as it was thrown aside, the soldier said to Tashama, "Come with me."

She stood partway in the cramped conditions, and Aleron said, "I must go with her."

"You, stay. The Karthlander woman is the only one the colonel has asked for."

"Not General Karam?" Tashama hesitated to leave the carriage.

The soldier grabbed her arm and pulled her out of the carriage. As Aleron tried to follow, a man poked a spear at his chest. "Return to the carriage and remain there." Another shoved the door closed while Tashama was led away in the dark.

She was soon brought to a campfire where cavalry officers gathered as they drank their evening mugs of ale. Her eyes searched for signs of the colonel, then, seeing him watching her from across the campfire as the flames cast twisting fingers of light across his stern face, she crossed her arms.

Handing his pewter mug to a junior officer, the colonel stood taller. "Her Royal Highness vanished without a trace."

"With Balthazar." Tashama nodded. The men grew quiet, and she could hear their doubts scattered in their thoughts.

"She would be twenty-three now."

"Yes," Tashama said.

"And eligible to marry and rule her people."

Tashama took a deep breath, then nodded.

He shook his head. "She is lost to us. Loran rules in her place and Valmor beside him."

"I am she and vow to eradicate this plague on our people, whom we know as Loran. There has been too much killing. The war will end."

Stifled laughs followed, but Tashama's eyes kept unbroken contact with the colonel's. "The general is not here," he said in response to her unspoken query.

Again, without speaking a word, Tashama asked the colonel, *"Where is he?"*

"He is leading our men in a charge against Oshon's cavalry as we speak on the Plain of Doredon."

One of the senior officers broke in, "Sir, should we let this woman know our plans?"

Tashama concentrated on the colonel further. *"Send word to him at once that I want to speak with him,"* her mind relayed to his.

The colonel turned to a lieutenant. "Send our swiftest messenger to General Karam. Give him word that Princess Tashama wishes an audience with him."

"But, sir," the senior officer said, "do we know this woman is truly Princess Tashama? There is no proof, and she's been found with Maldovians. Could she be a spy?"

The colonel looked back at Tashama when she commanded him to do so, and he said, "Release the Maldovians."

The senior officer grabbed the colonel's arm to everyone's surprise and led him from the campfire. He spoke to the senior officer in muffled tones, then the colonel looked back at Tashama and stared at her. She smiled, then turned to consider the other men who waited to see who would speak next.

Her focus shifted to a lieutenant, and he nodded to her. However, as he started to walk away from the fire, the colonel motioned for another officer to detain him. "Who are you?" the colonel asked Tashama as the wrinkle in his blond brow deepened.

"I will speak to General Karam. I have returned to this place to lead my people to victory. Only victory will be achieved by removing Loran from the throne and bringing peace to the region, not by destroying the Maldovians. Certainly, as you are from the 4th royal house, you should know this to be true."

"Tashama is no longer with us," the colonel said. "Return this woman to her carriage."

"And if I am Tashama and you have failed to notify the general of my presence here as you hold me hostage, do you not think he will have you demoted on the spot? The general and I were at the Maldovian compound as prisoners together even."

"Preposterous!" the colonel blurted out. "A Karthlander woman wouldn't have been taken there. He made no mention of you to me."

Sighing deeply, Tashama said, "So many say how things are a certain way here, and yet they know little of what they speak of." She turned to the lieutenant. "Tell the colonel you will lead the men as your father has done, but sooner than later, if I do not see the general."

The colonel glowered at Tashama. "You presume to..."

His speech was interrupted as a soldier ran into the camp. "My lord, one of our lieutenants rode out of here as if he were being chased by the dragon of Ramoria itself!"

"In which direction?"

"Toward the plain where General Karam clashes with Oshon's forces."

"Have him stopped at all costs!" the colonel said, then turned to face Tashama.

The flames' gentle light flickered off his green eyes like the emeralds that sparkled in the caverns of the mountains of Maldovia as she studied him. "They'll never catch the young man," she said softly.

"She's a sorceress, I tell you," the senior officer said to the colonel.

"There is only one per royal house," the colonel responded. "None of them have a female sorcerer."

"By morning's light," Tashama said, "General Karam will see me." Then she turned to return to the carriage, but one of the officers stopped her.

"The colonel hasn't released you," the major said.

"I am Tashama," she said, and the way in which she said it showed she delighted in saying so, "and the colonel has no say over me."

As the officers' voices stirred, Tashama turned her head away from the crackling fire.

"Return her to the carriage," the colonel said with a wave of his hand.

The lieutenant led Tashama away, and she studied him while his eyes avoided hers. "You need not be afraid of me, young man. I only want what's best for our people."

Two captains followed close behind, and she turned her head to observe them. She smiled. "None of you are from the 4th royal house. The colonel, though he doesn't believe in me, uses caution anyway just in case."

The captains exchanged glances. Tashama laughed. "You are from the 6th house." She pointed to the one. "And you, the 5th. The young lieutenant, here, is from the 7th house." She patted the lieutenant's firm grip on her arm. "This young man will be marrying Deloria, of the 2nd house, niece of Loran himself, soon, but I will not hold that against you. Do not tell her I told you this, or she will think the idea mine, instead of yours." At this comment, the lieutenant looked at Tashama, and she smiled back at him. "I have the gift."

Tashama and the lieutenant looked back at the two captains. One motioned for him to continue on his way, while the other hurried back to the campfire.

As Tashama entered the carriage, Aleron reached for her arm and pulled her close. "We must join General Karam and Oshon on the battlefield on the plain," she said.

He glanced over at Listra, and Tashama shook her head. "Listra must stay here and act as a diversionary force."

"Oh, Princess Tashama, I could do no such thing."

"You've aided me before."

"But with my own people. I could not face these Karthlander soldiers on my own."

"They will not harm you, Listra. I promise. You must slip away through the camp and run to the colonel's tent. He is of the 4th house and will have a blue flag waving in front of it. You must make a scene, then faint. Soldiers cannot stand to see a woman faint."

Aleron frowned at her.

"No, I have never done such a thing," she said, smiling, "but just the same, I've read how effective the maneuver can be." She turned to Listra. "You must do this, as Aleron and I must stop the warring of our people. I need all the soldiers I can get to help me rid Karthland of Loran's influence."

"All right," Listra said, but her tone of voice indicated her heart wasn't in the task she was given.

Tashama hugged her. "Go now, and quietly as you must make it to the colonel's tent."

Aleron shook his head. "I'm not certain."

"I've seen this is what must be done, Your Highness. Please help me in this, as I cannot do it without both your help."

Aleron opened a flap to the window and saw several officers conversing nearby. Tashama peeked out the other side of the carriage and found the soldiers so far away from the vehicle that she motioned in that direction. Listra walked out first, then, as she moved behind the horses that pulled the carriage, one of them whinnied, and Tashama motioned her to continue.

When Listra was out of sight, Tashama grabbed Aleron's hand and dashed toward a stand of horses as they were tethered in a long line nearby. He reached to untie a horse, and she pulled at the reins of a painted pony.

He helped her onto her horse, then mounted his own and walked into the dark, aware that the soldiers were bedding down for the night in their tents scattered all over the meadow, their conversation still cluttering the air.

Barely breathing, Tashama worried her heartbeat could be heard over the muttered conversations. She followed Aleron's lead because she hadn't a clue where the battle might be taking place, and they stopped their horses when a man said, "Who goes there?" He only spoke to a fellow soldier, and the other laughed.

"Drank a little too much ale tonight."

Their conversation drifted off as Tashama and Aleron continued on their way.

By the time the sky lightened slightly, Aleron motioned to the plain. Tashama nodded, then rode to where Oshon's men prepared for the day's battle while General Karam's men did the same.

The order was given to release a hail of arrows. Tashama perceived Carissian was nearby. Fearing he would see what she had planned and would have Aleron stop her, she dashed into the center of the meadow. Her hair and the horse's blond mane and tail flailed in the breeze, kicked up with his gallop.

She turned at the end of the battle line and rode like the zephyr back across the plain between the two forces. Stunned, several of the men lowered their bows, though their respective generals stormed through the ranks, urging them on without regard to the woman in their midst.

Tashama neared the halfway point across the battlefield. An enthusiastic Maldovian archer struck her in the shoulder with a well-placed arrow aimed at a Karthlander, and the Karthlander, in response, aimed for the Maldovian. But Tashama, determined to stop the war at all costs, kneed her horse forward to stop the arrow meant for the Maldovian.

The arrow hit her thigh, and she lurched forward, then pulled her horse to a stop in the middle of the field. She sat with her head held high as the blood trickled from her wounds while Maldovians and Karthlanders waited in silence. Then Aleron jerked his horse's reins from the officer who tried to keep him from aiding the lady. As he rode through his own ranks, Oshon hurried to speak with him.

Tashama watched them, then turned as General Karam was unmoved. As word was passed to the Karthlander's healer, he hurried to reach her with his bag of medicines in hand, while Aleron's healer did the same.

Both pleaded with her to dismount, but she declined. As one of General Karam's officers rode forth, then dismounted by Tashama's side, she shook her head.

"I won't leave this place until General Karam comes forth and agrees to end hostilities." Oshon and Aleron advanced toward them. "The Maldovians have already agreed to such a thing."

Aleron pulled in beside her and touched her wounded arm. "Tashama, let my healer see to your wounds."

"Not until General Karam agrees to cease this conflict."

Voices rose in discussion on both sides as the air heated with men's anger, and Tashama gripped onto her reins tightly as she felt her mind drifting. Carissian appeared beside Aleron. "Our healer must see to her wounds at once. The pain she's feeling..."

Tashama shook her head. "General Karam must come forward. We must be patient. He's just very stubborn."

"And you are not?" Aleron said. "You've lost a lot of blood, Tashama. Your cheeks have lost their color."

"We must wait."

The Karthlander healer reached up to break off the arrow in Tashama's leg as he feared waiting any further. As the arrow snapped off in his hands, the pain shot up through her leg. Tashama saw the sky grow white, then turn black.

THE NEXT MORNING, Tashama opened her eyes to find the Maldovian and Karthlander healers checking on other wounded soldiers. She rubbed her forehead for a moment, then sat up on the cot. As the bed creaked, Throckmorton, the Karthlander healer, looked her over. "My lady, you must lie down and rest." He hurried to attend to her as a Maldovian page ran from the tent hospital.

"What has happened?" She lay down.

He smiled. "Well, none of us would ever have thought it possible, but General Karam vowed for peace as soon as you fainted."

"Took him long enough." Tashama considered the bandages on her arm.

Aleron hurried into the tent with Carissian following two steps behind. "Well, it seems your plan worked after all."

"Can we work together to remove Loran from the throne?"

"Most assuredly. We've had discussions all morning, and we're all in agreement. In the meantime, we've also concurred that you will return to Banff, where you'll be safe during the duration of the conflict."

Tashama shook her head. "I will not be safe there as someone is still trying to murder me."

Aleron rubbed his chin as he'd failed to consider this. "Your proposal?"

"If our combined forces attack Loran's, we have a good chance of succeeding, but I must get into the palace. Valmor is the real threat to me, and I must exile him from here for good. If Valmor is gone, Loran will certainly fail."

"But Valmor is a powerful sorcerer. You've said so yourself, and you still don't even know what he's capable of."

"I know. I wish more than anything in the world that Balthazar was here with me now. He would know what to do."

"Oshon will lead my forces then. I will go with you."

"Sire," Carissian said, "do you not think..."

"I go where the lady goes, Carissian."

Carissian scratched his head. "She's confused and still suffers from her wounds."

"When can I ride, healer?" Tashama asked.

Both healers answered, "By tomorrow."

"Good, before sunset then, we will enter the palace grounds."

Shaking his head, Carissian said, "But, sire, as your advisor, I have to say the risk to both yourself and the princess is too great."

Aleron touched Tashama's cheek with his fingers. "You should never have darted in front of the troops as you did, Tashama."

"I hadn't intended to be shot, but I knew Carissian would soon realize what I had intended to do and would have had me confined. I had to take the chance."

"Had I been able to have stopped you," Carissian said, "I would have done so, but certainly by the time I could see your thoughts, it was too late."

"Had I been able to, I would have rushed after you to stop this foolish notion, but Carissian stopped me with one of his mind-control techniques." Aleron squeezed Tashama's good hand.

"I'm glad he did. No sense in both of us getting stuck with arrows after all, when one could do the trick."

"You, young lady," Aleron said, "will have to settle down as I cannot have a queen of mine doing such a foolhardy thing in the future."

Tashama smiled as Carissian's eyes widened. "Surely, Carissian, you had some inkling such a thing would occur."

"I thought you had some ability to project thoughts that were nothing more than a ruse."

"Not I, or at least I don't think I can," Tashama said. "Of course, only yesterday, I realized I had some mind-control ability over the members of the 4th royal house. It must be in the genes. And certainly, I didn't realize that I could understand the sprites as there was no such thing in Texas. But still, I thought everyone could understand their words. So maybe I have further powers that I haven't even discovered."

"But she cannot read our written word," Aleron said.

Tashama smiled. "Yet." She sat up in bed suddenly. "Listra!"

"She's here. The colonel and his forces brought her here an hour ago. Of course, the word has spread how you faced down the archers of both regiments to stop the war. For being only a woman, you have earned much respect."

"But Listra..."

"I was going to return her to Banff with you, but since she was also at risk..."

"No, she must come with us."

"To Karthland? But..."

"I have seen this, sire."

He nodded. "So far, your plans have worked."

Carissian frowned. "She has no plan I can see."

"You're right, Carissian." Tashama ran her hands over the folds of her blankets. "I have no plan, but when I arrive at Napolia, it'll come to me."

The Maldovian page waiting to be heard coughed, and Aleron motioned to him to speak.

"Sire," the boy said, "Princess Listra is waiting to see Princess Tashama, if you so desire."

"She may," Aleron said. He turned to Tashama. "I have other arrangements to make to get us to Karthland." He leaned over and kissed her lips. His mouth rested against hers for longer than he intended as she kissed him back.

Several of his wounded soldiers said, "Whoa," in response.

Aleron ignored the men and kissed Tashama's forehead. "Rest so we may ride tomorrow. I'll be back to see you in a little bit."

Aleron retreated from the tent. Carissian shook his head at Tashama.

"What?"

"What will you do?"

"You know already, I don't have a clue. But just as I freed my fellow prisoners at your compound and just as I freed the thieves in your tower, the situation will present itself, and then I'll know what must be done."

"If I could, I would join you, but I would put all of you at risk."

"Yes, I know. Even I might trigger the alarms that Valmor has in place in the event a sorcerer should infiltrate the castle. He fears Balthazar's return, of course. He knows nothing of my powers, as my mother and grandmother hid these from our people." She furrowed her brow. "Well, except he realizes I had something to do with the river that carried his men away."

"What about your hiding these powers from your people yourself?"

"Balthazar had often said I would have to use them to keep myself alive and well upon my return here. I don't have the luxury of just stepping into my role as ruler of Karthland as my ancestors had done."

"For being only part sorcerer..."

"Ah, but the part of me that is..."

"Who was the sorcerer in your family line?"

"Morkenza."

Carissian's eyes widened.

Tashama smiled. "Yes, he was one of the most powerful sorcerers of his time. Only he had a weakness––my grandmother."

Carissian said to Tashama, "But Valmor must know about your sorcery powers."

"No, Morkenza married my grandmother in secret on her twentieth birthday. She married her advisor as was necessary for her to rule. She had a mock wedding with a nobleman of the highest rank. But he was no more than a figurehead. Her duty was to Morkenza, her true love, and through their union, they had my mother." Tashama waved at Listra when she finally noticed her standing in the entrance of the tent.

Carissian bowed. "I must speak with you further, my lady, later."

"Certainly." Tashama grabbed Listra's hand as the princess hurried to greet her.

They exchanged light hugs so as not to cause Tashama further pain, then Listra frowned at her. "I have heard of the rash thing you did."

Tashama touched her bandaged shoulder and grimaced. "Well, had I known how much this would have hurt, I might have had second thoughts."

Listra sat in the chair the Karthlander healer offered her, then she leaned over close to Tashama so that no one could hear her words. "Why did you wish for me to go to the colonel's tent, Tashama?"

Tashama smiled.

"You knew, didn't you?"

"Yes. But we have more trials before anything can come of it."

"I thought we were returning to Banff."

"It's not safe for us there, yet."

"Then where?"

"Karthland."

"Ohh," Listra groaned. "Will I truly be more powerful than Daveal if I go with you after all of this is over?"

"Truly." Tashama reached over and squeezed Listra's hand. She would be her advisor, but she would wait to tell her once things were settled. If they were settled.

A figure loomed in the entrance of the tent. General Karam stood there. She nodded. "General Karam."

He bowed slightly but said nothing in greeting.

"Is everything all right?" she asked.

The healer watched him in anticipation. Turning back to Tashama, he nodded.

"Good, then if you have nothing further to say to me, I will speak to you later."

He bowed again with the greatest of effort, then hurried out of the tent.

Listra shook her head. "Seems he is not happy with the turn of events."

"He is sulking because he didn't think of the plan, but he will get over it."

~

With the aid of the colonel and some of his men, Aleron and Tashama made their way to Napolia. While the others waited in the colonel's home, Lieutenant Sanger led Aleron and Tashama into the palace.

"I'm not certain Princess Deloria will go along with us on this." Lt. Sanger shook his head. "If her uncle finds out she has aided us..."

"She truly loves you and will do anything you ask of her, if she's able," Tashama said.

Once they arrived at Deloria's quarters, she gave a start.

"Dismiss your maids," the lieutenant said to her. She stared at Aleron, wearing monk robes, and Tashama dressed in the Bachava order.

"What is wrong?" She gripped Sangar's hand firmly.

"Release your maids, and I will speak with you."

Deloria motioned for her maids to leave. "What's happening? Why are you here and not on the battlefield? Have you been relieved?"

"In Princess Tashama's bedchambers there's a sapphire necklace..."

Deloria clasped her hand to her mouth, and her eyes watered.

"Precious is our time, Deloria. We must retrieve the necklace at once."

Deloria studied Aleron and Tashama, then said to the lieutenant, "What have you done?"

Tashama spoke up. "Quickly, Deloria, I must have my necklace."

The young girl's eyes widened, then she quickly curtsied. "My lady..."

"We will wait for you, but you must hurry."

"Deloria." The lieutenant patted her hand while her green eyes reflected the terror she must have felt.

"He will kill us all," Deloria whispered. "It will matter not that I am Loran's niece."

Tashama shook her head. "It's too late. They come for me now." She said to the lieutenant, "You must find a way to bring the necklace to me, wherever I may end up." She grabbed Aleron's arm and hurried him down the hall.

"Where do we go now?" Aleron whispered to Tashama

When she saw the guards headed in their direction, she shook her head. "To prison, I fear."

EARLY THE NEXT MORNING, Tashama woke to find herself manacled to the wall of a small cell where two other men sat chained on an opposite wall. As she studied them, one of the men said, "What would a woman of the Bachava order be doing in here?"

"What are you in here for?" Tashama sat up straighter on the rock-hard floor.

Neither answered her, so Tashama reached up and pulled a pin from her veil. For several minutes, she worked on her chains while the men watched, then one finally said, "Murder."

Tashama looked up at them. "Both of you?"

The other nodded.

"You didn't answer my question," the man said.

"I'm overthrowing Loran."

The men sat in silence for a moment, then both laughed out loud. "You're doing a mighty good job of it."

"Thank you." Tashama undid her manacles. Tashama hastened to the locked door.

The two men stood up. "Free us too," the men pleaded in unison.

Tashama studied them, then shook her head. "Had you killed for a noble cause, I would have freed you, but you murdered for profit."

"We will call the guard."

Tashama poked her face through the bars of her cell and called out, "Sire?"

"Over here, Tashama," Aleron said from an adjoining cell.

She reached her hand out to his bars, but she could not reach his manacled hands. Tashama rubbed her forehead, then sat on the floor as she grew dizzy. She envisioned Balthazar's beard curling down to the tip of his sequined-toed shoes. Frowning, she whispered, "Balthazar." His image wavered before her as she reached out to him, but when she touched the figure, it vanished. "Balthazar!" she screamed.

"She's crazy," one of the men said.

"Tashama," Aleron called out to her. His voice deepened with concern.

Tashama rubbed her forehead when Balthazar appeared before her again. He drew symbols in the air, then spoke without a sound.

"Cannot you see I am imprisoned, Balthazar?" Tashama responded.

The figure spoke further, but the boots clanking in the hallway made her hook the manacles over her wrists. The young Maldovian thief in his blue shirt grinned at her when the guards brought him to her cell.

After shoving him into the room, one of the guards manacled him to the wall near Tashama. The guard turned to her. "I hope your being here doesn't upset the gods. I cannot imagine why Prince Loran would have locked up a woman of the order."

"Free me and save yourself," Tashama said.

The man shook his head and pulled the door shut, then locked it. "Better to be damned than lose my head."

Tashama turned to the thief and smiled. "How did you ever manage to get here?"

"We were promised a bounty to turn you over to General Karam for safekeeping. The bounty still stands."

Tashama shook her head.

The young thief pulled his tools out of his boot, then hurried to remove his manacles. When he walked over to Tashama, she set hers aside to his astonishment. "Hairpins. How did you manage to sneak those in?"

"I spent hours pick-pocketing the good citizens of Karthland as I was trying to get caught. They don't figure a member of the thieves' guild will pick pockets, so they never checked to see if I had any tools of the trade on me."

"Release us and we'll aid you," one of the murderers said.

Tashama considered the two men. "All right, if you go the opposite way that we do, it's a deal."

She picked the lock of one of the men's chains as the thief worked on the other. After they were done, he hurried to unlock the door. Jaran pulled the door open, and the four ran out of the cell. Tashama shoved her hands through the grate to Aleron, while the thief hurried to unlock the door.

She stared at the wizened old lady who lay quietly in the corner, then, as Aleron was released, Tashama said, "We must take the lady to see the healer."

"Can we not come back later, my lady?" the thief said, but Aleron had already lifted the woman in his arms.

The two murderers watched them. "You were to go…"

"We wish to see you overthrow Loran."

Tashama motioned to Jaran. "Unlock the other cells."

While the thief unlocked another door, Aleron chuckled. "Seems you have a propensity to free prisoners."

As Tashama handed out pins to several of the freed prisoners, she said, "Help the others now."

One of them took the old woman from Aleron's arms.

"What about the necklace?" Aleron asked.

"Safe and sound." Tashama pulled the necklace from the black bodice. "Deloria sneaked it out of my room and sometime in the night, slid it through the grate."

"Its purpose?"

"Why, sire, I've missed it ever since I left here ten years ago."

Aleron shook his head. "I thought it had some magical powers that would aid us."

Tashama smiled.

As the last of the prisoners were freed, the old lady pointed a crooked finger at Tashama. "You have returned, dear child. All will not be well."

"She is a soothsayer. She predicted the return of the rule of the first house. All of us thought she was crazy, except Loran and Valmor. They locked her away so she couldn't spread her tales," the man who carried the woman said.

"Take her where she'll be safe," Tashama said, then with the thief and Aleron, she headed for Balthazar's chambers.

"I thought you might set off the alarms," Aleron said.

"Not now." Tashama patted the necklace. "Elven magic."

Aleron chuckled. "It was magical. I don't understand why we weren't questioned while we were imprisoned."

"Valmor and Loran are on the battlefield fighting the combined forces of General Karam and Oshon. I'm sure Loran is trying to figure out how that ever happened. He's probably not even been told about the intruders in the palace. Those who captured us probably haven't a clue as to who we are."

"What do you intend to do now, Tashama?"

"I'm not certain. Something in Balthazar's chambers is drawing me. I've given the matter of Valmor much thought also. He has no power over water. Water must be used to defeat him."

As they arrived at Balthazar's chambers, Tashama recognized the familiar royal blue curtained bed trimmed in gold braid, while drapes hung from the windows in the same color scheme. A crystal ball rested on a gold stand next to one of the windows, and dusty books on potions and spells filled numerous shelves on one of the walls.

Two gold dragons held a bench in another corner of the room while a carpet of blue embroidered with the figure of Balthazar as he mixed a potion, lay across the gold-tiled floor.

Tashama studied the rug while Aleron ran his fingers over the spines of the sorcerer's books, and the thief stood guard. As Balthazar's figure changed, Tashama knelt at the foot of the rug. "What are you trying to tell me, Balthazar?"

Aleron walked over to the rug. "What is it?"

"Balthazar is trying to show me how to mix some kind of potion."

Aleron studied the rug, then hastened back to the bookshelf. He searched for a book on potions, then found one bound in purple and orange with gold lettering. He returned to Tashama. "It's the only one there with this coloration."

"The lieutenant is coming!" Jaran said from the doorway.

"Yes?" Tashama said to the lieutenant as he hurried into the room. He stared at Balthazar's figure, pouring liquid into a cauldron, then shook his head.

"Lieutenant?" Tashama said. "What word have you for us?"

"Oh, my lady, the guards have discovered the missing prisoners and are searching the palace room by room."

"Can you see that two of the 4th royal house come here at once?"

"My lady, you and King Aleron must leave here..."

"Two from the 4th royal house. No other will do," Tashama said, then turned her attention to watch Balthazar again.

"Yes, my lady," the lieutenant said and hurried out of the room.

Within minutes, the thief ducked back into the room. "The lieutenant is coming with two men."

"From the 4th royal house, I would hope," Tashama said. "You and King Aleron must hide momentarily."

"I will not leave you," Aleron said.

"Nor I," the thief added.

When the three men walked into the room, the two guards unsheathed their swords.

Tashama studied the older of the two, and he nodded, then sheathed his sword.

"What are you doing?" the other asked his companion.

"The princess has work to do. We will leave her in peace."

Tashama concentrated on the younger man, and he nodded. "We must guard Balthazar's chambers.

"Yes, they've already been searched, and we're not to let anyone in."

The two men hurried back out into the hallway and shut the door behind them as Aleron and the thief stared at Tashama. "Only with members of the 4th royal house." She turned to study Balthazar.

"That's good to hear," Aleron said.

Tashama smiled. "Had I been able to use such powers on you, Your Highness, there's no telling what I might have had you do."

Turning back to Balthazar's learning rug, she said, "All right, he's mixing the fine green powder of emerald crystals and ground tooth of dragon. I believe it's some sleep potion, or, hmm, a transformation potion. I never could keep the two straight."

Aleron turned to the section on transformation potions and showed them to Tashama. "Here's the transformation potions. It's number three." Balthazar waved his fingers in the air. Aleron turned to the correct page. "What are the ingredients?"

"The first two you already named, then there is the speckled mushroom of the fairy glade, a cup of the lake water of Curacao, a cup of Elorian elven ale, a dash of the poison of the prickling burs of the forest, a teaspoon of Mordavian tea, and a drop of sweat from the reigning sovereign of Karthland."

"Loran." She shoved her hair behind her ears. "Balthazar knows I'm not much good with spells." She took a deep breath. "We'll need to get the ingredients, then return here."

"And then?"

"Hopefully, Balthazar will guide us further." She turned to Jaran. "Can you lead us out of here? We need to return to the caves near where the Elorians live."

"Certes, my lady." Jaran bowed low. The thief soon led them to the nearest sewer system as Tashama wrinkled her nose. "The same man as ours designed your sewers. This is how I got into the city."

"We weren't always at war." Tashama squeezed Aleron's hand.

"About the ingredients, Tashama..."

"Yes, we must hurry to get them..."

"But the dragon's tooth..."

"They shed teeth all the time. I'm sure if the dragon is still courting his lady love..."

"Is it not necessary that the tooth comes from the dragon's mouth?"

"Heavens no." Tashama smiled at Aleron, then kissed his hand. "I wouldn't want such a task as that."

For a day, the three traveled to Ramoria and were warmly greeted by the Elorians.

"You came for Elorian ale," one of the leaders of the elves said to Tashama.

"He speaks." Aleron's raised brows indicated his surprise.

"They're pleased we are working together in an attempt to end the conflict. They have sent some of their bowmen to help our forces."

The king of the elves nodded. "We will feast and escort you to the emerald mines."

"Thank you, my lord." Tashama followed the men to a large area set under trees and stars, while Aleron and Jaran stayed close to her.

As they took their places at the honored head table, the queen leaned over to Tashama. "He has met all of the tests?"

"Nearly." Tashama smiled at the queen.

THE NEXT DAY, the Elorians escorted them to the emerald mines. The dwarves met them and offered the fine powder of emeralds... for a price. Then Tashama, Aleron, and Jaran continued with their escort to the dragon's lair.

"He has returned," Tashama whispered when his heavy breathing roared in a hush. "How can we safely find a tooth scattered about his lair when he is still here?"

"A female rejected him, and he is in the worst of tempers," the elf said.

Before anyone could stop him, the thief disappeared into the caves.

"Where is he going?" Aleron readied his sword.

"You'll never be able to fight the dragon," the elf said.

"He's a thief. If any can slip in undetected, the young man can," Tashama said.

They waited for ten minutes, then the dragon roared. The elf said, "He has been doing that several times a day. The wounded heart is the worst any creature can bear."

When they saw the thief running out of the cave, his colorless face showed he had failed in his mission. Tashama sighed deeply. "We must convince the female he is worthy."

She nodded at the elf, then headed south.

Aleron and Jaran joined her while the elves stayed behind. Aleron frowned. "They will not aid us?"

"They wish us every success."

"But they will not aid us?"

"They cannot interfere where the dragons are concerned. Unfortunately, if we cannot succeed, we will all have failed. If only a simpler potion would have sufficed."

"I take it there is a female in this direction?"

"The Elorians said she is the one who rejected their dragon, yes." Tashama surveyed the mountains for signs of her.

"If you can convince her she should unite with him, I will have to tell Carissian you are indeed more powerful than he," Aleron said.

"Ah, but have you ever asked him if he could do such a deed? Perhaps he can as well."

Aleron chuckled. "I don't believe he would think it was something his job required of him."

"What do you propose to do, my lady?" Jaran asked.

"Sweet words and comforting actions are what women like to receive from their prospective mates."

The thief scratched his head. "She is not human."

"What if we were to wound her slightly?" Aleron asked.

"Then the male will come to her rescue..."

Tashama took a deep breath. "If she did not finish us off, he would. Of course, their interest in each other would produce offspring, but it wouldn't do us any good."

"What if we were to steal something of hers?" the thief asked.

Tashama shook her head. "Same result, I'm afraid."

She studied the ridge looming before them and pointed at her silvery-green scales, the sun reflecting off them like a mirror of shimmering light. "There she is, just on the tip of that peak right in the middle."

"What is she doing?" the thief asked.

"Studying us," Aleron replied.

Tashama sat on the grass. "The male has done something to perturb her. No other males are around for miles...so the Elorians have told me. The dragons' urge to mate is as great as that of many of the beasts of the forests. But they're a sensitive lot and he might have offended her."

Aleron poked his boot in the dirt next to Tashama's knee as he smiled at her. "Such as?"

"He moved too quickly with her, perhaps? He demanded something of her that she wasn't willing to give up freely?"

Aleron shook his head. "Dragons aren't like people."

"I had one as a pet dragon once—Loralee." Tashama ran her hand over the top of the grass, allowing it to tickle the palm of her hand. "She was offended when I tossed a ball to one of my handmaidens, and the girl missed it, and it hit Loralee on the nose. She sulked for a whole day over the incident, no matter how much I tried to convince her it was an accident."

Tashama stood.

Aleron said, "What is it, Tashama?"

"She'd be the right age." Tashama pulled the pendant out of her dress and held it up to the sun. "They don't go very far from their home." As the blue sphere shone a light across the valley, Tashama studied the dragon's reaction. The dragon didn't move, and Tashama shook her head. "It would have been too good to be true."

"Look." The thief pointed at the dragon when she spread her wings.

"Is she the one?" Aleron asked.

"I don't know." Tashama held up the crystal to the light again. "Find some buttercups. If it is she, it is her favorite treat."

Aleron and the thief dodged through the field looking for the golden flowers. The dragon flew overhead, then hovered over Tashama.

"Loralee," she called out to her. "I've come home."

Aleron and the thief turned and watched in astonishment as the dragon sat down on the ground in front of Tashama. Tashama waited in place as the dragon considered her.

"Found some!" the thief said, and Aleron hastened to join him. After they gathered as much as they could, they walked back to Tashama.

"Does she understand you?" Aleron asked.

"Like a pet dog. They can learn quite a lot of our vocabulary."

"Can you tell her to give the male a chance?"

Tashama laughed. "That I cannot do." She leaned over with some of the flowers and offered them to the dragon. At first, the dragon just sniffed the flowers, then a sense of recognition reflected in her gray-green eyes. She nuzzled Tashama's cheek, then ate the offerings.

"She remembers me." Tashama ran her hand over the dragon's scaly skin, then reached up to rub her nose, just as though she were petting her horse's. "We must coax her to the male's lair. Find more buttercups, and I'll try to lead her toward the male."

Aleron and Jaran hurried to gather more buttercups as Tashama began to walk backward toward the cave. "Come, Loralee." The dragon clumsily followed her. Tashama smiled. "I remember when you could barely fly and were very awkward at that. Now you can fly like an eagle, but you are clumsy at walking."

When they reached the mouth of the cave, Loralee turned her head as the male dragon bellowed his displeasure, and Tashama smiled. "His heartache is winning her over." Tashama waited until Loralee entered the cave. "If they make up, we can get a tooth."

As soon as the female made her appearance in the male's lair, Tashama pointed at a tooth glistening nearby. Jaran hurried to get it, while Tashama watched the female touch her nose to the male's.

"Come, Tashama." Aleron took her arm and nudged her away.

"She will be happy with him." A tear rolled down her cheek and she hurried out of the cave with Aleron.

As more tears rolled down Tashama's cheeks, Aleron pulled her close. "She will be fine."

"Seeing her reminds me of all that I have lost." Tashama squeezed Aleron.

"You have me now." He hugged her with a firm grip. "You have me."

Then she spied a bunch of chili peppers and had an idea.

WITH ALL THE INGREDIENTS, but one, in Balthazar's copper kettle, the thief stirred while Aleron read the directions.

Tashama nodded as she studied the rug, then sighed deeply. "We have to get the drop of sweat from Loran's brow."

The lieutenant walked into the room. "We've prepared this hot, chili dinner as you've described, but I cannot see what good this will do."

"It will make Loran sweat and Valmor thirsty. Will Deloria aid us and wipe the perspiration from her uncle's brow?"

"She is afraid, but she has agreed to do it."

"Good, then the plan is all set. Nobody can resist good hot Texas-style chili...nobody."

The lieutenant folded his arms. "The servants who are loyal to you are ready to serve it as soon as you say."

"Good. And the colonel is ready to remove Valmor as he is incapacitated?"

"Yes, a ship awaits on our southern beaches."

"Everything is falling into place then. Come, we will watch from the hallway. Deloria will bring us the sweaty cloth, and we'll finish the potion. After that, you know the rest."

TASHAMA KNEW that the best-laid plans nearly always had some glitch. She hoped and prayed this time there would be no problems. She dreaded the notion that Deloria might be stopped as she tried to wipe Loran's brow.

She peered into the great hall as her puffy-cheeked cousin of the second royal house stuffed the chili into his greedy mouth. Tashama smiled when Aleron's breath touched her cheek while he observed the scene. Taking a deep breath, she attempted to relax her tense body when Deloria walked up to wipe her uncle's brow.

The pretty young blonde's hand shook slightly, and Loran grabbed her wrist suddenly. "Watch what you are doing with the cloth! You nearly poked me in the eye with it!"

Tashama shuddered as Valmor turned his attention from his meal to Deloria. Would the terror Deloria showed in her movements give her away? Her eyes darted toward Tashama, and Tashama shrank back. *Don't look this way, Deloria. Whatever you do, don't look this way.*

The room grew quiet. Valmor stood. "I propose a toast!"

Everyone rose from their seats.

"To our ruler, will he rule over Maldovia soon!"

"Here, here!" the courtiers shouted. Conversations continued in a muffled roar again.

As everyone returned to their benches, Deloria leaned slightly over Loran and wiped his brow again. He brushed her away. "What is your problem? Leave me!"

Tears rolled down her cheeks, and she tore out of the room in a mass of sobs. She ducked into the hall where Tashama stood and shoved the cloth into her hands.

Tashama quickly squeezed the cloth, but not a drop would emerge. She closed her eyes briefly. *I was never any good at potions.* After dumping the cloth into the mixture, she swirled it about, then pulled it out. She squeezed the fabric as hard as she could. A servant handed her a goblet, and she poured the mixture from the copper kettle into a cup of wine. "Go," she said, "but whatever you do, don't let anyone but Valmor drink it."

The man nodded and hurried to the high table with the drink. Aleron and the colonel's men all unsheathed their swords. Tashama gripped the wall with her fingertips. If he didn't drink it or the potion wasn't mixed right...she couldn't think of what might happen. It just had to work.

Valmor ate another spoonful of his chili, then motioned for a refill of his wine. The servant obliged. Valmor lifted the goblet to his lips, but before he drank it, he shook his head. "Another!"

The servant hurried back to Tashama. She had him add more wine. He returned to Valmor. This time, the sorcerer tossed the wine down his throat. Tashama barely breathed. *How long will it take, Balthazar? How long?*

The sorcerer slapped Loran on the shoulder to his sovereign's surprise. Deloria held her mouth to keep from laughing out loud, and the hall grew quiet again.

Valmor stood. "A toast!"

Tashama rubbed her forehead. "He's becoming unruly." She was afraid they hadn't gotten enough of Loran's sweat. Or she had mistaken what Balthazar had been trying to tell her.

Everyone rose, but Loran, who stared at his sorcerer, uncomprehending.

"To..."

Tashama turned to Aleron, who shrugged, his face hard and concerned as he held his sword at the ready.

Valmor pulled at his beard. "To..." He shook his head and guzzled his refilled goblet, then dropped to his seat.

"Hear, hear!" the confused courtiers said, then hurried to retake their seats.

Loran stared at his sorcerer. "What is the matter with you?"

Valmor grinned at him. "You know, I've never liked the way you snap your fingers to have me appear at your whim."

"He's not changing so that we can deal with him," Tashama said under her breath. "But what was he supposed to transform into?

The sorcerer punched Loran in the shoulder. "And I never liked the way you made fun of me when I was of the second house." He rose to his feet, then climbed onto his chair.

Tashama shook her head. "We have to do something."

Valmor stepped onto the table and then did a little dance in the middle of the dishes. Chuckles filled the room.

Loran stood from his throne. "Guards! Remove this buffoon at once!"

The colonel and his men rushed forward to Loran's surprise. Tashama took a deep breath. "They're no match for Valmor and his dark sorcerer ways."

"Look, Tashama." Aleron pointed to Valmor. "He's not doing anything about the colonel's men."

"Valmor!" Loran shouted as the men led him away.

"Maybe this was supposed to happen, my lady," Jaran said.

Tashama frowned at him. "Next, you will say what Balthazar has said to me all along."

"What is that, dear Tashama?"

Her lower jaw dropped as Balthazar limped toward her. "Balthazar!"

He groaned when she hugged him soundly. "Watch the ribs, my princess." He kissed her cheek, then pointed at the walking cast covering his foot, hidden mainly by the gown he wore.

"Balthazar." She tugged on the medallion dangling at his neck. "Valmor hasn't transformed."

"He has. Valmor is about four years old in your human years. If our men take him to the island now, he'll return to his own ornery way in a couple of days, only he won't be able to harm anyone further. He has no power over water...as I've found you've already learned."

Tashama gave the orders, and the colonel had the childish Valmor removed from the room.

She folded her arms as she considered her sorcerer. "You sent me to Maldovia. I know it was a mistake, but..."

He shook his head. "You found your mate and led your people to victory...all without hardly any of my help."

"You promised you would stay with me."

"I couldn't. Before I knew what had happened, I was lying in a hospital bed in traction. They said I had been drifting in and out of consciousness for several days. This was the first chance I had to break loose from my captors."

"You sent me to Maldovia on purpose?"

Balthazar smiled at Aleron. "You found your mate, did you not? The one you dreamt of for so many months before departing for here."

Tashama considered Aleron's smile. She took his hand in hers. "He has met all the tests. He is the one."

"To Tashama!" several of the courtiers shouted. "To the return of the first royal house!"

Tashama smiled as Aleron kissed her cheek. "You move men like no other...and me more than anyone else."

EPILOGUE

A leron was eager to participate in Tashama's coronation that day, with so much more going on than at his. He was thrilled for her. Balthazar had tracked down three of her friends from the farther reaches of their kingdoms—Princess Talamaya, Princess Mexia, and Princess Kersta. Everyone was delighted to be there with their friends.

Queen Talamaya had told them all about their wild adventures while retrieving the Scepter of Salvation and of marrying the barbarian king, as he was affectionately known to be. Princess Mexia had managed to help take over the mage school for sorceresses, and women were now allowed to attend, and she was married to a prince who co-led the school. And Princess Kersta had helped save Prince Argon's sister, all the while he had wanted Kersta for his own.

They were fascinating tales that included a grumpy dwarf adventurer and delighted everyone.

Even Tashama's dragon and her male companion sat high above on the parapets and flew down to give an exciting fire display.

Balthazar and Carission had become friends, exchanging

secrets between mages, which in and of itself was a remarkable thing.

Anyone in the two kingdoms who disagreed with the way things had gone, including Deveal and Oshon and his wife, was sent away to make their way in the world, even at the request to stay. Aleron couldn't have any of them remain who might still be a threat to his queen. Loran was made to pay the price for the ultimate betrayal of killing her parents and killing so many others in the nonstop wars.

Most of all, Aleron was glad that Balthazar had sent Tashama to him, which, in the end, decided taking her for his mate was the only choice he had—and the right choice all around.

"WHAT ARE YOU THINKING?" Tashama asked him as they participated in the royal feast that was combined with the coronation and their wedding.

Aleron had been so sweet, wanting them to have one big celebration for each, not together. But all life with him would be a celebration.

Besides, they planned another wedding celebration in Maldovia.

"That I found the one in my dreams, and I couldn't have been luckier."

"Oh, me too."

"You told Listra she would find a mate."

"The colonel whom she had fainted in front of? He will become a general, overseeing troops alongside General Karam. And how will her position be elevated? She is my advisor on women's issues, along with Balthazar."

"And Carissian?"

"He can remain your advisor."

Aleron laughed.

The prophecy had been fulfilled. Tashama had found her mate, discovered the murderers of her family, and led her people to victory. She returned home as she'd always said she would. Combining the two kingdoms was easy under Aleron and her rule.

Peace and prosperity spread across the land. The real challenge was changing the Karthlander and Maldovian's view of women. Overnight, the veils were cast aside. Deeper notions would take years to overcome, but Tashama prepared herself to meet the difficulties head-on.

But the first order of business was making sure they had heirs for the thrones for both kingdoms—definitely one of the most rewarding parts of their job.

"The dragons laid fifteen eggs today," Tashama said, taking a drink of his wine.

He smiled. "That's three more than yesterday."

"Without peace reigning in the region, it wouldn't have happened."

"I agree. If anyone wars on us now, we'll have two kingdoms to fight them off."

"Nobody would dare, love of my life."

"Nobody would. Can we slip off to your chambers yet?"

"You have been asking that since the coronation and wedding ended."

"Nobody will notice."

"Everyone will notice. But that's all right. Let's go, heart of mine. Let's make some offspring of our own."

And that was only the beginning of a loving relationship, which resulted in both of their prophecies coming true when they had a beautiful boy and a girl.

The End

ACKNOWLEDGMENTS

A heartfelt thank you to Darla Taylor and Donna Fournier for your invaluable contributions to making my book the best it can be. Your commitment to spotting errors is truly commendable!

ABOUT THE AUTHOR

USA Today bestselling and award-winning author **Terry Spear** has written over a hundred paranormal romance novels, young adult, and medieval Highland historical romances. Her first werewolf romance, *Heart of the Wolf,* was named a 2008 *Publishers Weekly*'s Best Book of the Year, and her subsequent titles have garnered high praise and hit the *USA Today* bestseller list. A retired officer of the U.S. Army Reserves, Terry lives in Spring, Texas, where she is working on her next werewolf romance, shapeshifting jaguars, cougar shifters, vampires, hot Highlanders, and having fun with her young adult fae and vampire novels, helping with her grandchildren and raising two Havanese.

For more information, please visit her website at: http://www.terryspear.com

Blog: https://terryspearbooks.blog/

Follow her for new releases and book deals: www.bookbub.com/authors/terry-spear

Twitter: @TerrySpear.

Facebook: http://www.facebook.com/terry.spear

ALSO BY TERRY SPEAR

Adult Titles

Romantic Suspense: Deadly Fortunes, In the Dead of the Night, Relative Danger, Bound by Danger

***

The Highlanders Series: His Wild Highland Lass (novella), Vexing the Highlander (novella), Winning the Highlander's Heart, The Accidental Highland Hero, Highland Rake, Taming the Wild Highlander, The Highlander, Her Highland Hero, The Viking's Highland Lass, My Highlander, Stolen Highland Dreams

Other historical romances: Lady Caroline & the Egotistical Earl, A Ghost of a Chance at Love

***

Heart of the Wolf Series: Heart of the Wolf, Destiny of the Wolf, To Tempt the Wolf, Legend of the White Wolf, Seduced by the Wolf, Wolf Fever, Heart of the Highland Wolf, Dreaming of the Wolf, A SEAL in Wolf's Clothing, A Howl for a Highlander, A Highland Werewolf Wedding, A SEAL Wolf Christmas, Silence of the Wolf, Hero of a Highland Wolf, A Highland Wolf Christmas; SEAL Wolf Hunting; A Silver Wolf Christmas, SEAL Wolf in Too Deep, Alpha Wolf Need Not Apply, Between a Wolf and a Hard Place, SEAL Wolf Undercover, Dreaming of a White Wolf Christmas, Flight of the White Wolf, All's Fair in Love and Wolf, A Billionaire Wolf for Christmas, SEAL Wolf Surrender, Silver Town Wolf: Home for the Holidays, Night of the Billionaire Wolf, You Had Me at Wolf, Joy to the Wolves, The Wolf Wore Plaid, Jingle Bell Wolf, The Best of Both Wolves, While the Wolf's Away, Christmas Wolf Surprise, Wolf Takes the Lead, Wolf on the Wild Side, Her Wolf for the Holidays, A Good Wolf is

Hard to Find (2024), Dreaming of a Highland Wolf (2024), Wolf Bound, Mated for Christmas (2024) , The Wolf of My Eye

SEAL Wolves: To Tempt the Wolf, A SEAL in Wolf's Clothing, A SEAL Wolf Christmas; SEAL Wolf Hunting, A SEAL Wolf in Too Deep, SEAL Wolf Undercover, SEAL Wolf Surrender

Silver Town Wolves: Destiny of the Wolf, Wolf Fever, Dreaming of the Wolf, Silence of the Wolf; A Silver Wolf Christmas, Between a Wolf and a Hard Place, Home for the Holidays, Jingle Bell Wolf

Wolff Family Lodge Wolves: You Had Me at Wolf, Wolf on the Wild Side, A Good Wolf is Hard to Find

Highland Wolves: Heart of the Highland Wolf, A Howl for a Highlander, A Highland Werewolf Wedding, Hero of a Highland Wolf, A Highland Wolf Christmas, The Wolf Wore Plaid, Her Wolf for the Holidays, Dreaming of a Highland Wolf, The Wolf of My Eye

Billionaire Wolf Series: A Billionaire in Wolf's Clothing, A Billionaire Wolf for Christmas, Night of the Billionaire Wolf, Wolf Takes the Lead

White Wolf Series: Legend of the White Wolf, Dreaming of a White Wolf Christmas, Flight of the White Wolf, While the Wolf's Away, Mated for Christmas

Red Wolf Series: Seduced by the Wolf, Joy to the Wolves, The Best of Both Wolves, Christmas Wolf Surprise

Greystoke Wolf Pack: Wolf Bound,

Wolf Novellas: Day of the Wolf, Seal Wolf Pursuit, Wolf to the Rescue, Night of the Wolf, United Shifter Force

***

Heart of the Jaguar Series: Savage Hunger, Jaguar Fever, Jaguar Hunt, Jaguar Pride, A Very Jaguar Christmas, You Had Me at Jaguar, The Witch and the Jaguar, Dawn of the Jaguar

***

Heart of the Cougar Series: Cougar's Mate, Call of the Cougar, Taming the Wild Cougar, Covert Cougar Christmas, a novella, Double Cougar Trouble, Cougar Undercover, Cougar Magic, Cougar Halloween Mischief, Falling for the Cougar, Cougar Christmas Calamity, Catch the Cougar (Halloween Novella), You Had Me at Cougar, Saving the White Cougar, Big Cat Magic

***

White Bear Series: Loving the White Bear, Claiming the White Bear, Bear of a Halloween, Protecting the White Bear

Grizzly Bear Series: Bear in Mind

***

Highland Wolves of Old: Wolf Pack, Wolf Alliance, Wolf Heir

Heart of the Huntress Series: Killing the Bloodlust, Deadly Liaisons, Huntress for Hire, Forbidden Love, Deadly Liaisons, Vampire Redemption, Primal Desire, Huntress Unleashed

Vampire Novellas: The Siren's Lure, Vampiric Calling, Seducing the Huntress

***

Comedy Romance: Exchanging Grooms, Marriage, Las Vegas Style

***

Science Fiction: Galaxy Warrior

Young Adult Titles

The World of Fae:

The Dark Fae

The Deadly Fae

The Winged Fae

The Ancient Fae

Dragon Fae

Hawk Fae

Phantom Fae

Golden Fae

Falcon Fae

Woodland Fae

Angel Fae

***

The World of Elf:

The Shadow Elf

The Darkland Elf

Warrior Elf

***

Blood Moon Series:

Kiss of the Vampire

Bite of the Vampire

Night of the Vampire

The Vampire Chronicles Series:

The Vampire in My Dreams

Demon Guardian Series:

The Trouble with Demons

Demon Trouble, Too

Demon Hunter

Non-Series for Now:

Ghostly Liaisons

The Beast Within

Courtly Masquerade

Deidre's Secret

The Magic of Inherian:

The Scepter of Salvation

The Mage of Monrovia

Emerald Isle of Mists

Tashama